THE PLACE WE WERE MADE

LAUREN JONES

For Callan.
My love.
There's nothin' like you and I.

CHAPTER ONE

Something bad is happening. I knew it the second my brother showed up for dinner. Thirty minutes ago, I was setting the table and through the dining-room window I saw a sleek, black sedan pull up out front. It idled for a few seconds before Alex stepped out, phone to his ear and a duffle bag in his other hand. I love my brother and I'm excited to see him. But I also know he's supposed to be in New York with his band working on their next album. The fact he's on this side of the country and not the other has my palms sweating.

"What's happening?" I nudge Alex's arm as our mother places several dishes of food on the table in front of us. Now a rich garlic smell complements the tension in the room.

"I'm here for dinner." He shrugs as he pulls the fancy serving dish of mashed potatoes toward himself and shovels some onto his plate.

"Are you staying here?"

"Yes, he's staying for two days before he has to be in New

York." Mom huffs as she takes her seat. "Not everything is a conspiracy, Kit."

Alex looks back to his plate. Clearly, he's a dead end so I try my luck with my sister, Bea, who sits opposite me. Her shoulders are back, and her jaw is tight. She's about to crack, so she chooses that moment to use the bathroom.

"I'll be back in a sec." She stands up so quickly, the fine linen napkin Mom issued us with upon arrival falls to the floor.

"I don't think everything is a conspiracy," I grumble, even though Mom isn't listening, and Dad and Alex are squabbling over who gets the bigger chicken leg. Can no one else see how weird this is?

Alex is passionate about his music. Sometimes, to the detriment of his personal life so it's strange he would bail on his bandmates when their album is already overdue. And it's strange our Sunday night dinner didn't start off with Dad trying to get us all out to the garage to look at whatever old piece of radio equipment he disassembled over the weekend. No part of this event is adding up.

At that moment, the front door opens and my older sister, Eve, drops her bag on the table in the entryway with a thud. "Sorry I'm late. Traffic was a nightmare."

Eve being late actually adds a sense of normalcy to the evening.

She shrugs off her fitted black blazer before carefully removing her Louboutin pumps. They cost her a fortune, crush her toes, and reward her with severe cramping in her feet after wearing them all day. She's never been happier with a purchase.

"We haven't started yet," Mom says as Eve turns around and sees Alex. He stands and pulls her into a hug.

"What happened to you, Evie?" He holds her at arm's length and inspects her. "Last time I was here, you were working at that essential oil store and trying to convince us all not to wear shoes."

"I'm in real estate now." She smooths the wrinkles from the front of her cream silk blouse. "And I love it. I think this job might be the one."

Mom scoffs, and even though Eve ignores it, the muscles in her cheek pull tight as she clenches her teeth. My older sister isn't as lucky as the rest of us. She's never known which career to pursue and, as a result, has explored many options.

"Can we eat yet?" Dad grumbles, his fork poised over the chicken he won.

"Of course," Mom confirms as Bea returns to the table.

Eve takes her seat as I study my family members' expressions for clues. Why didn't Bea bring her boyfriend, Jamie, and where is Darren, Eve's fiancé? Even Spencer, Eve's best friend, isn't here. She's been a staple at our dinners since her parents bought the house across the street twenty years ago.

Strictly biological family means this is serious.

"Where's Spencer?" I ask Eve.

"At work, I guess. I think she's on a deadline." She shrugs.

"It's just family tonight, Kit," Mom says.

Alex shifts in his seat, and something dawns on me. "Wait. Is someone dying?"

Dad disregards my remark and glances at Mom, who is wearing that barely-holding-it-together facial expression. The one she reserves for door-to-door salespeople and Mrs. Hastings, the woman in her volunteer group who called her bake sale idea "gauche".

"No one's dying," Bea pipes up. I stare at her, and she shrinks in on herself. She knows exactly why we're here and she didn't tell me. After twenty-six years on this earth together, plus nine months in the womb, she has now decided that keeping secrets from each other is something we do. I narrow my eyes at my twin, and her cheeks turn pink.

"It smells great, Mom," Bea stammers, but I cut in before Mom can accept the compliment.

"I don't understand why Alex is here and why we're using the special occasion tablecloth and why Dad has done his hair."

Dad presses his hands on the salt-and-pepper strands at the crown of his head. He hasn't had a haircut in five months and usually does nothing to contain the unruly mess it's become. Tonight, it's smoothed at the sides and far too shiny because he hasn't mastered measuring out a dime-sized amount of gel.

"Oh yeah, this *is* the special occasion tablecloth." Eve moves her plate to inspect the woven floral pattern beneath it. "I thought you threw it out when Alex spilled gravy on it."

Mom's eyes grow wide. "He what?"

"It's over there, under his plate," Bea points out, completely ignoring the daggers Alex is staring at her.

"Is that why you insisted on sitting there?" The sorrow in Mom's eyes is palpable as she looks at Alex. The golden child is looking a little tarnished now.

"It was an accident," Alex explains.

"It's a family heirloom." Mom's lip is shaking.

"It's a tablecloth." Eve laughs.

Mom's eyes snap to her eldest daughter, her shaped brows drawn, and her lips pressed tight. "My great grandmother sewed the lace trim by hand."

"But it's a tablecloth." Eve folds her arms across her chest. "It's to protect the table from having food spilled on it. Also it's white so that is a poor design choice."

How has a years-old gravy stain usurped the purpose of this gathering? I look back to Bea. She's the weakest link and there is a chance I can exploit it with some twin telepathy. She immediately knows what I'm up to and becomes invested in re-positioning the beans on her plate.

"I can't believe you didn't tell me what's happening!" I hiss across the table.

She drops her fork with a clatter. "I don't know what's going on."

"Yes, you do," Alex chimes in, only to immediately regret it when a chunk of carrot narrowly misses his left ear.

"Beatrice, don't throw food," Mom barks. "And stop lying."

"I'm not lying."

Eve scoffs, "Yes you are."

"I knew it!" I point at my twin. "Now tell me. Is someone dying?"

"No!" Mom and Dad say in unison.

"Then why are we all here?"

"We'll talk about it after dinner," Mom drapes her napkin over her lap with shaking hands.

I glance around at the faces of my family members. They can't look at each other and I'm reminded that this table holds memories like a vice. On four separate occasions, we've sat here and been informed of a grandparent's passing. Alex announced he was moving to LA over this matching floral serving dish set and we sat in these very seats when Dad told us they found a mass on his liver in my junior year of high school. A family-only dinner with this tablecloth is a bad omen.

"Bea, did something happen between you and Jamie?" I look at my sister. "Because if he hurt you, I'll scalp him. Alex will help."

"I will," my brother confirms, his voice deepening.

"Nothing happened with Jamie," Bea sighs. "Please don't scalp him."

I release the grip I have on my butter knife. "Then I am really confused about what's going on?"

"Just hurry up and tell her," Eve says.

Alex puts down his fork and looks at Mom. "Yeah. It's time."

"After dinner," Mom says. Her tone is sharp.

"Mom, do it now," Bea chimes in. "I'm tired of keeping it a secret."

"I said we'll discuss it after dinner."

All three of my siblings talk over each other, imploring Mom to explain everything, but she holds out. The chatter is overwhelming and when it reaches fever pitch, Dad slaps his hand on the table, causing Mom to emit a surprised squeak.

"Stop beating around the bush, Elaine," he grumbles. "Kit, we're selling the house. We told Bea two weeks ago because she showed up when the realtor was here. Alex found out a month ago because we thought he'd want to visit one more time before it sells, and Sheryl Hastings from number fourteen knows because she's always sticking her nose in our business."

"Doug!" Mom scolds.

"What? She was going to find out, anyway. They're putting the for-sale sign up in the morning."

"I wanted to approach the subject with a little more tact."

Dad frowns. "Oh, and Eve found out because her brokerage is handling the sale."

I turn to Eve, who lifts her shoulders in reluctant confirmation.

"Wait, wait." My head spins. "Why are you selling the house?"

"Downsizing." Mom brushes off the question and Dad rolls his eyes. "You kids have all moved out, so there's no sense in hanging onto such a large house."

Such a large house? Bea and I shared a room until we moved out, and we had a strict morning schedule to ensure everyone had equal time to get ready in our single bathroom. We outgrew this house when Mom gave birth to Bea and me. Now it's the perfect size for an older couple.

"That makes no sense." The temperature in the room feels like it's rising exponentially, and I briefly fan my face with my napkin. "Where are you going to move to?"

"We'll find somewhere. Now, can we just eat dinner and not worry about this?" Mom exhales like she's run a marathon.

"Isn't the whole point of this dinner to talk about it?" Alex lifts his shoulders in a casual shrug and Mom's eyes widen, her mouth slack. Yet another betrayal from her favorite child.

"Yes, it is." Dad's tone is rigid once again, and he looks back at Mom. "It's time to tell them, Elaine."

Eve's brows draw together. "I'd also like to know where you're going. Because I keep sending you listings and neither of you will commit to anything."

"I haven't decided where to go," Dad says flatly, and my siblings and I share a collective look of further confusion.

"So, that's it? You're selling our childhood home to go nowhere." Alex rubs his chin.

"Yes," Dad lies.

Eve's head drops back, and she lets out an exaggerated breath. She's seconds from leaving and I'd like an explanation before that happens.

"What about the block parties? The Stewarts just put in a pool and the invitations for Christmas in July have gone out," I ask. "And what about the Larsons? They're your oldest and closest friends. You can't leave them."

Alex chuckles under his breath. "I'd sell the house at a loss to get out of Christmas in July."

Mom ignores Alex and looks at me. "Kit, I know it's a shock, but we'll get through it as a family."

I sag back into my chair. "I still don't understand. Why sell the house when you don't have somewhere else to go?"

Mom and Dad share a look that makes me think they do know where they're going. Mom is always talking about visiting her sister in Florida, and Seattle's extended bouts of rainy weather often get her down. She's also fallen out of love with her guest services job at the Pacific Grand Hotel, and she's started ditching her weekly book club. A knot of panic forms in my stomach.

"Everything will be fine, Kit." Dad's tone is slightly more nurturing.

"Yeah," Bea agrees. "We'll just do Sunday dinner at the new house."

Not sure how to do that when a third of the family is in Florida.

"Your dad's right, Katherine. Everything is going to be okay." Mom's eyes are soft as she stares across the table at me. "It won't be that big of a change. You and Bea are happy in your nice little apartment, and you've got a great job at the bank."

That's not the point. Also, "great" isn't the adjective I'd use. I'm a loan officer, so my day mostly consists of disappointing people. "Stable" would be more accurate.

"Is it a financial issue? Because I'm sure we could help. At least Alex can," I offer on behalf of my brother.

Mom holds up her hands. "It's not a financial issue."

"Are you moving to Florida, then? I know how much you love it down there, but it's so far away. What about all the memories we have in this house? Seattle has an average of one hundred and fifty-two sunny days per year...that's pretty good!"

"What? We're not moving to Florida," Dad says.

"And it's not about the weather," Mom adds.

"Then why sell the house? It's in a good area. All your friends live nearby, and Dad's commute is practically nothing."

Eve reaches out and pats my arm. "She's right. It *is* a great area, and it's expected to boom in the next five years. Hang on to the house for longer and you could make a lot more money."

"It's not about money." Dad's tone is firm.

"Then what is it about?" Bea chimes in. "Because I don't think you should sell it either, and if it has nothing to do with money and you love the neighborhood, why is this place suddenly not good enough?"

Bea holds Mom's gaze for a long time, almost like a challenge. Waiting for her to offer a more plausible explanation but instead her face falls. Tears spring to her eyes as she drops her fork and it clangs on the side of the plate, splattering the heirloom tablecloth with more gravy. Alex looks momentarily relieved, until Mom speaks.

"Your father and I are getting a divorce."

The room falls silent, and you could cut the tension with one of Mom's fancy butter knives.

CHAPTER TWO

"The sale has nothing to do with any of you," Dad says. "It's about the division of assets."

That's it? Our home, our family and their marriage come down to the division of assets? That hurts more than being told it *is* our fault.

"Whose fault is it?" Eve's voice has a razor edge. "Because you told me you were just selling the house. Not that your marriage is over."

"It's complicated, Eve," Mom says.

Eve doesn't look at Mom. Her attention is fixed on Dad, who has taken to pushing food around his plate.

"What did she do, Dad?"

"Eve!" Mom snaps as Dad looks up. He doesn't spring to her defense, instead he silences Eve with narrowed eyes.

"I need a minute," Bea whispers.

"Beatrice, please." Mom's hand shakes as she holds it over her heart.

Bea stands, hurries through the kitchen and out the door to the backyard. Mom lets out a small whimper.

"I'll talk to her," I assure my mother, even though my shock level matches Bea's with what's unfolded tonight.

It's a clear and cool night with the sweet smell of rain hanging in the air. The overgrown grass is soft underfoot and the lights of the neighboring houses cast enough glow to light the way to the old treehouse at the back corner of the property.

Bea climbs the weather-beaten ladder and when she reaches the top, holds her hand out to help me up. I grip her arm and maneuver myself to sit beside her, dangling our legs off the edge of the mossy decking boards.

"This sucks," Bea says, her basic observation hitting the crisp night air with a slight puff of steam.

"Mild understatement," I reply as I lift my thighs and tuck my hands beneath them to stop myself from picking at my cuticles.

"I only knew about the house, and Mom made me promise not to tell you."

"Sounds like something Mom would do."

Bea yanks on the sleeves of her knitted sweater, pulling them down to cover her hands. "How did we not see it? I mean, Dad doesn't say much, but Mom is an open book. I can tell the day she's had by the number of wrinkles on her forehead."

"True." I chuckle. Dad has always kept to himself, but the one thing that's written all over his face and in every facet of his body language is how much he loves Mom. You can hear it in his voice and in the way he holds her every chance he gets;

how when he gets home from work, he kisses her temple before he drops his keys on the bench. It's like muscle memory. He's conditioned to show her how much he cares for her.

"This is so out of left field." I exhale. "And selling the house is too final. Why can't they keep it until they're certain they don't want to be together?"

Bea takes my hand and I close my eyes as the night air brushes my cheeks. The smell of that incoming storm is getting stronger.

"I don't want to lose our house." Bea looks around the yard. "Our entire childhood is here."

That thought cuts close to the bone. No matter where we go, or what we do together or independently, this is home. It's the place we always come back to. It's the place where we can just be us.

As though summoned, Alex and Eve step out the back door and cross the yard. Alex has two coats hanging over his arm.

"Put these on and move over." He holds our respective coats out, and Bea and I shuffle over to make room.

"This sucks," Alex says as he settles beside me. Eve follows, our older siblings bracketing us and huddling close.

"Mild understatement," Bea mumbles.

Eve frowns as she cradles my twin, and the air is thick with her unspoken thoughts.

"So, neither of you knew about the divorce?" I ask my older siblings.

"Dad told me they wanted to sell the house and Mom said she wanted to tell the rest of you herself," Eve answers.

Eve rarely does what Mom asks of her, so Dad was the one who made her keep the secret.

"What about you?" I address my brother, who holds a hand up defensively.

"I didn't know. I swear."

We huddle in silence, but even in the safety of our tree-house, my mind continues to race. My parents are solid. They're in love and have been since they met as twenty-year-olds. They had it all, they still have it all.

"Is anyone else wondering what Mom did to make Dad finally leave her?" Eve couldn't hold her tongue forever.

"Evie," Alex scolds. "Don't say shit like that."

"It's true, though. Didn't any of you notice they've been snapping at each other for almost a year?"

"They have not," Bea disagrees quickly, but I stew on it for a moment and place the last twelve months under a micro-scope in my mind.

Dad's been working for the same logistics company since he left high school and even with the long hours, he always made time for Mom on the weekends. For the last year, however, he's been busying himself with tasks like building a garden bed along the back wall of the house, painting the exterior trim, and tinkering with any electronics he could find in the house. He also got really into meat smoking and compound-butter-making around Thanksgiving last year.

It's like he's been looking for something to do.

How did I not notice this before?

"Everything is going to be okay," Alex says softly. "We're all here and we aren't going anywhere."

Bea reaches over and cradles my hands in hers. She

squeezes tightly while Alex rubs my shoulder. His words are only a partial comfort because he'll be gone again soon. I am thankful for my sisters, though.

"Mom's already asked if I can take the property photos," Bea admits. "I'll have to use the wide-angle lens to convince the internet there's extensive space for entertaining in this yard."

It cuts a little deeper knowing Mom has already contracted Bea's services as a professional photographer to sell our home.

"I told Dad to rip up the carpet in the dining room," Eve adds. "The hardwood under there is beautiful."

Alex looks up at the stars and lets out a heavy sigh. "I'm going to have to come clean about the hole in the wall behind the headboard in my room."

Bea raises a brow. "How did you put a hole in the wall?"

"I'm not telling you."

"Eww." I turn up my nose.

Eve laughs. "Wait, is that why you asked Mom to leave your room exactly as it was when you left?"

He shrugs. "I intended to fix it at some point."

Alex doesn't have the skills to execute such a task. Eve vocalizes that thought and she and Alex squabble while I stare out over the backyard in silence.

"It's going to be okay," Bea whispers, noticing I'm not engaging in the conversation.

I sincerely hope she's right, because we're in uncharted waters now.

"We should go back in," Eve says. "They're probably fighting."

"Kit and I are going to stay out here for a little while." Bea continues to hold my hand.

Alex and Eve go back into the house, and through the back door, I see Mom in the kitchen. She pulls Alex into a hug while Eve leans against the counter with her arms folded. When Mom turns to her, she leaves the room.

"This might be the last straw for Mom and Evie," Bea whispers. "She's definitely on Dad's side."

I hate the thought of taking sides, but this isn't a surprise to anyone. Eve and Mom have never seen eye to eye. Mom has tried to connect with her eldest daughter, but Eve pushes back. Aside from shared genetics, they have nothing in common and keeping Mom at arm's length is more like sport for Eve. Mom will never stop trying though. She's always been about her children. She convinced Dad to buy Alex his first guitar and attended all his shows. She used to drive me to the skate rink so I could hang out with my best friend, Danny and she spent hours sewing costumes for Bea's middle school dance recitals. She was always front and center with the camera too. But things never really clicked with Eve. My sister had hobbies, heaps of them. In fact, she bounced around from one activity to the next so fast it gave us all whiplash. Mom tried to instill in Eve the importance of seeing things through. It never stuck though.

I turn my face away from the house. From this height, I can see over the fence into the Larson family's backyard. They've lived on this street as long as we have, and even though all the Larson kids moved out a while ago, I'm left with fond memories of growing up alongside them. When Bea and I were eleven, Alex pulled the nails out of four fence palings at the back of the yard to make a swinging door big enough to sneak through. The primary purpose of the backyard trap door was so Miles Larson, Alex's best friend, could smuggle booze into the treehouse. That came in handy when Eve was sixteen and she and Spencer tried to turn the treehouse into an exclusive club for their school friends. The cover charge was astronomical for a structurally questionable box you couldn't stand up in. Still, our treehouse had a rep on the street for being the ultimate hangout. A rep Danny, the youngest Larson, and I improved with a coat of arctic white paint on the internal walls. We wanted to open up the space, really make it pop. Unfortunately, we forgot about proper ventilation and both almost passed out from the fumes.

"You know Danny's back, don't you?" Bea says, noticing that I'm staring over at the Larson's house.

I tilt my head to one side. "To see his parents?"

"Permanently. He's living at Fletcher's place."

The pit in my stomach doubles in size. "I've been calling and texting him for months. He never responded."

Bea shrugs. "With the injury and breaking up with Alissa, I'd say he'd want to be home."

"He broke up with Alissa?"

"Yeah. Months ago, but I only found out yesterday."

My throat grows tight and I stumble over my words. "How long has he been back?"

"Only a week. I think," Bea responds and even though her tone is casual, her words are like a hot poker being shoved down my throat. Is he intentionally staying with his brother so he wouldn't run into me?

As kids, Danny and I were inseparable. His love of hockey

meant we spent most of our time at the community rink. I attended all his games and, in return, he tolerated my school debate tournaments.

When we weren't at the rink, we were watching games on television or smacking a puck, tennis ball or crumpled soda can across the Larson's back deck. The bench at the far end was my goal, while Danny aimed at two chalk markings on the wooden fence at the other end. We'd have to redraw the chalk lines every time the Seattle rain washed them away. Until the day Mr. Larson painted the lines on the fence for us.

When we graduated high school, Danny went straight to college in Minnesota and joined a college hockey program. He was always talented, but everything changed when the scouts noticed. He was only there for a year before he got drafted and signed a contract with Philadelphia. It happened fast, and I still remember every second of the phone call. He could barely string a sentence together. He was overwhelmed.

Our contact slowed after that. Late night calls turned to infrequent texts until we started going months without contact. It only took a couple of years for him to establish himself in the national league. By that time, he'd met his girlfriend Alissa, and he'd signed a five-year contract with New York. He was living his dream…until it all fell apart.

Our friendship fell apart too and I haven't recovered.

CHAPTER THREE

I love being a twin. I tried to explain what it's like to Danny, but all I could come up with was: it's like having a built-in best friend. I feel like I'm part of an exclusive club with only two members and it comes with a sense of security and importance.

At least that's how I felt until the day Bea brought home Jamie Chambers. Watching them together, I experienced an odd sensation. I could see Bea was happy, but instead of a shared rush of dopamine, I felt something else. Like someone had poked a little hole in my soul and our shared magic slowly began to leak.

It created a small hurdle in getting to know Jamie, the Englishman. However, after spending some time with him, I've learned that he's kind, driven and genuinely cares for my sister. I can't ask for anything more than that.

"What's this for again?" Jamie asks as we approach the bar, Whiskey Double.

Bea beams as she takes his hand. "All the Larson kids are in one place for the first time in a while and I wanted to get a drink before they fly up to Alaska for Fletcher and Hallie's wedding."

I'm already panicked, knowing Danny will be there.

"Aren't Hallie and Fletcher hosting a reception when they get back?" Jamie scratches his clean-shaven chin.

"Yes they are and I've already RSVP'd on your behalf." Bea pinches Jamie's cheek as he holds open the door to the bar and ushers us inside.

I'm immediately overwhelmed, my muscles tense as the wall of sound hits me—laughing, shouting, karaoke and the music accompanying it. My head is swimming.

Then I see Danny.

That's when the room and my head go quiet.

Bea takes over, steering me toward the table. I stand to the side, waiting, hoping Danny will jump up, pull me into a rough hug and tell me how good it is to see me again. It's what he used to do and my body itches for it.

He doesn't move. Instead, he gives me a lazy nod. It's the same nod he gives Jamie, a man he's never met before.

"Hey, Kit." Leah, the only Larson daughter, pushes her way between Jamie and Bea to provide a replacement for the hug I was hoping for. "It's so good to see you again."

"It's good to see you too. I love the blazer."

She turns from side to side and pushes the folded sleeves of her neon pink blazer up to her elbows. "Oh. You're sweet."

Leah is always well dressed, and tonight is no exception. She perfectly pattern clashes a polka dot blouse with a hound-stooth skirt and her chocolate hair falls in waves around her shoulders. She's a picture of grace and style in a dimly lit bar that exclusively serves deep-fried food.

At the table, her husband, Ben, is deep in conversation with Fletcher Larson. Fletcher's fiancé, Hallie, is chatting with Nolan, the oldest Larson sibling. As a father of three, it's rare to see him out of the house on a weeknight. Miles is the middle child and he owns Whiskey Double. He and Alex were best friends and bandmates until they moved to LA together. I don't exactly know what happened but, a few months after the move, Miles gave up music and moved back to Seattle. He and Alex haven't spoken since.

"Here, Kit." Bea pats the end of the booth and I sit, even though I would rather have taken the seat beside Danny that Jamie has now occupied.

It doesn't matter because, for the first ten minutes, it's impossible to have a conversation with anyone over the noise in the bar. I busy myself reading every word on the menu, even though Miles keeps dropping food off at the table. Leah is talking about a vodka campaign she and Bea are photographing, and Jamie is deep in conversation with Nolan about income tax rates in the UK. Danny doesn't engage with any of the singular conversations—judging by his winces, he's listening to the off-key karaoke singer on stage.

Bea notices my waning interest in the evening and brings me into her discussion with Leah about Instagram engagement. I only use my account to post an occasional photo from my morning run along the waterfront. As a result, my involvement in the conversation fizzles out and I look back to Danny. He hasn't changed since we saw each other last, except he has slightly longer hair and he's lacking a smile.

Like his brothers, he has a defined jaw and heavy brows, though he sports a thick scar on his upper lip, to the right of his nose. That was my fault. I pushed him off his parents' back deck when we were seven, and he landed face first on the garden edging. The scar above his left eyebrow has nothing to do with me, though. He took a hit to the head after his helmet came off at a junior club game when we were fifteen. I remember how much my knees hurt when I jumped the boards and slid down next to him. There was so much blood on the ice. I thought he was dead until he rolled over and started laughing. Something about the panic on my face was hilarious; I didn't talk to him for three days.

What a waste of three days.

I'm lost in my thoughts when he looks up and I glimpse his gunmetal eyes.

They set him apart from his family. Judy Larson provided the rest of her children with the same dark hair and amber-brown eyes, while Danny got his dad William's dark-blond hair. But he's the only one in the family to have those stormy eyes. A beautiful genetic anomaly.

"Can you help me with the next round?" Jamie leans down beside me, bringing me back to the present. I agree and he moves to the side, allowing me to lead the way to the bar.

"You don't look like you're enjoying yourself," he says as we wait for Miles to see us. "Is it because of Danny?"

Of course Bea told him. If the last three years have taught me anything, it's that whatever Bea knows, Jamie will know a few seconds later. It doesn't bother me because, from time to time, Jamie provides useful insight into certain situations. Like renegotiating the lease on our apartment when the landlord tried to raise the rent or analyzing my handful of low-stakes romantic relationships.

"He's acting like I don't exist." I let out a labored breath. "Why is he doing that?"

Jamie pats my shoulder. "I've been sitting next to him this whole time, and he's barely said a word to any of us."

"He's always been quiet," I admit. "But not so much with me."

"In my experience as a sometimes-moody individual, often the simplest reason is the correct one." He taps his temple and winks. "He's probably tired or not in the mood to socialize. Or hungover. Never discount a simple hangover."

I discount that immediately. Danny isn't a drinker. He's never taken it further than a few beers at a backyard party out of fear it would affect his ability to train or play.

"I can drop you back at the apartment if you'd like?" Jamie offers, and I glance back at the table. Everyone is laughing and chatting, except for Danny. Though Hallie appears to be working hard to get a word out of him.

"Do you think Bea will be upset if I leave?"

"I don't think so," Jamie says.

I place my drink order with Miles and wonder if he knows Alex is back in town. Eve probably told him, but I doubt he would care anyway.

When we return to the table, I offer a flimsy lie about my need to be up early in the morning so I can leave. Leah asks me to stay a little longer but doesn't push it when I decline. Danny says nothing, he just dips his head in farewell when Jamie offers to drive me home. Part of me thought Danny would offer me a ride. It would give us a chance to clear the air, but apparently I have grossly misjudged the state of our friendship. Which is incredibly unfair considering I was the one who tried to maintain contact the entire time he was gone.

It's a seventeen-minute drive to the apartment, and when Jamie pulls up outside the building, he cuts the engine and leans back in the driver's seat. He was quiet on the drive and now he stares vacantly at his hands as his thumbs press into the leather steering wheel.

"Is everything okay?" I ask.

He lets out a hurried breath, like he's been waiting for me to ask. "I have to go back home. My dad called yesterday to tell me my gran has taken a turn and might not have much time."

I don't know much about Jamie's family, but I know how much he loves his grandmother. He sends her mystery novels and every second Friday video calls her to discuss the plot twists at length. He even had custom t-shirts made that have "*Across-the-Pond Book Club*" printed on the front.

"Jamie, I'm so sorry." I drop my hand from the door handle. "You should definitely go home."

"What about Bea?"

"What about her?"

"Well, I'd like her to come with me."

"Have you asked her?"

He shakes his head. "It's not a good time."

"It's not, but I can hold the family together for a week or two, and I'm sure Leah can handle the work side of things."

Jamie stares at his hands, squeezing the wheel tighter. "I'll likely be gone a while."

"More than a few weeks?" The thought of Bea leaving sends a rush of panic up my spine.

"Possibly," he says. "My father is talking about retirement, and my brother and I will need to discuss what happens with the company going forward."

From what Bea has told me, Jamie and his brother have been preparing their entire lives to take over the family's property development company. Jamie's extended stay in the US wasn't planned but he has still been an integral part of the growth of the business. He should definitely get a say in what happens to it.

"Well, you can spend some time with your grandmother and have a meeting with your brother, then come back. Bea could even fly over for a visit while you're there."

As the headlights from a passing car light up the interior, I see Jamie chewing on his lip.

"Jamie?"

He swallows hard. "Yep. Sounds like a plan."

CHAPTER FOUR

With the divorce and house sale out in the open, the family dynamic has, as expected, deteriorated. Mom and Dad were relatively amicable for the announcement, but they aren't on good terms. I haven't realized how cold they are with each other until I spend the weekend at the house, helping clean out the attic. Dad keeps to himself, but leaves the room when Mom comes in, and they only seem to speak to each other when absolutely necessary. I want to know what reduced their thirty-five-year marriage to this, but, deep down, what I really want is to know who I should be more angry at.

"I miss this room." Bea stares at the ceiling with her hands folded on her stomach.

Being twins, Bea and I shared everything, including a bedroom. Mom made it her mission to match almost every-thing about us as well. The same hairstyles, the same toys, and the same outfits. Alex called it the Gemini Curse—like our shared appearance meant we had the same interests and personalities. One look at our bedroom would tell you otherwise. Bea's side of the room is a veritable garden of wildflower wall decals above her twin bed. The stars she painted on her white, French-country-style nightstand have faded with time, but the top is still cluttered with hair clips, nail polish bottles, and her old Polaroid camera. My side is neat as a pin. There's nothing but a lamp on the clean white nightstand and the bed has hospital corners.

Even though we tried to radiate our individuality, Mom would still buy us matching clothes, and from time to time Dad would get our names mixed up. It was the driving force behind Bea bleaching her hair without permission when we were seventeen.

"Those comforters aren't getting better with age," I joke as I lean on the door frame. "You don't even like purple."

"No, I don't." Bea sits up, inspecting the room from a different angle. "Hey. I just remembered something."

She slides to the floor and inspects the baseboard beside the closet door. "Which one did we hide the letters in?"

"The next one over. With the bent nail on the right." I point at the baseboard in question.

Sixteen years ago, Bea and I ripped it off the wall using a screwdriver and a soup spoon because we wanted a place to hide our secrets. By torchlight, we used one of Mom's good steak knives to saw a rectangular hole into the drywall behind the board. I remember waiting until morning and being used as a decoy to get everyone out of the house so Bea could hammer the baseboard back on. She used the heel of a boot, hence the bent nail and the fact it's barely attached to the wall.

Bea grips the timber, her manicured nails wedged between

the board and the wall, and with a grunt our time capsule is exposed.

"I still can't believe we sawed a hole in the wall." Bea laughs as I join her on the floor.

"It was pretty brazen for a couple of ten-year-olds."

"God, I feel old now." She says as she reaches into the cavity and pulls out four folded pieces of paper. I know exactly what they are. The one sealed with a heart sticker is Bea's letter to her future self. It contains all the things she wanted her grown self to know. I never read it out of respect for her privacy, but I remember her writing *"Dear Thirty-Year-Old Bea"* with a heart above the *"i"*. The letter with the cloud sticker is mine. It's not a letter, so much as a reminder of all the things I needed to have achieved. A college degree, a stable job and perhaps a marriage to a certain blond-haired neighbor. The third, with no sticker, is a list of all the things Bea and I wanted to do before we cracked open the baseboard again. The fourth letter, sealed with a star, lifting at every point, is for Danny. It was the last addition before we attempted to reattach the board eight years ago.

Bea takes her letter and unfolds it, laughing before she even makes it to the second paragraph.

"Wow. I was dramatic."

"Only in print." I use her momentary distraction to slide Danny's letter under the bed. Next, I pick up our list, brush off the dust, and unfold it carefully.

"'*Katherine and Beatrice Reilly's list of things to do before we're old,*'" I read the heading out loud as Bea leans over to inspect it. "The title is a bit wordy."

Bea chuckles. "I can't remember a single thing we wrote on that list."

"Number one is to host a dinner party."

"Really? There has to be something better."

I clear my throat, adopt an authoritative tone, and continue reading. "Sleep under the stars, spend money on something that won't last, get a tattoo, dance in the rain, stay up all night and watch the sunrise."

Bea takes the list, and as she skims it, her mouth pulls into a frown. "I've done all this stuff."

"Not all of it," I say, facetiously.

She's silent for a moment, re-reading it. "I'm not kidding. I really have done all of this."

Bea continues to scan the page, in search of something she hasn't done. It's not an extensive list and Bea is more adventurous than me—I'm not surprised she's done it all and I've done nothing.

"When did you stay up all night to watch the sunrise?" I ask, recalling one item on the list.

"I'd been seeing Jamie for a month. We'd parked outside a restaurant and he told me how uninspired his plan for the date was. Dinner and a movie, so admittedly cliché. I told him to surprise me. He started the engine and we just drove. Ten hours later, we held hands and watched the sunrise on a beach in California."

The smile on her face makes me frown. I remember this disappearing act. I was worried sick about her, and now I find out she lied about where she was. She told me she was staying at Jamie's house, not hopping two state borders when she could have watched the sunrise from our balcony.

"That's stupid," I say.

"No, it's romantic, and we spent twenty hours in the car getting to know each other. We talked about everything. Our families and our future. I decided, somewhere outside Portland, that I was going to spend the rest of my life with him."

"What if the car broke down? Or he left you at a gas station? Or he took you into the woods and strangled you?"

Bea chuckles again. "Stop listening to murder podcasts."

"You told me you were at his apartment, but you weren't even in the state."

"You would have freaked. Anyway, I didn't get murdered, and three years later, I'm still with Jamie," she says. "How about you stop worrying about what I'm doing and cross some things off the list yourself?"

"I'm not getting a tattoo."

Bea pulls herself up to rest on her elbows. "Don't start with that one. Start with the dinner party."

I picture our two-bedroom apartment and the tiny dining table, with just three chairs and a broken fourth chair pushed against the wall.

"Beatrice." Mom's voice sails through the hall. "I found a box of old school supplies. Can you sort through them?"

"Coming," Bea calls out. She grunts loudly as she pulls herself off the floor and smooths the wrinkles from her sundress.

"You're not that old," I laugh.

Bea's face crumples and presses on her stomach. "It's not that. I'm just not feeling well."

"Tell Mom. It might get you out of cleaning the hall cupboard."

"Good thinking." She winks before leaving the bedroom.

When I'm certain that Bea and Mom are both focused on their tasks, I snatch Danny's letter out from under the bed and stuff it back into the wall. I don't remember every word I wrote, but I'm certain it isn't suitable for general consumption. Leaving it locked behind the baseboard is currently the safest place for it.

With my childhood secrets secured, I head down to the treehouse. Dad has finished mowing the lawn and when I ask how he's going, he pulls me into a hug and tells me not to worry about him. He holds on longer than ever, smelling of freshly cut grass and drug store aftershave.

"What's that?" he asks, dipping his chin at the paper in my hand.

I unfold it and hold it up for him to read.

"Ah yes, the list. The top-secret list that sat on the dining table for two days waiting for the glitter to dry." Dad squints as he reads. "I take it you rediscovered that broken baseboard?"

My eyes widen. "How do you know about the hiding spot?"

"Your mother has been asking me to fix it for a decade, Kit-Kat." He sighs. "I checked it out the first time she asked, saw that it was full of letters and left it alone."

My adolescent heart sinks. "Bea and I thought it was a secret."

"Not a good one. You mangled that nail trying to reattach it. Your mom would skin you alive if she knew what you did to that drywall."

As we cut the hole, I'd had the same thought. I could picture the vein in Mom's forehead swelling to a startling degree before she took away everything Bea and I loved. I'd already come up with contingency plans on how I could sneak over to Danny's place if it came to that.

"Why didn't you say anything?" I ask.

"Well, you were smart enough not to hack into the wall near an outlet and if you wanted somewhere to hide your love letters to the neighbor kid, I wasn't going to stop you."

He shrugs in a delightfully casual way, and I spring forward and wrap him in another tight hug. It takes him by surprise, but he hugs me back and pats between my shoulder blades.

When we break apart, his eyes are wet.

"Everything is going to be okay, Dad."

He wipes sweat from his brow and looks around his immaculate backyard. "I hope so."

CHAPTER FIVE

O n Wednesday, I finish work and drive straight to the
house for a "family dinner" before Jamie flies back to
the UK. I don't know what Mom hopes to achieve by insisting
on this delusion, but Dad makes up plans with a guy from
work to get out of it and Eve was never going to attend
anyway. Mom thought if I extended the offer, she'd have more
luck. I sent the text as requested and three hours later received
a one-word answer.

No.

I wish I could decline, because it's uncomfortable watching
Mom try to pretend everything is normal. To Jamie's credit, he
avoids any hot-button topics, but Bea carries most of the
conversation. Still, I don't make it to dessert and excuse myself
as soon as possible so I can gather my thoughts in the treehouse. For as long as it's still our treehouse.

As I pick at the splintered decking boards, I wonder how
I've missed out on all the experiences Bea has had. I've never

felt this distant from her before. I'm hit with the same pangs of jealousy I had when she started spending more time with Leah back in college. That list has both our names at the top, but I let myself be left behind.

I take the list from the pocket of my jacket and unfold it. A decade-old sprinkling of glitter falls onto my jeans as I flatten it and study the words. Bea's handwriting is sweeping and expressive compared to my neat block lettering. Always in the lines. Always in my comfort zone.

I thrive on structure, but this hollow feeling in my chest begs to differ. This list was meant to change that and maybe it's not too late.

I skim the list and start formulating a plan on how I'm going to execute each item. My eyes are drawn to *"meet someone famous"*. I could easily achieve this if I counted my brother or Danny. Even Fletcher's star is on the rise since his book hit the *Times* best sellers list. Using any of these connections feels like a cop-out, though. I want to meet someone famous on my own, not because I live next door to a family that has produced a decent number of successes.

There is no criterion on how famous they have to be, so I set the bar at the same level as Bea. Her brush with fame came a few months ago when Rebecca Reid was in Seattle promoting the *Blood of Gold* TV show. She only met Rebecca because Hallie's dad and Fletcher literally wrote the books the show is based on. Now I wish I'd powered through the migraine I had that night.

"Hi," a little voice sings out. "There's a door in your fence."

Gemma, Nolan Larson's eldest daughter, pushes the loose

palings and slips through, coming to a stop at the bottom of the treehouse ladder. "Do you know about the door?"

"My brother made it," I explain as, without invitation, Gemma climbs the ladder and sits beside me, legs dangling over the edge.

"I'm Gemma." She grins.

We've met before, at last year's Halloween party. She wouldn't remember me. She was busy throwing a tantrum because her furry spider legs wouldn't stay attached to her shirt. Her mother, Estelle, ended up using an entire roll of duct tape to secure them.

"Kit." I hold out my hand and she shakes it firmly. "Shouldn't you be under supervision?"

"Uncle Danny is watching me."

I instinctively look across to the Larson's yard, but I can't see Danny.

"I don't think he's doing a good job."

"I asked him to make me a sandwich and then I snuck out. What's the point of being inside on the couch, watching cartoons, when I can do that at home? We don't have a tree-house in our backyard."

I nod. "That's fair. Mind you, this treehouse isn't what it used to be. It had a roof and a disco ball at one point."

"That is so cool." Her eyes widen. "What else did it have?"

I look over the fence again. "Danny's probably worried about you."

She adjusts, pushing her legs out behind her and lying on her stomach so she's hidden by the walls. "He's slow at making sandwiches. I've got time."

I study the girl for a few seconds. She looks like her mother, with light-brown curls and freckles on her cheeks. She's all knees and elbows, though, and tall for her age. She carries herself like she's desperate to grow into her own body.

"You know I have to return you to Danny, right?"

Her mouth pulls into a frown. "Not yet, please."

"If you disappear, he'll never get another babysitting gig."

I smile at the crease that appears between her eyebrows, but she doesn't have time to respond before her name is being shouted from the neighboring house. I look up to see Danny hurrying out into the yard.

"Gem!" He calls out again and I wave to get his attention. He notices and I point at the spot beside me. Gemma is huddled into a ball with her head down.

"Did he see me?" she whispers.

"Yes, for sure. You might need to find a better hiding place."

We watch as Danny strides across the yard, pushes through the loose palings and comes around to the treehouse.

"Gem," he says sternly, and it's all she needs to get to her feet.

"Sorry, I have to go." She groans. "But I liked talking to you, Kit."

"I liked talking to you too, Gemma."

Danny reaches out to help her down the ladder. "Come on, Gem. Uncle Fletch is coming over soon and he's got ice cream."

"That's why Uncle Fletch is my favorite." Gemma winks, and the second her feet hit the ground, she takes off through the trapdoor and back into the Larson house. I stand up and brush any dirt off my jeans before climbing down the ladder.

"You alright?" Danny says, in a tone that's more a grunt than a greeting.

"Yeah, why?"

"I don't know. You're just sitting in the treehouse by yourself."

"It's peaceful." I shrug. "And I was sitting with Gemma."

"Gemma doesn't make things peaceful."

"She's entertaining though," I say with a knowing smirk.

We stand in silence for a few seconds and Danny makes no move to leave. He just stands there, hands in pockets, waiting for something to happen. I don't know what to do or what I want to happen. The opportunity for a heartfelt reunion has passed after he practically ignored me last night.

"How long are you in Seattle for?" I ask.

He shrugs. "No idea."

He may have grown his hair and filled out but he's still a man of few words. I always loved that about him. I especially loved the little crease between his eyebrows that let me know he was rehearsing what he wanted to say in his head. It was to make sure he got it right and it made me value his words so much more.

"So your parents are selling the house?"

"Yeah. We're going to miss all those block parties."

"No you're not, Mrs. Hastings' potato salad isn't edible."

I grin at the accuracy of the statement before we fall into silence again. I want to talk about hockey and what his plans are now that he isn't playing professionally. He should be utilizing every contact he's ever made to find a way to stay involved in the game. The old Danny wouldn't fold, but he isn't the old Danny anymore.

"I heard about the divorce, too," Danny lowers his voice. "I'm sorry."

"Thanks," is all I can muster in response.

A deep crease forms between his eyebrows and he rubs his hands together

"How's your knee?" I ask.

He looks at his right knee and extends his leg as much as he can. "Fine."

I've read the articles and had a lengthy discussion with Danny's mother about the two knee reconstructions he went through. The first one almost guaranteed his career was over. The second one made it a certainty.

I remember watching the game on TV. Seven minutes into the season opener against Vancouver, he hit the boards so hard the sound of it made me sick. When he got up and put weight on his knee the look on his face killed me. His eyes were so wide and the veins in his neck were visibly protruding. It wasn't pain; it was panic. Panic that everything he'd worked for his entire life was in jeopardy.

I called him eight times in the weeks that followed the Vancouver game. All unanswered and unreturned. I just wanted to know that he was okay. I guess he didn't want me to know anything. By the end of the season, they released him from his contract due to injury and still he didn't contact me.

I open my mouth, poised to ask why he came back when he has a life in New York and why, after all this time, talking to me seems like the last thing he wants to do.

"Dan!" Fletcher's head appears over the fence. "Oh, hey Kit."

"Hey." I give Fletcher a wave.

"Dan, do you want ice cream?"

Danny nods at his older brother before turning back to face me. "I'll see you later."

"Yeah," I say as I tuck my hands in the back pockets of my jeans. "See ya."

I watch as Danny crosses the lawn toward the Larson home, and with every step he takes I feel emptier.

I wish he'd climbed up the ladder and sat with me. Even if we sat in silence.

CHAPTER SIX

I n the day leading up to Hallie and Fletcher's wedding reception, Bea is at the salon having her roots retouched, because heaven forbid the world know her hair is naturally black like her siblings', and not caramel blonde.

My prep for the wedding is more logistics based. I've Googled the address, street-viewed it and identified a number of appropriate parking locations. Bea said it won't be a huge gathering, but we have differing opinions on what "huge" constitutes. In light of this, I've chosen sensible shoes with a low heel in case we have to go with parking option F, which is a four-block walk from the house.

I'm committed to parking option A, and on the drive over I explain all the options to my twin. She's unfocused and her thirty-eight-dollar concealer isn't hiding the bags under her eyes. She was up all night. I could hear her rustling around in the kitchen then rustling around in the bathroom. She's been distant since Jamie left. More than once I've caught her staring off into space while she waits for her phone to ring. I understand the feeling. When Danny moved away, I used to wander the house aimlessly, knowing I had something to do, but never able to remember what it was. When I noticed Bea was staring at her phone, I bought two clocks and hung them on the wall in the living room, one showing our time and one showing Jamie's. Bea loves it. I even called Jamie and he assured me he's added Seattle to the world clock on his phone so he knows when to call her.

"Well parking option A and B aren't happening so we're going with C," I explain as I pull the car into a vacant space seven houses down. Seven houses might not sound like much, but Bea didn't take my advice on suggested footwear and our trek to the house is slow and wobbly. By the time we reach the front door, Bea's face is pale, but she forces a smile as Judy and William Larson welcome us in.

"I'll be back," she whispers before disappearing down a long hallway, likely looking for a bathroom. Every time I try to talk to her about the divorce, she goes pale and has to excuse herself. High amounts of stress have always made her sick.

"Is she crook or something?"

I look up to see a tall man with blond hair has strolled in from the party out back, beer in hand and a concerned look on his face.

I tilt my head. "Crook?"

"You know. Crook as in sick. Looks like she's about to chunder." His Australian accent is thick and his explanation hasn't cleared anything up. Judging by Judy's smile she has absolutely no idea what he's saying either.

"Hey, Kit." Hallie strolls into the entryway dressed in a

simple long-sleeved gown with a boat neckline. Her dark hair falls in waves down her back and she has her usual rosy glow. "I see you've met Wes."

Wes holds out his hand. "Nice to meet ya."

I give his hand a shake as my phone vibrates in my other hand. It's a text from Mom letting me know she's already here. Dad, for obvious reasons, has decided to forego the event and I didn't miss the disappointment in Mom's eyes when she told Judy a few days ago. Mom is never one to RSVP late, so it was clear she was holding out hope Dad would come around.

"Your dress is stunning, Hallie," I say.

Hallie steps back to give me a look at the dress and grins as she buries her hands into the folds of thick, white fabric at her sides.

"It has pockets." She demonstrates this by pulling out a small bracelet made of blue and yellow beads.

They got married last week in a small ceremony in Fairbanks. It was family only and even though Judy insisted on some kind of reception, Hallie looks thrilled to give her wedding dress another outing.

Hallie and I are still discussing the functionality of pockets when Bea returns from the bathroom with a little more color in her cheeks. She introduces herself to Wes, hugs Hallie and is also made aware of the wedding dress pocket situation. We're then ushered to the backyard which has been lit up with string lights crisscrossing overhead.

Bea claps her hands in delight. "Kit, look! They look like stars." It's the happiest she's looked all day, and I can tell she's adding them to her mental Pinterest board.

Bea and I find Fletcher and offer our congratulations before we're intercepted by Miles.

"Have you seen Spence or Eve?" he asks as he pulls at the tie Judy made him wear. Bea swoops in and fixes it but the second she steps back, he loosens it again.

"Miles. Can you just leave it?" Bea scolds, but Miles isn't one to back down.

While they're arguing over the tie, I catch a glimpse of Spencer's shiny chestnut hair moving through the crowd.

"Spence." I wave my arm and she moves toward us. She takes the wine glass Miles offers and he uses his now free hands to remove the tie completely.

"Hey, girls." Spencer grins. "How are we tonight?"

"Bea's already vomited," I explain, and Bea widens her eyes.

Miles laughs. "For real?"

A little crease appears on Spencer's forehead when she looks at my sister. "Do you want some water?"

Bea waves off the offer. "I'm fine. It's just an upset stomach. I need to eat something."

Miles directs her attention to a passing waiter, and they both trail after him, still arguing over the tie. I shake my head and exhale as I look back to Spencer.

"Have you heard from Alex?" she asks.

"Yeah, he called yesterday to see how we're all going. I think he feels bad about leaving right after Mom and Dad announced the divorce," I say.

"Yeah." She takes a sip of her wine. "I can't imagine how tough this is for all of you. Eve is refusing to talk about it."

She is? Even with Spencer?

I've tried to broach the subject with my older sister a couple of times, but it never gains any traction. She's not speaking to Mom at all, and even Bea barely gets a reply. I assumed she'd be confiding in Spencer.

"I'll get Alex to call Eve. He'll be able to help." I try to play off the divided state of our family.

Spencer fiddles with the stem of her wine glass. "Eve isn't coming tonight because your mom is here."

"That's a bit childish isn't it?"

Spencer doesn't get the chance to answer because Miles has returned with a fistful of canapés. They're so squished, I can't work out what they are, but it doesn't stop Spencer from taking the offering. Bea reports back with her own spread of food, though she had the forethought to get a plate.

"God, this house is incredible. It must be worth a bundle," Bea says through a bite of tomato tartlet.

"Yeah, we don't talk about that," Miles says. "Mom's been trying to work it out, but Fletch has been cagey about it. Something to do with Hal not wanting to flash her dad's money."

I hang around with Miles for a little while and field some questions about refinancing the loan he has on the bar before excusing myself to find Mom. She's seated at one of the corner tables and for the next twenty minutes I try to make conversation while she stares vacantly at her Tom Collins. When the speeches are over, she excuses herself to use the restroom and misses the part where Hallie and Fletcher briefly dance to a Cat Stevens song.

She still isn't back when the guests inundate the removable wooden dance floor with drinks in their hands. Bea is all too thrilled to join Leah in dancing to late nineties pop songs, so I take the opportunity to slink off and find a little silence to recharge my social battery.

I enter the ground floor of the house, navigating the cavernous hallways, living spaces and a massive library before I find a spare bedroom.

The darkness is like a warm hug, and with the noise of the party dulled, I'm able to relax.

"Trying to escape?" a deep voice rumbles.

My hand flies to the wall and I flick on the light to see Danny seated on the end of a king-sized bed, his face crumpled by the sudden brightness.

"Fuck, you scared me." I clutch my chest. "What are you doing in here?"

"Enjoying the quiet."

"Want me to get Gemma?" I quip as I give the room another cursory glance. The space is as large as my kitchen, dining, and living rooms combined, and decorated to match the ultra-modern aesthetic of the rest of the house. A cluster of empty vases of varying heights sit on the sleek dresser and the color palette is capped at three shades. Danny hasn't settled in, though. His clothes are folded in a suitcase on the floor of the walk-in closet.

"Not interested in partying?" he asks as he shifts on the bed to allow ample sitting space for me.

"Mom is struggling to celebrate a wedding. It's all about divorce these days."

"Fair," he says as he crosses to the dresser to collect his cell phone and a set of headphones. He plugs them into the phone as he sits back on the bed.

I fold my hands in my lap as Danny taps the phone screen before offering one of the white, plastic headphones. He used to do this all the time. When we weren't firing pucks at a fence, we were listening to music.

Now I'm confused by the gesture. Is he going to completely ignore the fact he completely ignored *me* for the better part of two years?

"I'll keep the volume low," he assures me.

I take the offering, twisting it into my ear as a gentle melody comes through. Acoustic guitar followed by a crisp yet soothing male voice. He sings about a broken heart, the taste of cigarettes and lies.

Danny smiles at me and I've forgotten how much I adore it.

We listen to several songs by the same artist. It releases the build-up of tension that's slowly been twisting me into knots for the last few weeks, and when the playlist ends, I pluck the headphone from my ear and hand it back.

"Why did you stop talking to me?"

My palms are sweating and his face flashes with a look of dread. He knew I was going to ask and that's why he's been keeping his distance. That's why he's hiding in this room and why he had me listen to music.

He's saved from answering when Wes steps into the room.

"Hey Kit, your sister's looking for ya. She's really under the weather and wants to bail."

It takes a second to decipher the code Wes has spoken in, but Danny's entire body relaxes when I stand to leave.

CHAPTER SEVEN

The car ride home feels infinitely longer than it is. Bea is lying on the back seat, trying to keep her stuffed mushrooms down while Mom rides a rollercoaster of matrimonial emotion.

"It was so beautiful and they're so in love," she rambles on. "But wait till it isn't all fairy lights and people making speeches about you. That's when the work begins. Suddenly you've got four kids and the most satisfying part of your week is emptying the lint trap in the dryer."

I dig my trimmed nails into the steering wheel. "Is there something you need to get off your chest, Mom?"

Bea groans loudly.

"It's important to empty the lint trap. It can cause fires, girls. Remember that." She points at Bea, who lets out another groan.

"I meant, is there something you need to get off your chest

about Dad?" I reiterate. "I already know about the lint trap. Every second Thursday I check it, because Bea never remembers."

"Couldn't even tell you where it is," Bea mumbles.

Mom immediately sobs, and I reach over to take her hand.

"It's okay. I'll show her where the lint trap is."

Mom ignores my attempt at a mood-lightening joke.

"He was the one who wanted to work on it. He begged me, you know. And I know I made mistakes. Of course I did, but he said we'd salvage it. That he'd get over it, but he didn't even try. He just clammed up, too consumed by resentment to actually deliver on what he promised."

I'm surprised to learn all it takes is a bottle of wine to get Mom to open up about the implosion of our family.

"You know he stood me up seven times for couple's therapy?" she continues. "Seven times, I had to sit opposite Dr Daphne Partridge and apologize for wasting her time."

"Dr Daphne Partridge?" I raise an eyebrow. "The relationship expert on Seattle Public Radio?"

"Yes. *Dating with Dr Daphne.*"

"Mom, I don't think she's a real marriage counselor."

"She's not," Bea moans. "Spencer wrote an article about her being a scam artist."

Mom clutches the gold chain around her neck. "She has an office downtown. I've seen her diploma on the wall."

"All fake." Bea pulls herself up and hands Mom her phone. "Here's Spencer's article."

Mom squints at the brightness of the screen and reads. "*Dr of Deception: The Daphne Partridge Story.*"

I flick the indicator and turn onto our street. Logistically speaking, it would have made more sense to drop Mom off first, but Bea is green and I'm not willing to risk my upholstery for any longer than necessary.

"Oh my goodness." Mom gasps. "She ran the same scam in Phoenix under the name Dr Nancy Drew."

"Didn't overexert herself with that alias, did she?" I deadpan. In the rear-view mirror Bea smirks for a second before her face falls again.

Mom hands the phone back to Bea and stares absently at the dashboard. "I feel deceived."

"Look on the bright side, Mom. There's probably a big class-action lawsuit you can join. Recoup some of the money you gave her." I pat her hand.

Mom contemplates this while Bea crawls out of the car and up to the apartment. I'd scold her about eating wedding cake when she already wasn't feeling well, but she's too defeated for the lecture.

Instead, I lecture Mom on how important it is to thoroughly research health providers before giving them money. She frowns as she twists the wedding ring on her finger.

"I doubt a professional could save my marriage, anyway," she whispers as I pull up in front of the house.

Dad's car is in the driveway with the trunk open, and Eve is dragging a suitcase over the threshold.

"What's going on?" I slide out of the car and Mom looks on with a blank expression.

"I don't know." Her voice shakes.

"Evie?" I call out as my sister hoists the suitcase into the back of Dad's car. "What are you doing?"

"Moving Dad out. Being here isn't good for him."

"Evelyn, please." Mom takes the suitcase out of the trunk and places it back on the driveway. "I need to talk to your father."

"I don't want to talk to you," Dad says as he steps out of the house with a second suitcase in his hand. Eve moves in between him and Mom.

"Eve, let them talk." I sigh as Mom steps around her.

Eve's nostrils flare. "You haven't told the twins what's going on, have you?"

Mom's eyes go wide. "Please don't."

"That's enough!" Dad's voice booms across the front lawn and we all fall silent. "Girls, go inside."

Eve looks hesitant before she strides back into the house. I follow and step around her to watch what's unfolding through the dining-room window.

"What's going on?" I ask as she sits at the table. Her arms are folded and her expression is so prickly it looks painful.

"Ask your mother," she snaps as she pulls out her phone. I look back to the driveway. Mom has her arms wrapped around herself as she pleads with Dad. He stands opposite, passive, hands by his sides, not a hint of emotion in his body language.

"Tell me what's happening, Eve."

"No. She needs to take responsibility for what she's done. She should have to look you and Bea in the eye and say the words."

Eve's eyes are glistening, but she looks at me with conviction.

"Where's Dad going?" I ask.

"I don't know. But anywhere is better than here."

My stomach hardens like a stone as I watch my parents on

the driveway beside the large FOR SALE sign. Mom is sobbing and Dad won't look at her.

He can't leave. It's too final. Once he's gone, it'll be easy to stay gone.

"We have to stop him." I hurry toward the door, but Eve reaches out and takes my arm.

"No, we don't. He deserves better." Her tone is venomous.

I look at my sister, her large eyes not conveying her tone. She's scared like the rest of us. She's just too proud to admit it.

"There are two sides to every story." I yank my arm from her grip.

I was a high school debate team champion. There are three boxes at the top of the stairs packed with trophies to prove it, but that's the best I can come up with.

"Sure, there are two sides. Mom's lies and the truth."

Anger rolls off Eve in waves as she strides out of the house. She and Dad climb into the car and Mom does nothing to stop it. She isn't sobbing anymore. She's completely still with her arms hanging at her sides.

It takes a few minutes, but I coax her back into the house. She's shaking like a leaf and as she leans against the kitchen counter, a torrent of questions bubble up in my throat. I settle for the most obvious.

"Mom, why is Eve so angry with you?"

Mom stares at the marble countertop for a moment. "Because she doesn't understand."

For another hour, Mom mumbles to herself as she wanders the house, ever so slightly moving various ornaments and cushions. I wait on the couch, hands folded and staring at the pristine surface of the coffee table. She'll talk eventually. She has to.

When she scrubs the sink for a second time, I genuinely believe she's forgotten I'm here and have the sad realization that we're done for tonight. She isn't going to process anything, so I make my presence known with a gentle hand on her shoulder and guide her up to bed. Her eyes are bloodshot and she's so exhausted it takes less than a minute for her to fall asleep.

I wish Alex was here. Not because he's useful in a crisis, but with Bea sick and Eve in a blind rage, I need someone who understands all of this.

"How bad is it?" Alex answers on the first ring.

"Really bad," I whisper into the darkness of our backyard from my perch in the treehouse. The neighborhood is quiet and the Larson house is dark and empty. "Dad moved out tonight."

"Okay." Alex's voice is calm and even. "I'm here and I've got time to talk."

He probably doesn't, but he knows there's nothing else he can realistically do.

"It's all falling apart now, Alex." I try to steady my own voice. "And there's so much more going on, but no one is telling me anything."

"I understand," he says. "I'm sorry I'm not there to help you through this."

That's his guilt rearing its ugly head. I saw a text Bea sent him, begging him to come home while we all work this out. I wish she hadn't done that. All it achieved was applying a massive amount of pressure.

"Talk to me, Kit."

I swallow past the lump in my throat and shift my weight on the decking boards.

"Eve said all of this is Mom's fault."

"What does she think Mom did?"

"I don't know. Eve wouldn't tell me. She said that's Mom's responsibility."

Alex sighs. "Eve and Mom have never seen eye to eye on anything. I'm sure it's not that bad."

"What if this is Mom's fault?" I hold my stomach. "I'm trying to help her but what if she did something really bad."

Every muscle in my body tightens at the thought. Mom wouldn't do anything to hurt Dad. She isn't that kind of person at her core.

"I'm still really upset about losing the house, too," I say.

Alex is silent for a moment and a rustling down the line suggests he's shifting to a more comfortable position. "Why is it important that we still have the house?"

My eyes fill with tears, but I lean my head back to stop them from falling.

"Because you already left. When you come back, where will you come back to?"

Where will any of us come back to? Where will we celebrate Christmas? This house is a tangible collection of memories. The chipped tile on the bathroom floor from where Bea dropped the bottle of perfume she spent two months saving for. Or the faint scorch marks behind the stove when Dad tried to cook dinner while Mom was recovering from her appendectomy. Dad lost an eyebrow and I've never seen Mom laugh so hard. It was probably the pain meds.

Alex exhales, and I can hear the chatter of his bandmates in the background.

"As much as I hate to say it. Seattle isn't home anymore, and the house is just a house. It holds a lot of memories, but you hold them too. They aren't going anywhere."

I take a deep, rattling breath. "None of this makes sense to me, Alex."

"That's because you're all logic and none of this is logical."

He's right. None of this is logical, and after witnessing Mom and Dad's fight on the lawn tonight, this new reality is even more foreign. They've never behaved that way toward each other.

"Can you talk to Eve?" I ask. "She's being really hard on Mom and it's not helping."

"I'll talk to her. If she'll listen."

She won't but I feel better knowing that Alex will do what he can to help. I wipe the tears off my cheek and shake my shoulders to reset.

"Anyway. How's New York? And the album."

Alex takes a beat before he responds. "It's fine. It's good. I'm working on it."

He sounds agitated, like the question has caught him off guard. I've worried about my brother every day since he moved to LA. I don't know if it was the fame, the lifestyle, or the people he surrounded himself with, but it was a hard transition. He overindulged in certain vices and after two stints at an addiction recovery facility he is doing much better. That city still feels dangerous though and when he said he'd be spending time with his band in New York to work on the album we were all relieved.

Someone calls Alex's name, and he covers the mouthpiece, muffling the response.

"Kit, I'm sorry, but I have to go."

"Don't apologize," I assure him. "I shouldn't bother you when you're working."

"Bother me anytime." He says before the call disconnects.

CHAPTER EIGHT

Two days after the wedding, no one has heard from Dad. Eve isn't answering my calls and Mom is refusing to leave the house. Between the family tension, Jamie being away and a sudden downturn of new clients at work, Bea's stress levels have reached such a high, she's bedridden.

Now I'm caring for Bea, making sure Mom eats and trying to locate Dad. I'm a hairsbreadth from snapping, so when I return to work on Monday my tolerance for people is at basement level. Not ideal when I have to spend all day at Pacific Northwest Savings and Loan, and client #834621, also known as Patricia Bennett, is narrowing her eyes at me from across my impractically small desk.

The blood has drained from her knuckles and her nails are leaving impressions on the leather of her purse. I've explained why the bank denied her loan application—but she is looking at me like I've robbed her blind and spat in her cereal.

Patricia and her husband have applied for a mortgage. Her

husband works at a deli counter and Patricia prefers volunteering and hosting a true crime enthusiast group on Facebook, so the hours she works at the accounting firm aren't enough to make them desirable candidates for a $950,000 mortgage. I've done my job and I can't change the outcome.

Patricia grinds her teeth. "This has nothing to do with our financial situation. You made up your mind about us the second we walked in here."

It's actually the opposite. Her manicure is fresh and her professionally lightened hair is immaculate down to the root. Her purse is designer and so are her shoes. The issue is they spend their minimal income on the appearance of an affluent lifestyle.

"I assure you, Mrs. Bennett, I have made no judgments about you as a person."

Pressure builds behind my eyes because this is the third mortgage application I've rejected today, and none of the reactions have been easy to deal with. Though I appreciate Patricia isn't crying like Miss Dennings. I'm not prepared to deal with unpredictable emotional outbursts and I don't understand what a sick cat has to do with her desire to buy an overpriced apartment two streets back from the waterfront.

Patricia scoffs. "I'd like to speak with another loan officer. You're not equipped to handle our account."

I'm more than equipped and honestly, we don't need a complex computer system to analyze these accounts. They have taken out credit cards to pay for expensive restaurant meals and have deferred several payments on their BMW. Patricia frequents a boutique in downtown Seattle, and her husband has several charges for website subscriptions that I doubt Patricia would like to know about.

"I'm sorry you feel that way, but you'll get the same outcome regardless of who processes the application." My palms are flat on the desk. "You're welcome to reapply, but I would suggest a change in spending habits and an increase in income before you do. That way, when you reapply, you'll have a higher probability of being approved for the loan. We recently launched a free budgeting service for our existing customers. We can analyze your finances to see where you can reduce personal spending."

Patricia's hand moves to her decolletage, pressing the gold chain into the pale silk of her blouse.

"You are incredibly rude," she looks at the nameplate on my desk, "Katherine Reilly. There's nothing wrong with our spending."

I glance over at my computer. The screen displays the Bennetts' account and in the three seconds I stare at it I can see five charges deemed frivolous. I turn the screen to face her, trying to hide my irritation.

"Mrs. Bennett, as you can see, there are charges for restaurants, online cosmetic companies, and designer clothing stores. Mr. Bennett's card has also recorded sizable cash withdrawals at gentlemen's clubs in the Seattle area, and you've missed payments on all eight of your credit cards."

Patricia looks at her husband, then back at the hard evidence of her poor choices glowing on my computer screen. I feel a rush of satisfaction. Her denial and excuses hold no weight. I turn the screen back to face me and swallow against the clawing sensation in my throat. The rush is gone, and the annoyance hits me again like a tidal wave. There's nothing more anger-inducing than someone denying the obvious truth. It's like nails on a chalkboard.

"I'm not trying to be rude. We've rejected your application and I've explained why as best I can," I try to remain calm but Patricia is hell bent on winding up again.

"This is fun for you, isn't it?" She hisses. "Do you enjoy your little power trips? Cutting people down when all they're doing is trying to achieve their dream."

"Then I suggest you get a more achievable dream."

Her cheeks redden. "You rude bitch."

The sensation of rational thought leaving my body is a momentary high.

"I am not a bitch. I'm doing my job. If anything, you're a bitch."

The come down from the high is instant and as Patricia's watery eyes widen, I hear the tell-tale swish of polyester alerting me to the arrival of the bank manager, Brian French. His lip is quivering and beads of sweat form on his forehead, like he's watching a horror movie scene unfold. I wish he'd caught the start of the conversation. That would make things far less incriminating for me.

Patricia stands from her chair, bag clasped in her hands. "Roger, we're leaving."

Mr. Bennett pulls himself up and casts me an irritated glance. He's in for an uncomfortable car ride home, and that knowledge brings me joy.

Brian French steps into my office and gathers the loan application from my desk. He escorts Mr. and Mrs. Bennett over to one of my colleagues, continuously muttering apologies on my behalf. He shouldn't waste his breath. We both know how it's going to play out. In less than twenty-four hours, the Bennetts' second mortgage application will fail. A further waste of bank resources.

"Katherine." Brian rushes back to my office and closes the door. "What the hell was that? Did you really call a customer a bitch?" He lowers his voice as though he'll be struck down for saying the word.

"They don't meet the bank's lending criteria and apparently that makes me a bitch."

"So you turned it into a slinging match?" Brian's eyebrows chase his receding hairline. "Do you not see how inappropriate that is?"

This is the most forceful I've ever seen Brian. It makes him appear less bug-eyed and clueless.

"She called me a bitch. I was pointing out that calling me a bitch was rude and inaccurate, as she was the one that was behaving like a bitch."

"Stop saying bitch."

"But that's the word she used."

Brian pinches his nose and I worry he's on the verge of tears. "I know, I know, but that doesn't mean you get to say it back to her."

I fold my hands on my lap and look down at my desk, feigning remorse. In the four years I've worked here, Brian has always been nice to me and frequently compliments my hard work. On multiple occasions, he's called me a model employee, but I'm not myself at the moment.

"Katherine, I'm sorry." Brian sits in the chair that's still warm from Mrs. Bennett.

"What are you sorry for?" I raise a brow at him.

Brian shifts his weight and drags his hands down his thighs, leaving sweat patches on the beige fabric. "You can't speak to customers that way."

It's happening. I'm about to be fired. This is my first reprimand in all my time here. Don't I get two verbal warnings before adding a written warning to my personal file? Unless Brian categorizes this as gross misconduct?

"You're a wonderful employee, but customer service is an important part of this job and I can't turn a blind eye to this."

Good on Brian for finally growing a pair, but fuck, I'm definitely getting fired.

What would Eve do in this situation? She'd tell him she isn't fired and she'll see him tomorrow. It would probably work on Brian, considering how much he's sweating, but I'm not confident enough to carry that with any conviction. Instead, I think of Bea, her kind soul and her openness. I should be honest for a change, and hope Brian appreciates it.

"I shouldn't have spoken to Mrs. Bennett that way." I look Brian in the eye. "I'm just dealing with a lot of personal stuff right now."

Brian's brow furrows. "What do you mean?"

Yuck. I didn't think this through, and now the thought of divulging personal information to Brian makes me uncomfortable. I'm not sure what I'm more frightened of, judgment or pity.

"My parents are getting divorced and selling our family home. My sister isn't talking to any of us because she thinks we're all siding with Mom. I can't even find my dad. My brother is away, so he can't help, and my other sister is so sick she can't get out of bed. I'm holding down the fort here, Brian, and to be honest, it's killing me."

The words come out of my mouth in a garbled rush and my cheeks burn with embarrassment.

The mottled tone of Brian's skin gets pinker. "Right. Okay."

"Sorry," I say. "But you asked."

Brian rubs the balding spot on the crown of his head. "Maybe you should take some time off? Our three new staff members are finishing their training next week, and Janine can cover your workload until then."

Brian's hands continue to rub sweaty circles on his pant legs as he mentally assures himself that my absence can be managed.

"How long will I be on leave?" The pitch of my voice changes and I clear my throat to correct it.

Brian looks around the gray-toned interior of the bank. His brown eyes shift from one cubicle to another. "I'll need you back by mid-July."

"That's months away."

I wasn't expecting such leniency but considering I haven't had a decent vacation since I started working here, I won't rebuff the offer.

"It will be unpaid, of course, and you'll have to be back when Janine goes on maternity leave."

I stumble over my words. "Thank you. I really appreciate it, Brian."

"Right then. Good luck with everything." Brian follows this with a curt nod and a swift departure.

CHAPTER NINE

Without a job, my morning is more productive than
ever. I go for a five-mile run along the waterfront,
make eggs for breakfast, convince Bea to eat them before she
drags herself to a meeting and I get Mom to the grocery store.
Sure, she browses two aisles, purchases a case of red wine and
goes back to the couch, but at least she got some fresh air on
the walk to the car and back.

By lunch, I'm back home, drafting an email to Mrs. Schaffer, who runs the front desk at the ice rink Danny and I lived at
when we were kids. I volunteer there occasionally, and with
this leave, I can help her out with the skate class schedule like I
promised months ago.

"Kit," Bea calls out as she enters our apartment. "Are you
here?"

"Yes," I respond as she rounds the corner of the entryway
and drops her keys on the kitchen island.

She's pulled her hair back in a severe bun and paired an

oversized white button-down with high-waisted jeans. From the neck down, she's her usual professional self, but even makeup can't hide what this stress is doing to her body. I made her promise to come home immediately after her meeting and I've got fresh pajamas and two bottles of water waiting in her bedroom.

When her meeting wrapped up, I sent a text to let her know about my forced leave. I wanted to tell her last night, but whenever something bad happens to me, her face crumples with sympathy, and I feel compelled to match that level of emotional intensity. I've had a good morning, so texting meant she could get all the crumple-face out of her system before we're together again.

"Talk or just sit?" She's out of breath and her eyes are heavy as she hovers in the middle of the living room. I've dodged crumple-face, but she looks worse than before. She's holding a dining chair for support.

"Go to bed," I instruct as she shuffles over and drops onto the couch beside me.

"Not yet. I want to know how you're feeling about this leave thing."

"I'm fine. It's weird not having somewhere to go, but I like having a break from customers."

Bea slouches back into the cushions and closes her eyes. Her voice becomes breathy, like she's finished a marathon. "Maybe you can explore other options?"

"Like what?" I wander to the freezer, retrieve a bag of frozen peas, and place it on her forehead.

"You don't have to be a loan officer, Kit."

"Yeah, I know. But I'm good at that job."

"You haven't tried anything else." Bea's mouth turns down at one corner. The expression she always makes when I've done something predictable.

"I haven't needed to. I studied finance at college and now I'm working at a bank. It's a stable career," I assure her. "This is just some time off to sort through everything else that's going on."

The sigh she lets out is dramatic. "Stability doesn't make it enjoyable. You could take some extra time and find something you're passionate about. You've got savings."

I do. Since my first job at the movie theater, I've divided my paycheck into three categories: bills, savings, and other living expenses. Now, more than ever, I'm glad I stuck to this strategy.

"I emailed Mrs. Schaffer before you got here. I'm going to help her at the rink a bit more."

Bea pulls her hair from its bun. It falls around her shoulders in a wave, but the indentation from the hair band makes her look disheveled.

"You should take Danny, too. He might like to visit his old stomping ground." She yawns and her lids partially close of their own accord. I really don't want to talk about Danny.

"Time for bed." I slap her gently on the thigh. "Jamie's flight lands in six hours and we need you to feel better."

———

At six o'clock I make the trip to SeaTac to pick up Jamie. He's only been gone two weeks, but it feels like months.

"I don't know what's wrong with her," I tell him as I take

the downtown exit. "I've never seen her this sick. She said the doctor told her it's food allergies, but it's definitely stress."

"I'm surprised you got her to the doctor."

He's not wrong. Bea is notoriously terrified of doctors. On our eighth-grade field trip to the Pacific Science Center, she lied about her appendix and it nearly ruptured.

Upon our arrival home, Bea has showered and looks a lot more human. I busy myself making dinner, desperately to avoid any form of eye contact with what's happening on the couch. There's lots of murmuring and hands moving around, which continues until there's food on the table and I have to clear my throat dramatically to get their attention.

"This looks great," Jamie says as we sit down to a stomach-friendly meal of grilled chicken and plain rice.

"Thanks, Jamie," I reply, but he and Bea are already murmuring about how much they missed each other. I can't explain the irrational jealousy that takes hold when I look at them. I wanted Danny to miss me like that.

"I'm going to cross everything off that list!" I announce as my fork hits my plate with a clatter.

"List?" Jamie looks puzzled.

Bea takes a second to explain, then Jamie goes off on a tangent, wishing he'd met Bea when they were younger. They would have been high school sweethearts, apparently. I wrangle their attention with a few snaps of my fingers.

"What are you going to start with?" Bea asks.

I hurry to my room, grab the tattered list off my night-stand and return to my seat. "Host a dinner party. It's first on the list and the easiest."

Jamie takes the list and skims it.

"Are you sure you don't want to get a tattoo?" He grins and I snatch the paper back, roll it up, and slap him on the arm with it.

"This is going to be fun." Bea squeals. It's nice to see some color return to her cheeks. "We can help you with the food and you can host it at Jamie's place."

"Hold on a minute, love. Do I get a say?" Jamie interjects.

Bea shrugs like her hands are tied. "I'm afraid not because we can't host it here. There isn't enough space."

Jamie grumbles and Bea slips off her chair and flaps her hand at him, signifying that he needs to push his chair back. He observes the wordless request and Bea settles on his lap.

"I appreciate you helping my sister with her project." She leans down and kisses Jamie on the cheek.

"I can't say no to you." He stares at Bea for a lot longer than necessary. "I love you so bloody much."

They rub the tips of their noses together, and I clear my throat. Again.

"Yes, Jamie. Thank you for offering help of your own volition."

"Well, I'd hardly say—"

"So nice of you." I smile.

For the rest of dinner, Bea and I plan the menu for the dinner party. I've always loved cooking; it's a list of ingredients with step-by-step instructions and an almost guaranteed outcome. Glorious.

"Duck?" Bea looks confused. "Isn't that hard to cook?"

"I've never made it before, but I'll practice before the party."

The menu conversation goes on so long Jamie falls asleep

on the couch. Bea keeps glancing over at him and from the concerned look on her face, something's going on.

"Is his grandmother okay?" I lower my voice even though the TV's on and Jamie is snoring.

"Not really," Bea says. "And the meeting with his brother didn't go well. They can't agree on anything."

I don't know much about Jamie's family. Not for lack of trying. Whenever I've asked about them he seamlessly changes the subject.

"He has to go back," I say, ensuring the inflection in my tone is not a question.

She looks back over at Jamie. "I don't want him to go."

"He'll be back, though. Won't he?"

Her shoulders lift, and her eyes shine with tears. "I don't know. I guess, at some point."

I reach over and take Bea's hand, feeling the heaviness of her heart in mine.

She wipes her eyes. "Ugh. I don't know why I'm getting so worked up over it. He's back now and we've been apart before."

It's true. Last year, Jamie went home for two months. Bea was insufferable.

"You're allowed to get upset about him leaving. I'm pretty sure it means you like him."

She looks over at Jamie on the couch. The static-y texture of the couch cushion has fluffed his usually smooth waves of dark hair, and his mouth hangs open. Every few seconds his throat makes a sound like coarse gravel being forced through a wood-chipper.

"How could I not be in love with that?" Bea giggles.

CHAPTER TEN

O ver the next week, the dinner party responses trickle in. It's all the Larson children and their spouses, because aside from Bea and Jamie, they're the only people I see semi-regularly. I invited Eve and Spencer and it broke my heart a little when Spencer RSVP'd and said she'd be attending alone.

The other guest list hurdle was Danny. I analyzed all the interactions I've had with him since he came back, trying to decide whether to invite him. The conversations we've had were as deep as a kiddie pool. It doesn't feel like we're friends anymore, because he isn't the same person he was when he left.

I guess I'm not really the same person either.

When he left, I went through phases. There were depressive episodes where the entire city felt like it had left with him. I couldn't get out of bed and everything around me, down to the lines painted on the Larsons' fence, was a dagger twisting in my heart. Then I went through the hard-partying phase and did a fantastic job pretending I was holding it together through that first year of college.

Bea picked me up after every stumble. She didn't ask questions when a stranger called her from my phone after finding me passed out on their front lawn after a college party. She helped me smuggle boys out of the house on Sunday mornings, and she didn't say a word when I asked her to come with me to the doctor because I was worried my one-night stand might end up in the picture for a lot longer than intended. That scare certainly sobered me up. When Danny stopped answering my calls, Bea was terrified. I'd lost him all over again and she couldn't handle me destroying myself for another year.

But now he's back and while we're not what we used to be, not inviting Danny would raise questions from his siblings.

"Wow, this looks amazing." Bea inspects the place settings on the long timber dining table that bisects Jamie's apartment. "Kit, are these peonies real?"

"Yep. I picked them up from the florist an hour ago. Jamie should be back with the wine in a minute, and I need you to make sure the towels in the bathroom are clean. There's some linen spray in my purse if you need it."

Bea sets to work on her task while I make little spirals out of lemon peel for the cocktails. There are three on the menu and I've stashed laminated copies of the recipes in the silverware drawer should Jamie or Bea need some guidance. The kitchen is off limits to guests, which is a challenge considering the apartment is open plan and the kitchen is the architectural focal point.

Hallie and Fletcher are the first to arrive, with Danny tagging along. He gives us a nod as he crosses the threshold and Bea ushers them over to the table so I can get back to work. Jamie also turns on the charm for our guests. He no longer appears under duress and is actively taking part.

Miles, Spencer, Leah, and Ben soon arrive, followed closely by Nolan. He's without his wife, instead accompanied by a wide-eyed Gemma in a sparkly dress.

"Hope you don't mind me bringing Gemma. The boys are sick, so Estelle's home with them."

Gemma gravitates to my side, grips the edge of the counter, and zeros in on the perfectly scored and seared duck breast.

"What's that?" She points an accusatory finger at my masterpiece in progress.

"Duck," I say.

"Yuck." Her freckled nose wrinkles.

"You haven't tried it yet."

"I don't want to. I'll have chicken nuggets instead."

"This isn't a McDonald's."

She looks me dead in the eye. "Can I see the menu, then?"

I bark out a laugh. I like this kid.

"Are you helping or hindering?" Miles places his hands on his niece's shoulders.

"Mostly hindering," I admit, and it earns me a scathing look from Gemma.

Miles steers Gemma out of the kitchen as I slide the tray of duck breasts into the oven. That's when Ben makes his way over. He asks polite questions about the food and compliments me on the savory citrus smell of the sauce bubbling on the stove. I can't field his questions while making the orange jus.

"Ben, Leah's volunteering your painting skills for Nolan's spare room," Danny says as he enters the kitchen area. "I heard it involves stripping some wallpaper, too."

"Not again," Ben groans. "I helped re-tile the guest bath. Isn't that enough?"

Danny shrugs as Ben hurries over to his wife, inserting himself into the conversation.

"Thank you for that," I say as Danny leans on the bench.

"I can keep running interference?" he offers. "Or dice something?"

He points at a bulb of garlic that doesn't need dicing of any kind. With cooking, Danny is a student of chaos, and there are a thousand ways he could destroy this dinner by helping.

"Absolutely not." I snatch the garlic and sit it on the other side of the cutting board. He watches my movement and opens his mouth in surprise.

"Okay. Just thought I'd offer." He backs away slowly and rejoins his siblings in the living room. I know I messed that up, but I don't have the capacity to engage with him right now. There is too much going on and if I look away for even a second, I could ruin this entire meal.

Bea casually strolls into the kitchen, consulting the laminated cocktail recipes like it was her purpose all along.

"Everything okay?" she whispers.

"Yeah. Why?" I look over at Danny and swallow the lump in my throat when his eyes meet mine. He's stiff, acting like he doesn't belong, even though he shares DNA with most of the room.

Gemma tugs on his sleeve, her face pinched, demanding his attention.

"You snapped at Danny over garlic," Bea points out.

"I didn't snap. There's a lot of components to this dish and he's all thumbs."

"Okay."

"We've seen each other twice since he got back. He could have spoken to me then, not waited until I have four different components of a complex dish all being prepared at once."

"That's true."

I pick up the cheese grater and savagely drag a block of Parmesan over it.

"And Mom can't bring herself to shower anymore. Eve won't answer any of my messages, and Alex is too busy to talk."

"It's a lot, I know."

I continue grating. "I can't find Dad. And if I can't find Dad, how are we supposed to fix the divorce issue? He doesn't want to talk to Mom. Who, according to Eve, is the reason their marriage ended. But, hey, if you want clarification on that, you'll have to ask Mom because Eve wants her to look us in the eye when she tells us how she fucked everything up."

My pulse is pumping so hard I can feel it in my throat. "And he should have called me back."

"Who?" Bea asks.

"Danny!"

"There it is." Bea rubs my back and I realize the entire room is watching.

I clear my throat, but Bea steps in. "Danny, could you do me a favor and head across the street to the convenience store and grab some ice cream? Jamie was supposed to get it, but he's English, so…" she trails off.

Jamie raises a brow. "What does that have to do with anything?"

"Thanks, Danny. I really appreciate it." Bea is all smiles as she glides from the kitchen, taking the guests' attention with her.

I hurry back to the stove in time to see that my orange jus has turned into a congealed mess on the bottom of the saucepan.

"Fuck."

———

An hour later, the appetizers are gone and I'm plating up the duck. It's roasted to perfection, and I remade the sauce, but the potatoes aren't as crispy as they could be. Everyone takes turns in assuring me the food is perfect, and when it's time to serve the homemade blueberry cobbler, I usher Leah out of the kitchen so she doesn't see there are now two tubs of vanilla ice cream in the freezer.

When the night finally ends, I promise myself I'm never hosting a dinner party again. It's too much pressure, and all I'm left with is an erratic heart rate and a sink full of dishes. The effort was not worth the reward. Why did I put this on the list? It seemed like something a grown-up would do and I'd wanted to be grown up so badly.

It's almost eleven and silence settles on the mess in the

kitchen. Danny is hovering at the kitchen island when Fletcher stops beside him.

"Ready to go?" Fletcher claps Danny on the shoulder. He doesn't immediately respond to his brother, instead he looks at me.

"I've got this," I say as I scrape partially chewed duck off Gemma's plate and it lands in the trash.

Danny turns his head to his brother. "Take Hal home. I'll see you back there."

Fletcher thanks me for dinner and puts his arm around Hallie as they leave.

"You can pack the dishwasher," I say to Danny.

He gets to work and I clear the remaining glassware from the table while hushed, angry voices coming from Jamie's room punctuate the entire process. Jamie got a phone call right after dessert and Bea couldn't wait until everyone left to discuss it.

I return to scrubbing the baking dish in the sink, trying not to zero in on the conversation in the next room.

"Why did you have this dinner, anyway?" Danny asks as he bumps his hip against mine. He used to do that when trying to get information out of me. It's like we've slipped back in time for a moment, and it calms me.

"When we were kids, Bea and I wrote a list of all the things we wanted to do in our lives. Hosting a dinner party was number one."

"I remember the list," he says, nudging me out of the way to take over scrubbing the dish. I don't have the upper body strength of a professional hockey player, so he puts my efforts to shame. "I don't remember what was on it, though."

He wipes a hand across his forehead to get the hair out of his eyes. His t-shirt lifts, exposing part of his stomach and a pattern of black ink.

That's new. He never said anything about getting a tattoo.

"There are all kinds of things on the list," I explain. "Conquer a fear, dance in the rain, see something from a new perspective. That kind of stuff."

I'm still thinking about the tattoo. He would have told me if he was planning on doing something like that. How long ago did it happen?

"How many things have you crossed off?"

"As of tonight, one."

"It's a start." He nods in approval. "Can I see the list?"

"I don't have it on me."

He tries to hide a look of disappointment "Another time, then."

We return to our respective duties and eventually the dishes are done and we've returned the apartment to normal.

"Thanks for your help tonight."

"I can help you with some of the stuff on that list, too," he offers, and I'm one hundred percent sure he's realized the context of my earlier outburst.

"You don't have to do that."

"I want to," he insists. "And you'll need help, since Bea will be busy."

"Busy with what?"

Danny frowns and his brow creases with confusion. "With the move to London."

CHAPTER ELEVEN

I t feels like my bones are shifting. My ribs are contracting, squeezing my heart and lungs until they're ready to burst. My built-in best friend, my sister, is leaving.

"London." I repeat the word over and over as I pace. "You're moving to London."

Bea stands and tears fill her eyes. "It's only for a year. So Jamie can be with his family."

My heart keeps skipping, and deep breaths aren't helping. With everything going on with our parents and her business, a year-long trip to London shouldn't be an option.

"What about the studio? It's coming into wedding season. You're already booked."

"Leah and I have talked. We have a few freelance photographers we can use, and I'll be able to help with the business side of things from London."

I'm silent for a long time and continue my pacing. At least

she's considered some of the logistics. I'm almost proud of her for that.

"Kit, please tell me you're okay with this. I need you to be okay with this."

Sweat beads on my forehead. It's not okay. We've never been apart for this long. I don't know what I'll do without her. Especially with Eve and Mom not speaking, Dad still missing and Alex being away. The whole family is crumbling.

"I'm in a really difficult position here," Bea whispers as the tears spill onto her cheeks.

She can't go. I need her here to help hold the family together.

Bea keeps her distance, her hands pressed flat against her thighs to stop from trembling. She is really going. If she wasn't, she would be holding me and telling me everything is fine. She isn't holding me because it's not fine.

"A whole year?"

Her eyes are wide and unblinking. "The timing is bad, I know."

I reach out, pulling her into a pleading hug. "Please, Bea."

We hold each other for far too long. Eventually her body relaxes and I close my eyes. The smell of her freesia perfume fills my nostrils and I already miss her. A year is too long.

"When are you leaving?" I ask as we break apart.

"In a few weeks."

The room falls silent save for the muffled sound of the traffic on the street below. The apartment already feels too big and our time too finite. The next few weeks will be a torturous countdown.

"I don't know what I'll do without you," I whisper as we sit on the couch.

"I don't know what I'll do without you, either." She wipes her eyes. "But this might be good for us, Kit. It gives us a chance to learn how to exist outside of each other."

I look at my hands in hers, taking in the thin, white scar on the back of my left hand. When I was seventeen, I reached into the kitchen drawer and didn't see the knife facing backward. Our parents were at work, so Bea drove me to the hospital to get stitches. She said everything was going to be fine, even though she was shaking and crying.

"I don't want to exist without you." I lay my head on her shoulder. "But I want you to be happy."

I mean it, but it doesn't make it hurt less.

———

Over the next few days, Bea takes care of Mom to give me a reprieve. I want to use the time to catch up with Dad and Eve but when I call neither of them answer. After a few more tries, I get less worried and more angry about the radio silence. I've done nothing wrong, and I haven't taken sides. For the entire afternoon it weighs on me. I pace the apartment for a while before stalking Eve's social media for clues on what she's doing. When that comes up empty, I rearrange my closet. This results in the bracket of my overstuffed shelf being ripped from the wall and I'm presented with another task to get my mind off Eve and Dad.

By dinner time, I've fixed the shelf and every item of

clothing I own is neatly folded. There is also a growing stack of winter wear for Bea to take to London. I'm curating the selection when the deadbolt on the front door clunks.

"Bea!" I call out as I hurry into the living room. "I found some cute sweaters for you to take with you. Or as Jamie would say, jumpers."

"Kit," Bea says, and I look up from the crewneck in my hand to see Danny and Bea standing in the kitchen.

"Danny?"

"Hey," he says as he tucks his hands in his pockets. He's too big for my tiny kitchen and towers over Bea, who gives his arm a gentle pat.

"Good luck," she whispers before scurrying off to her bedroom and closing the door.

"I'm sorry about the other night," he mumbles. "I thought you knew."

"Yeah," I say. "It was a shitty way to find out."

"I know. I'd been talking to Jamie and I thought if he was telling me, Bea would have told you."

Bea is obviously listening to everything because I can see her shadow under the bedroom door. "I don't really want to get into it now," I say, dropping the sweater on the arm of the occasional chair.

"Yeah. Okay." He looks at the floor and drags the toe of his boot over the join where the kitchen tile meets the carpet.

"Follow me."

I turn and walk back into my bedroom. The walls are paper thin, but it will give us a modicum of privacy—to make Danny feel comfortable, of course. I'll just telepath what's going on to Bea in real time.

I close the door behind him, and he steps over the dust and wood on the floor.

"What happened here?"

"My closet shelf collapsed, but I fixed it."

He looks into the closet, inspecting the newly attached bracket. His hands are still in his pockets and his shoulders bunch. It's like he's landed on an alien planet and isn't confident he can tolerate the atmosphere yet.

"Did you come all the way here to apologize for spilling the beans on London?" I fold my arms across my chest. "You could have texted or called. If you remember how to do that."

"I deserve that," he says. "You're right to be mad at me."

I shake my head. "Not mad. Just heartbroken and confused."

For the first time since he's been back, he really looks at me, holding my gaze. I'm not ready for it.

I want to hold him. I want to hold him for so long I'll never be able to get the smell of him from my body.

"Why did you do it?" I say. "Why did you shut me out?"

He opens his mouth, then presses his lips together.

"You left me and you said nothing would change. That we'd still be friends. And then you ghosted me."

"I know."

It's hard to scold him when he looks this beaten down already.

"I wanted to know you were okay. That's all." I take a step closer.

"I wasn't okay," he admits.

"Then you should have told me that."

"I know."

"When you left, I thought about how much it sucked that you were going to miss everything. But it was going to be fine because we'd talk every day and tell each other everything. But you stopped caring."

He steps toward me and I feel tears well in my eyes. "I didn't stop caring."

"Then why didn't you call?"

"Because I'm selfish."

"I wanted to be there for you."

Danny opens his arms wide and pulls me into him. I wrap my arms around his midsection and feel the heat that radiates off him. It spreads through my body and makes my fingers tingle. This is what I've wanted ever since I heard he was home.

"Kit." He rests his cheek on top of my head and holds me for a long time. I close my eyes, listening to his heartbeat, and prepare myself for the moment he pulls away.

"Will you let me make it up to you?" he says. "Because I've got an idea for one of the things on your list."

"Which thing?" I continue to cling to him as a crackle of nervous energy runs up my spine. He better not be talking about the tattoo.

"See something from a new perspective?" he says. "Or whatever it was."

"Yeah, that's one of them." My heart swells inside my chest that he remembered something on the list.

"Can I help with that one?"

I grin with an embarrassing level of enthusiasm. "Yes. Please. I don't know what to do for that one."

"Okay. Let's go." He pulls back, still holding my upper arms.

"Now?" I raise a brow. "Where are we going?"

"You'll find out when we get there."

CHAPTER TWELVE

I spend a solid fifteen minutes insisting Danny tell me where we're going. It's strictly for outfit reasons, but that doesn't cut it.

"What you're wearing is fine," he says, giving my leggings and faded green t-shirt a cursory glance.

He's wrong. The only thing this get-up is suitable for is scrubbing the tile grout in the bathroom.

Danny's wearing Converse and an unbuttoned red flannel with a gray t-shirt underneath—but he always wears something like that, so it's not an indicator of what occasion he's dressed for.

In the end, I throw on jeans, my dusty pink cable-knit sweater and some white sneakers.

"Finally." He exhales as I reappear from my bedroom.

"I would've been quicker if you told me where we were going," I grumble.

"You've always been slow."

"I like to be prepared."

"Slowly." He bumps my shoulder, and we continue to bicker on the walk to his car. It's another timeslip, like the one in the kitchen at the party. A tiny moment where I catch a glimpse of what we used to be, and experiencing it now, grown up as we are, makes my heart thrum.

Two minutes into the drive, I've worked out that we're headed downtown. He hasn't given me any clues, and with every innocuous turn, the list of probable destinations gets shorter. It's silent in the car, save for the gentle hum of the radio, and I give up the push for information. He's proud of himself, but when we pull up outside an upscale café, I have a sneaking suspicion about where we're headed.

"It's two blocks away," he says as he slides out of the car. I follow, falling into step beside him as we head down Cherry Street toward Columbia Center and the Sky View Observatory.

"It's not the most original idea," Danny mumbles as we climb into the elevator and move to the back to allow more guests to enter.

"I've lived here my whole life and never been to the observatory. So it is a new perspective for me."

"Check it off the list," Danny says as the elevator takes us seventy-three floors up.

We arrive on the observation deck and though I've never feared heights, I'm a little queasy when we approach the glass. Danny stands beside me, silent, hands in pockets as he looks out over the skyline. I've never found him particularly hard to read, but right now I can't even speculate on what he's thinking. There's no wrinkle in his brow, tightness in his jaw, or tells from his body language. The best I can figure is that he's enjoying the view, judging by the softness in his eyes.

"Thanks for helping with my list," I say as I retrieve my phone from my pocket and open the camera app.

"It's the least I can do."

He steps back, looking over my shoulder as I lift my phone and snap some photos of the expanse of buildings that bolster the skyline. The Space Needle stands out in the distance and, like the list intended, I've never seen it from this perspective before.

"Ready to go?" I ask after we spend an hour milling around to get our money's worth.

"Whenever you are," Danny says, and I lead the way to the elevator.

When we step inside, Danny leans against the back corner. We've exhausted his desire for conversation, and as the elevator descends, I settle in the opposite corner.

I'm about to thank him again for bringing me here when, with a sudden jerking motion, the elevator grinds to an abrupt halt and we both stumble forward.

"Shit!" Danny hisses as the lights go out and the dim emergency light in the roof panel turns on. My first thought is that Danny hates enclosed spaces. Which is Miles and Alex's fault. They locked him in a steamer trunk as a prank when he was eight and accidentally snapped the lock. I sliced my hand open with a screwdriver trying to remove the rusted hinges so we could get him out.

"It's okay. We're okay," I assure him as I cross to the

control panel and hit the call button. There's a loud buzzing sound followed by a man's muffled voice through the crackling speaker.

"Hi, there is something wrong with the elevator. We've stopped." I work hard to keep my tone even.

"Looks like a power failure," the maintenance tech says. "We'll have you out shortly."

Danny doesn't take any of this in and when I turn back to face him, he's pressed against the wall and his fingers are digging into his thighs.

"They're working on it." I rush over to him, taking his hand and helping him to a sitting position on the floor.

"We're okay?" he asks.

I nod as I sit beside him. "They'll have us out in a second. It's a really minor power issue. Nothing to worry about."

"Okay. Okay." His voice shakes, but he leans his head back against the wall and takes a few deep breaths.

After a few minutes, they haven't given us an update on the power failure situation and Danny is getting tenser. We've reached the point where deep breathing isn't cutting it and I doubt he'd be interested in looking at the photos I took from the observatory again.

"I was the one who broke your hockey stick when we were thirteen," I confess as the emergency light flickers.

His eyes open wide. "What?"

"I didn't mean to. I tripped, and it got stuck between the decking boards. I was holding the handle, and it just snapped."

"I didn't talk to Miles for weeks."

"Yeah. I asked him to take the fall because I didn't want you to be mad at me."

"Dammit, Kit. I loved that stick. It cost us the championship that year."

I slide over so our shoulders are touching. "No, it didn't. Your three best players were out because they got caught smoking weed behind the rink after training. You scored three goals and took it to a shootout."

He takes another shaking breath and closes his eyes. "I fucked my ankle, too."

"Thankfully, it was only a sprain," I remind him.

"You slept on the floor beside my bed for a week."

"Yeah, in case you needed anything. Your mom had her hands full with Nolan's wedding."

He opens his eyes again, and his head rolls to the side to look at me. "You didn't have to do that."

"I wanted to be with you."

Part of me has belonged to him since he snuck over the fence, climbed the treehouse ladder, looked at me from under his mop of blond hair and asked if I'd be his friend.

We shook hands, and my innocent little heart made a promise without understanding the gravity of it.

He takes my hand in the most natural way. It makes me wonder what would happen if one of us said what we're really thinking? Or had the guts to show it?

"I'm sorry I made things difficult for so long," he says.

I can see the sincerity in his eyes and it feels like our souls live in this quiet in-between. So much is swirling right below the surface, but our lifelong friendship keeps it at bay. Maybe I should push forward? Tell him all the things I've been afraid to tell him because preserving our friendship was the only thing that mattered.

It's my turn to take a deep breath and when I do, he says the last thing I want to hear.

"Still friends?"

His smile is apprehensive, and my battered and bruised heart is trying so damn hard to beat normally in the face of this disappointment.

"Always," I say as I rest my head on his shoulder.

We're only stuck in the elevator for another ten minutes before the power returns and it moves again. Danny almost bolts from the building and his knuckles are white as he grips the steering wheel on the drive home. I do my best to distract him with a conversation that doesn't relate to hockey or elevators.

Unfortunately, Danny steers our stilted conversation toward something I'm not interested in sharing with him. My parents' divorce.

"I didn't see that coming," Danny admits as he turns onto my street and pulls up in front of the apartment building.

"None of us did."

"Do you know what happened?"

I drag my hands down my thighs. "Nope. Mom and Dad aren't saying anything and Eve knows what's going on, but she isn't saying anything either."

"What about Alex?" he asks.

"He knows less than all of us, and I don't want to bother him while he's recording."

Danny agrees, but he seems distracted. I open my mouth to ask if he's okay as Jamie's car passes us and pulls into a space two cars up. Bea's at work, so I don't know what he's doing here or how he's going to get into the building.

"Jamie's here." I frown at the interruption. "I should go."

"Okay," Danny says as I climb out of the truck. I hesitate, hoping that he'll suggest we see each other again, but he says nothing.

I close the door and turn toward my building as Jamie approaches with a large pink box in one hand. He appears to be muttering to himself, like he's practicing lines.

"Hey, Kit," he says as I open the building door. "I hope you don't mind me stopping in. I wanted to talk to you."

He's sweating. I didn't know I was this intimidating.

"Sure. Come on up."

Jamie follows me to the apartment without saying a word. I've never seen him nervous before.

"What's in the box?" I ask as I drop my keys on the counter and shuck off my coat.

"A peace offering," he says, opening the lid to show off an assortment of brightly colored cupcakes with candy stuck to the frosting.

"Why are you giving me a peace offering?" I walk over to the couch and Jamie follows, cupcake box in hand, and places it on the coffee table.

"I assume you're mad at me," he says as he sits beside me, his hands grip his knees, then the edge of the couch cushion, then back to his knees.

"A little."

He doesn't look at me. "I'm not trying to come between you and Bea."

"But you are."

"She isn't trying to hurt you. She just wants to live her

life." He fiddles with the zipper on his jacket before his restless hands settle on his knees again.

"I never said she couldn't. We've just never really been apart before."

I've already done the research. There are several airlines that offer non-stop services to Heathrow. I can visit her anytime I want over the next year, and I remind myself of that every time I think about her leaving.

"My family and the next phase of my career are over there, and Bea understands that. We can't be apart, though. We just can't do it."

"What about Bea's family and career?"

He nods. "It wasn't an easy decision."

"But you're expecting her to press pause on her whole life to go with you."

"We don't see it that way. We made this decision together, and I don't want you to feel like she chose me over you." He runs his fingers through his hair and his breathing accelerates.

"Jamie." I put my hand on his arm. "You need to calm down. Don't get all worked up over this. I know it's not your fault, and I understand why Bea wants to go with you. This is a lot to get my head around, though, especially with what's going on with our parents."

Jamie wrings his hands. "I felt like shit when I asked her. It put her in a terrible position."

"No, it didn't. She would have gone even if you hadn't asked her. She would have just followed you to the airport."

Jamie barks a laugh. "She would, wouldn't she?"

"Yep. She might be all sweet and cute, but she knows what she wants and she'll get it."

I lean forward and take a cupcake from the box. It's bright pink and covered in rainbow sprinkles.

"And please don't bring cupcakes again," I say as my living room rug gets showered with sprinkles. "They make a mess."

He looks down at the rug and his mouth presses into a line. "Indeed. Donuts next time, then."

CHAPTER THIRTEEN

"Do you really need to take your birth certificate?" I ask as I work my way down Bea's list of things to pack.

"What if I need to prove my identity or something?" she calls back from the bedroom.

"You have a passport and a driver's license."

She pokes her head out of her room and frowns. "Okay. Take it off the list."

I put a strike through another six items without her permission. They sell shampoo in London, so she doesn't need to take three bottles with her, and her blatant disregard for luggage limits is bothering me.

"Which coat?" She steps into the living room, holding up two beige coats. "Left or right?"

"They're the same." I raise a brow.

"No, they aren't. This one has the detail on the cuffs." She holds out the left one and then switches to the right one. "And this one has this stitched panel in the back so it's more cinched at the waist."

Of course, how did I not notice the back and cuff details while they're crumpled in her fists?

"They're both great. You can't go wrong with either."

She drops her arms in a huff. "Ugh. You're worse at this than Jamie."

"Not with organizing your travel documentation." I grin as I pull out the sleek, tan document wallet I bought as a going-away present. "I've got your passport, flight confirmation, insurance information and at the back here is a fun little pocket that holds a flash drive with digital copies of everything in the wallet."

Bea's interest is clearly waning as she sags against the door frame, though she does show some enthusiasm when I show her the flash drive pocket.

I'm slipping the drive back into its spot when my phone vibrates across the table.

"You're free to go." I release my sister as I pick up the phone.

"Hey, Spence," I answer. "How are you?"

"Good, good." Her voice is hurried and coupled with the background noise, it's hard to hear her. "I found your dad."

"What?" I inadvertently shout. "Where?"

"He's staying in the apartment above Whiskey. Eve arranged it with Miles."

Bea hurries back into the living room, eyes wide.

"Thanks for letting me know, Spence. I'll be there soon."

I hang up the phone and look at my sister. "Dad's staying in the apartment above Miles's bar."

Bea gives me a resigned nod. "Of course he is. Why didn't we think of that?"

I snatch my keys off the table. "I'm going to see him."

"Should I come too?" Bea asks as she drops her beige coats over one of the dining chairs. "Is Eve there?"

Since Dad wasn't the one to tell me of his whereabouts, he's clearly skittish about seeing family members. "What if Eve is there? He might feel ambushed."

Bea thinks on it for a second. "Sure. You're probably right."

"I'll text you when I get there," I say as I hurry out of the apartment.

On the drive over, I cycle through all the things I want to say. Starting with how pissed I am that he dropped off the map after the wedding reception. He hasn't called to check on Mom, and Bea and I have done nothing that warrants being cut off. I've tried to remain impartial because when this smoke clears, I want our family to be amicable, even if it's not in one piece.

By the time I get to the bar, I'm pretty worked up. A hot flush creeps up my neck as I enter the building and see Spencer and Miles in a heated argument at the end of the bar.

"I promised Eve. She's going to cut off one of my toes now," Miles moans.

"She is not," Spencer fires back, but her expression softens when she sees me. "Kit."

"Hey, give me the key." I hold my hand out to Miles, who stares at it for too long. "Or I'll cut off your toe right now."

He grumbles as he pulls a key from his pocket and places it

on my palm. "I'd like to go one day without being threatened by one of the Reilly women."

"Today is not the day," I say as I rush out of the bar and around to the side of the building.

The apartment above Whiskey Double has had a few residents over the years. The most permanent of which was Fletcher. It's been vacant since he moved in with Hallie, and I can't believe I didn't think of it as the perfect hideout for Dad. It's pretty smart on Eve's part.

I slide the key into the external door and yank it open before hurrying up the stairs to the landing.

"Dad!" I call out, banging on the apartment door. "Dad, it's Kit."

A few moments later, the door swings open, and my disheveled-looking father stands on the threshold. He's bleary eyed and dressed in the gray pajama set Bea got him for Christmas last year.

"Kit, what's going on?" He rubs his left eye.

"Nobody knows where you've been. Mom's a fucking mess. Alex keeps asking if you're okay because you haven't answered any of his messages and Bea's about to leave for London."

I move past him and plant myself in the center of the small apartment.

"I told Eve and Miles to keep this between us," Dad groans.

"Why?" I bark. "You have a wife and children that are worried about you. You can't just leave us all behind. It's so selfish."

His unruly hair falls into his eyes. The once black strands

are graying and his beard has filled in. It's the first time I've ever seen him with this much facial hair.

"I needed a break."

"A break from what?"

"You need to leave, Kit," he says on the intake of a deep breath. "Now is not the time to hash this out."

He looks small and frail. He's not a tall man, but he had a presence. The little creases around his eyes from a lifetime of smiling now make him look tired. He's a shadow of the man he used to be.

"I'm sorry," I soften my tone. "I didn't mean to barge in like this. I've been worried about you."

"I know, but I need some time."

"You don't have to explain all this to me. But can you at least talk to Mom? None of us want to lose the house, and if the problem is fixable, can you hold off on taking such drastic action?"

He shakes his head. "It's done, Kit. We can't go back, and I'm sorry that you're stuck in the middle."

What does he mean they can't go back? Maybe Mom was right when she said he refused to work on it. His words are so resolute but he's not coping, judging by the ketchup stains on his pajama shirt.

He can't meet my eyes and it turns my gut to stone.

"Why did you leave?" I ask, wanting the truth, but still gripping to the shred of hope that my parents just grew apart.

"Please tell me the truth," I whisper.

"Kit, it's complicated, and trust me when I tell you, knowing everything won't make it easier."

I drag my palms across my cheeks, only to have more tears

appear. How do I tell him that knowing the truth will make it easier for me? Of course it's complicated. Relationships are, but what pushed this one over the edge?

"Is she okay?" he asks. "I didn't want to leave the way I did."

"She's not okay, Dad." I can't sugar-coat this. "She's barely eating. She's used all her personal days at work because she can't bring herself to leave the house."

Dad sighs, like he expected this.

"This sort of thing doesn't happen to our family," I say. "We're good. We've always been good."

"I know," he says, eyes firmly fixed on the heavily scuffed floorboards.

My heart crawls into my throat and anxiety builds, hot and painful, in my body as I drop into a chair at the small dining table. It's littered with electronics catalogs and what must be the last few print magazines in existence.

"I'm sorry I haven't been there for you," Dad says as he places his hand on my back. "But I need to sort my head out."

I turn around to look up at him. His eyes shine with tears and I pull myself up to hug him.

"We'll get through this," he says.

I stay with Dad for a long time. We don't talk much, instead we watch *Law and Order* reruns and he cracks a few jokes about how unhelpful the witnesses are at the start of each episode. When he yawns, I check my phone and see that it's after midnight. He has to start early in the morning.

"Please don't shut me out," I say. "And let Mom know you're okay."

He agrees and, at his behest, I promise not to tell Mom where he's staying.

Key in hand, I wander back to the bar, intending to apologize to Miles for my earlier threat. It's kind of him to let my dad stay in the apartment, and I'm happy that Dad's safe.

"Everything alright?" Miles raises a brow as I place the key on the bar.

"It will be...hopefully," I say. "I'm sorry about before. I was a bit on edge, but I really appreciate you helping Dad like this."

"It's no problem. He's been keeping me company on the night shifts."

I cock my chin at the bottle of vodka near Miles's left hand and look around the bar while he pours me a drink. It shows no sign of slowing for the evening.

"Here you go." Miles slides the glass toward me and refuses the ten-dollar bill I hold out.

"Please take it. It's the least I can do."

"Your money's no good here," he calls back as he rounds the end of the bar and disappears into the kitchen.

I sip my vodka and lime and listen to the off-key crooning of the heavily intoxicated karaoke singer currently wobbling around the stage. One of her eyes is closed, and she keeps pressing buttons on the screen of the karaoke machine, causing the music to skip. It forces me to down the rest of my drink in one gulp, but as I slide off the stool to leave, Danny steps inside.

He's wearing sweatpants and a black t-shirt with a plaid jacket thrown over it. His sneakers are untied, and no matter how much he runs his hand through the front section of his hair, it won't cooperate.

"What are you doing here so late?" I ask as he leans on the back of the stool I vacated.

"Miles called me."

I whip around to see Miles's face peeking around the wall that blocks the kitchen door from view of the bar. He slinks back when I frown at him.

"You drove all the way here from Fletcher's?" I say to Danny.

He blushes. "Miles told me about your dad and said you'd been up there with him for a while. I wanted to make sure you were okay."

My heart swells so suddenly that if it wasn't for my ribs caging it in, we'd have a serious problem.

"Thank you," I say, knowing he won't want me to make a big deal of the gesture. "Dad and I talked and hung out a bit. He said he needs some time but he's going to talk to Mom."

"That's good." Danny's voice is still gravelly from sleep, and he lazily drops onto the stool.

"You didn't need to drive over. I was about to leave."

He waves it off. "I'm here now. Let's sit for a minute."

I sit on the stool beside him. We're facing each other and his knees bracket mine. I reach over to pinch the leg of his sweatpants.

"Were you asleep?"

"Yes."

"Well, now I feel worse about you coming here for nothing."

He puts his hand on my knee and leans forward. The

crease between his eyebrows appears and he stares at his hand on my leg for a moment.

"Not nothing. I get to see you."

Something has shifted. I can feel it. Even if this is just him trying to make up for the last two years, it has my heart thrumming.

"Since we're here." I paint on a sweet smile. "Want to cross something else off the list?"

CHAPTER FOURTEEN

I t's hard to maintain this level of false bravado when I'm shaking so much.

"Is this the worst item on the list?" Danny asks as he hovers behind me, microphone in hand and looking like he'd rather be shark-diving with the cage door open.

"I think the tattoo is the worst. But this is a close second."

"Which song?" Miles asks as he presses a series of buttons on the karaoke machine.

"A short one," Danny mutters.

"That doesn't require much vocal range," I add.

Miles scratches his chin as he sifts through the karaoke catalog. My hands are so slicked with sweat I can barely hold the microphone.

"Push this button when you're ready." Miles points at the machine as a single spotlight draws all the attention to Danny and me. A break in the rain has driven most of the patrons to tables outside so our audience is a group of middle-aged women on a girls' night out, an elderly gentleman with wing sauce in his beard and the dregs of a bachelor party that are arguing over who's paying for the cab home. It's terrifying.

I give the microphone one sharp tap before bringing it to my lips. "Can you hear me?"

The elderly man makes a grunting noise before his head drops to the table with a thud.

"I'm Kit and this is Danny," I say into the microphone. "We're going to sing one song."

A loud whooping noise comes from the back—Miles clapping his hands. It does nothing for my confidence, in fact we now have the eyes of the bachelor party.

Danny leans in and whispers, "It doesn't need this much preamble."

With a sharp nod and the burning sensation of stomach acid rising in my throat, I press the button on the karaoke machine.

The song plays and I recognize it before the words scroll across the screen. It's a pop song with repetitive lyrics and large instrumental sections. The perfect choice. But that doesn't stop me from fumbling my way through the first verse.

My palms are still sweating, but by the second verse, I'm getting into it. The bachelor party cheers us on and the elderly man is lucid enough to clean the food out of his beard and sing along.

The song finishes and I'm enjoying myself. So much so that I don't want to get off the stage.

"Alright. Let's go," Danny says as he slides his mic into the cradle on the side of the karaoke machine.

"One more? Please?" I beg.

The bachelor party hollers, and I point at them. "See. They want more."

"More of you. Not me."

The bachelor party calls out again, and I grin. "Please. If you close your eyes and listen to the music, it's pretty fun."

I hold his gaze for a few seconds until he finally closes his eyes.

"Fine. One more and we're done."

"Thank you." I grab his mic and hand it back to him before finding another song for us to sing.

Danny regrets this immediately when a wave of new patrons arrive at the bar. It's packed, and the sudden appearance of an audience is nerve-wracking, but it meets the list item criteria of facing a fear.

Our second song is a train wreck compared to the first. We're two beats behind from the outset and Danny nearly falls off stage trying to dodge the spotlight.

"Okay, that's two songs." Danny returns the mic for a second time. "That's all you get."

My heart is thrumming as I follow Danny off the stage to a lackluster round of applause. Some new arrivals have been wanting to take the stage and a guy in a worn leather jacket grumbles and says, "Finally."

Miles drowns out the comment by whooping as we approach the bar.

"Thanks for the support." I grin as I bump the fist Miles holds out.

"Can we go home now?" Danny yawns and takes his jacket from behind the bar.

"Yeah, alright." I pat him on the back. "You earned it."

It's even more crowded now and people have gathered around the entrance. We step out, weaving our way through the bodies, with Danny leading the way. The crush of people is uncomfortable and the smell of sweat and cigarettes sours the fresh night air.

"Hey," a gruff voice calls out. "Aren't you Danny Larson?"

I scan the crowd for the source and see a broad man in a Vancouver jersey making his way toward Danny.

"I asked you a question," he calls out when Danny puts his head down. "You're number twenty-eight. Larson, hey?"

He's blocking the narrow path to the sidewalk, and Danny turns to face me. He takes my hand, searching for another route out of the maze. When he finds one, I tuck in close and we work our way through the crowd again. It's not the first time someone's heckled Danny. He took that kind of heat during every game when a play didn't go the right way.

"Did that hit fuck up your brain *and* your knee?" The heckler laughs, and as we walk away, his voice is still close. He's following us.

Danny doesn't respond and I'm glad. It's after two a.m. and I want to go home.

"Ignore it," Danny mumbles as we clear the crowd and reach the sidewalk. Still, the voice follows.

"You know we celebrate that hit, right?" he calls out.

I try to block it out, but his voice is grating. His sardonic laughter is worse. Danny is trying to herd me away, but with every burst of laughter from the guy, more fire ignites in my blood.

"He can't say that to you!"

Danny puts his arm over my shoulder. "Don't worry about it."

"I watch the clip over and over," the man carries on. "The sound of you hitting the boards is my brother's ringtone."

I spin around, duck under Danny's arm, and march toward the heckler.

"What the fuck is your problem?"

The man continues to sport the most infuriating grin I've ever seen.

"I've got no problem with you, sweetheart." He chuckles and the sound of it sends wild impulses to all my extremities.

"Kit!" Danny calls, but I ignore him and step into the heckler's space. I'm genuinely repulsed by everything about him. The smell of bourbon on his breath and the stench of the cigarette hanging from the side of his mouth.

"I asked what your problem is?" I lower my voice, hoping it sounds more menacing.

"I don't have a problem. I want to thank him for being a waste of eighteen million dollars."

"How much was your last pro hockey contract worth?"

Danny calls again from behind me. "Kit, come on."

"No. I genuinely want to know what gives him the right to talk to you this way. He doesn't know you."

"I don't need to know him, sweetheart," the guy sneers. "Because I know he ain't the greatest thing since Gretzky, like everyone said he was."

"Sorry, I missed the part where we asked for your thoughts on the subject."

He drops his cigarette on the ground and grinds it into the

pavement with the toe of his boot. "You know you're really startin' to piss me off, honey."

"How about you stop calling me honey and sweetheart and apologize for being a dick?"

"I ain't apologizing for shit. It's not my fault he fucked his career and can't handle criticism."

"Criticism implies you have something constructive to say. From what I can tell, you're just some brainless asshole who must feel so small and emasculated in life that you need to publicly shame someone for getting injured."

The color drains from the man's face as his brain slowly registers what I've said. It's gratifying that it takes so long.

"How about you back off? You crazy bitch."

I laugh. "Oh okay. So it's fine to harass Danny, but the second you get called out, you're suddenly the victim and I'm a crazy bitch."

He looks over my shoulder at Danny.

"Come and get your dog, Larson," he grunts. "She won't stop barking."

A small group of women nearby gasp in unison as I turn my head away to suck in the moderately fresh air. My skin is prickling all over. I'm angry about a hundred different things, and for some reason I'm certain that shutting this man up will fix everything. If it doesn't, then at least I tried.

So I throw my fist as hard as possible into the heckler's face.

The pain that radiates through my hand is blinding, and I let out a squeal.

"Fuck." Danny is at my side, his wide eyes on the man with blood pouring out of his nose.

"Oh shit," I groan. "I think I broke my hand."

The full attention of the crowd has settled on us and near the entrance to the bar, someone makes a whooping noise.

"You broke my fucking nose!" the man splutters as he looks down at his blood-soaked hands.

"You deserve it. You piece of shit," I bark as I take a step toward him. He stumbles back before turning around and pushing back through the crowd. I'm thankful. I can't sacrifice another hand for Danny's honor.

I turn to Danny. "Could you take me to the hospital, please?"

CHAPTER FIFTEEN

The emergency department is busy. Danny checks me in, I fill out all the forms, and then we're told to wait for the doctor. The triage nurse didn't seem concerned about me, so every time someone walks through the door with blood dripping from them, I become a lower priority.

"You need to work on your technique." Danny looks at my hand. Which is wrapped in ice and sitting gingerly in my lap.

"I wasn't that concerned about technique. I just wanted him to stop saying those things."

He lifts his shoulders in a lazy shrug. "Doesn't bother me."

"Why not? He was being cruel."

"I've played in front of crowds that boo me for the entire game."

"That's not fair. You don't go to their jobs and boo them." I adjust my hand and wince. Danny leans forward, hands out and ready to swoop in and help.

"It's fine," I assure him, and he settles back in his seat. He's still watching me though, like I lied on the pain scale when the nurse was questioning me.

I watch the swinging doors that hospital staff keep emerging from. It's been two hours now and every time someone in scrubs walks through, my chest flutters. Unfortunately, my name is yet to be called.

I adjust my hand again, because my thigh is freezing, and it triggers a jolt of pain. "Fuck. This hurts."

Danny slides off his jacket, rolls it into a ball and rests it on his leg. He then gently guides my hand to sit on top of it. "Better?"

"Thank you." I say as I breathe in the smell of recycled air and disinfectant. The elevation has helped, but I really want to go home. Danny said I should at least get an X-ray to make sure it's not broken.

"Katherine Reilly."

I look over at the swinging doors. A small woman holding a clipboard is glancing around the room.

"Here," I call out as I get a firmer grip on my icepack and stand up.

"I'll wait here," Danny says.

The doctor is smiling at me, but my good hand trembles.

"Can you come with me?" I ask.

Danny stands up, takes my good hand, and we walk toward the doctor.

It takes another hour before I'm discharged. The doctor looks at my hand and orders the X-ray to rule out a fracture, and both the doctor and radiologist enjoy the story about how I got into this pickle. In the end, it's a sprained thumb and soon it's tightly bandaged, and I'm on my way.

"Limited movement for forty-eight hours," I groan as we exit the building. "And it's my dominant hand, too."

"You should have thought about that before you assaulted someone," Danny says.

I huff. "Don't say assaulted. It makes me feel like a criminal."

"You are."

"I was defending you."

"I appreciate that," he says. "But you got hurt and it could have been much worse."

We drove my car to the hospital, and even though I probably shouldn't drive, I offer to take him back to the bar to get his own car. He doesn't dignify this suggestion with a response and when we arrive at the car, he opens the passenger door and tells me to get in.

For the first part of the ride, we listen to the late-night radio announcer stumble through his program. It's annoying, so I switch it off and turn around to look at Danny. His eyes are heavy, and I feel guilty for making such a mess of his night. I can't believe he showed up at the bar so late just to make sure I was okay after talking to my dad. Not only that, but he sang karaoke, and waited with me at the hospital while I dealt with the consequences of my poor decisions. He's serious about making things up to me.

When we arrive, Danny pulls the car into the only vacant space on my street and walks me to the front of my building

"You can stay here," I offer as he pulls out his phone and opens the rideshare app.

"It's okay. I need to get home."

"Then I'll wait with you."

"It's cold. Go inside." Danny doesn't look up as he speaks. His phone screen illuminates his pinched expression.

"No. I want to stay out here with you."

He looks at me, and the corners of his mouth lift. "Driver is five minutes away."

"I can handle five minutes in the cold."

I shuffle over a little so we're standing closer. My coat is plenty warm enough, but I tuck my good hand in my pocket and lift my shoulders toward my ears.

"Alright, come here." He puts his arm around me and I cuddle into his side. It reminds me of sitting in the stands at the rink with him. He'd scold me for never wearing a warm enough jacket and no gloves meant he held my hands. I knew what I was doing.

"Thanks for punching that guy," he whispers.

"I'd do it again. Sprained thumb and all."

"I know you would. You're more like Eve than you want to admit."

"I'm a delicate balance between Bea and Eve."

Danny's nose wrinkles. "You're nothing like Bea."

"Except that we're literally identical."

"She's way nicer than you," he jokes, and I slap him on the arm. "Careful, you'll break your other hand." He tenses his upper body and I roll my eyes.

"Oh, stop it."

A soft laugh rumbles through him, and I commit this moment to memory. The cool night air is mixed with the smell of his cologne. It's faint now, though, aged off his skin, but it's a musky cedar smell. He never used to smell like that. He used

to smell like two-in-one shampoo and the off-brand fabric soft-
ener his mom bought in bulk when it was on sale.

A few minutes later, a notification dings on his phone.

"Shit." He frowns as he looks at the screen. "The driver
canceled."

"Just come upstairs. Bea's probably at Jamie's, so you can
have my bed and I'll sleep in her room."

He thinks on it for a moment before we enter the building
together. I don't understand his reluctance to stay the night. We
used to sleep over each other's houses all the time when we
were younger. Sharing a twin bed, no less. Though he would
tire of my inadvertent kicking and end up sleeping on the floor.

"Hey, the rink is having their sign-up day tomorrow for the
next beginner hockey program," I say. "I told Mrs. Schaffer I'd
help. If you want to come with me, I'm sure she'd love to see
you."

I do my best to distract him as we ride the elevator; he's
plastered to the back wall and trying not to let it show that he's
anxious.

"You still volunteer there?" He lifts his head to look at me.

"Just when I can. I haven't had much time over the last few
years." I say, trying to hide the guilt of my waning commitment to our once favorite place.

We exit, and Danny stands close as I open my door. My
eyes land on Bea's keys on the kitchen counter.

"Oh, Bea is home." I take off my coat. "Looks like you're
getting kicked in the shins all night."

He doesn't laugh and I half expect him to pull out his
phone and try to find another ride.

"I can take the couch."

I look at the two-seater and back to Danny. "Shall I fold you in half?"

"You've got a point," he laughs as he takes his coat off as well.

I brush my teeth and get ready for bed in our impractically small bathroom and when I return to my room, Danny is on the left side of the bed, eyes closed and fully clothed, except for his shoes. He's lying on top of the blankets, but I lift my side and slide under the covers.

"I'm supposed to be taking Gemma to the sign-up tomorrow. She wants to join," Danny says into the darkness.

"Following in her favorite uncle's footsteps."

"Something like that."

I roll onto my side, lifting my bandaged hand up to rest on my pillow. "So you'll be volunteering?"

He says nothing but lets out a sigh. In the dim glow of the city outside, I can see his eyes are open.

"Danny?"

"I don't want to go back there," he whispers.

"Why?" I match his somber tone. "You used to love it there."

He continues to stare at the ceiling. "Go to sleep, Kit."

"We can talk about it," I say, gently. "Your injury."

He rolls away from me. "Go to sleep, Kit."

I lift my hand to touch his shoulder but think better of it. If there's one thing I know about my oldest friend, it's that he'll only talk when he's ready.

And I can wait.

CHAPTER SIXTEEN

I don't know what time Danny left, but the combination of exhaustion and pain killers had me dead to the world. I reach over and lay my hand on the mattress. It's stone cold.

I shouldn't read into it. He wanted to go back to his bed. But as I delicately push my injured hand through the sleeve of my bright blue ice-complex volunteer t-shirt, I sense we won't be sharing a bed again and disappointment radiates through me.

"What happened to your hand?" Bea says as I awkwardly tug my left shoe on.

"Nothing. It's just a minor sprain."

Jamie gives me a knowing look from across the table. Obviously he caught Danny leaving my room and is desperate to ask questions.

"Are you sure you're feeling okay?" Bea's eyes soften with concern.

"Yeah. I'm fine. Just running late." I'm out of breath as I kiss her on the head and sprint out of the apartment.

When I arrive at the rink, Mrs. Schaffer is talking to a group of parents in the small dining area by the snack bar. She waves hello and I mouth an apology before she points at the reception counter.

"Sorry I'm late," I apologize to a teenage boy currently manning reception. His face is pale and his eyes wide. Clearly he was thrust into this role on account of my absence and the second I take over he hurries away without so much as a glance back.

Reception on sign-up day isn't that taxing of a job. All I have to do is answer a few questions about class timetables, program costs and equipment fees. It's all outlined in the brochures stacked on the counter. Once a brochure is issued, I direct the kids over to the equipment hire desk so they can pick up some skates and head to the ice to do laps until their legs give out.

As easy as it is, I'm not quite firing on all cylinders today, so it requires slightly more mental dexterity than I have the capacity for. My thumb hurts and my head is manifesting a rapid drumbeat when I hear my name being called.

"Kit! Kit!"

I look over to see a small arm waving wildly behind a group of boys pushing each other around.

"Hey, Gemma," I call back and watch as she lectures one of the boys who bumped into her. He looks terrified and when she's done scolding him, she makes her way over to me.

"Did you finish your sign-up?" I ask.

"Yep. I'm in the B group for the Tuesday afternoon and Sunday morning classes."

"That's great," I say as I look around the crowded space. "Did Uncle Danny bring you?"

She shakes her head. "Nope. Dad and Grandma brought me."

My heart sinks. I was confident that he wouldn't show, but that doesn't make it less disappointing.

I paint on a smile. "Are you going to have a skate?"

"Yeah, but I want red skates. Do they have red skates? Dad said they go faster."

I fight the urge to point out the obvious. "You'll have to check over at the equipment desk."

There are no red skates, but I tell her to hold out hope while I write in the notebook under the keyboard, suggesting we invest in a couple of pairs of red skates for the equipment stock.

"Thanks Kit!" She grins as she bounds off.

I'm only manning the counter for another half an hour before Mrs. Schaffer takes over again.

"I thought young Mr. Larson would be with you today," she says as she straightens the brochure stacks. "His mother said he was back in town."

"He was planning on it." I shrug. "Something must have come up."

She continues to tidy the desk. "Such a shame, what happened to him."

I know little about the end of Danny's career, but I won't admit it to Mrs. Schaffer. As much as I wish he'd open up, it feels like we're starting over and I don't want to rock the boat.

Mrs. Schaffer doesn't notice my reluctance to talk about Danny because a warm smile breaks across her face. "I'm so proud of him."

That goes without saying. I remember the astronomical hire fee for the electric lift to hang his number from the rafters. It was after he went pro and the junior team retired his number. Half the reason I continued volunteering at the rink was to feel like he was still here. It never worked. It made me miss him more.

When my shift ends, I head up to the stands and watch Gemma on the ice. I'm stalling for sure because I told Mom I'd be over for dinner, and since I spent time with Dad, I'm at more of a loss about how to handle the divorce. They're both miserable, so any blame I was looking to lay has evaporated.

In the crowded stands, I find a secluded spot halfway up. I spot Nolan a few rows down. He's watching his daughter, who's hovering close to the boards with a couple of other girls and pointing up at Danny's number above them.

"Mind if I join you?" I look over to see Judy standing at the end of the row.

"Sure." I wave her over and she takes a seat beside me, folding her hands in her lap.

"He wanted me to tell you he's sorry," she says.

"Sorry for what?"

"For not being here," she clarifies. "He feels terrible about disappointing Gemma, too, but he's not ready to come back yet."

My heart sits heavier in my chest. I understand why he doesn't want to be here. He doesn't have to send an apology with his mother.

Judy's shoulders drop. "I've barely spoken to him about it. Every time the subject comes up, he either changes it or walks away."

"He hasn't spoken to me about it, either," I say. "It's going to take some time."

"I really want to help him." Judy tilts her head back and blinks away tears. "But I don't know what to do."

"I don't think there's anything we *can* do. Everything has always been about hockey, and I can't picture him doing anything else. I can't imagine how he feels about it."

She wipes her cheek and we sit in silence for a few moments, watching Gemma skate around the rink. She barely wobbles, and it reminds me of the first time Danny got on the ice. He was a natural, like the skates were an extension of him.

I was too scared to join and watched from the side as he laced up. When he got me on the ice, I was so frustrated that I couldn't do it. I'd wished I was born with the same skill or at least have the confidence he did. Instead, I clung to the boards and worked my way around until, after many sessions, and with Danny beside me, I let go.

And fell flat on my ass.

To this day, I remember the pain that spiked through the heel of my hands and my wrists as I came down. I wanted so badly not to cry as the cold seeped through my clothes and chilled my skin. I wanted to be good at this, because my best friend was good at it and I didn't want to share him. We were so young, and I already knew hockey was going to be a big deal.

After my fall, Danny helped me up off the ice and held one of my hands while I held the boards with the other. We spent the entire session like that, and the next two sessions after that. He attended the sign-up day a month later and joined the hockey program. They issued him with number twenty-eight—my birthday, so it must be lucky. At least we both thought it was, until his last game.

We've both come a long way since he wore that number for the first time.

"I had coffee with your mom this morning," Judy says, bringing me back to our conversation. "She seems better."

"She's getting there," I say. "Thank you for spending some time with her. I think she's getting tired of me hovering all the time."

"Nonsense. She loves having you around." Judy pats my knee.

"I just want her and Dad to at least talk to each other again. They're both miserable, so I don't understand why they won't talk it out."

Judy exhales. "It's probably more complicated than any of us realize."

She's right, of course, but I'm still rattled from my talk with Dad.

"It was a shock to hear about it, though," Judy says. "She seemed happy."

Mom was happy. I don't remember a time when she wasn't, but maybe I wasn't looking hard enough.

CHAPTER SEVENTEEN

B ea broke the news about London to Mom while I was at the hockey sign-up, and when I stopped by to see her, she was in a downward spiral. Out of guilt, Bea stayed with her for the last two nights and called this morning to ask if I could go to the house today to keep Mom company.

"Should we tell her where Dad is?" I ask Bea over breakfast. "He was supposed to call her, but that hasn't happened."

She chews on her lip for a second. "Well, I mean, Dad needs his space, but Mom should know. She's worried about him, and it's making things worse."

Mom has repeatedly asked, point blank, if we've seen or spoken to Dad. Keeping his whereabouts to ourselves has become less like secret-keeping and more like calculated deception.

"Speaking of sharing secrets, are you going to tell me how you broke your hand?" She narrows her eyes.

I move my bandaged hand into my lap and out of sight. "Like I said, I slammed it in a car door."

Her gaze is frosty. "Really? Are you sure you didn't punch someone who was heckling Danny about his injury and then spent hours in the ER before bringing Danny back here to stay the night?"

"Fucking hell, Jamie." I exhale.

"Danny sang like a canary when Jamie caught him sneaking out of your room in the morning." Bea picks up her bowl and slurps the dregs of discolored milk and crumbly cereal bits. "Broken hand aside—"

"It's sprained."

"Sprained hand aside. Have you heard from Eve?"

"I called her yesterday, but she didn't answer," I say.

"I'm so sick of this. Why is she alienating herself from the rest of us? We're all in the same boat."

I wish it was that cut and dry, but the way Eve is handling this whole thing is true to her nature. She's always been quick to take sides in any argument and she'll die for the cause. It's admirable, and when it's your side she's on, it makes you feel invincible.

"Mom and Eve aren't good, though." I fold my arms across my chest. "You know how much pressure Mom puts on her."

"Yeah, because Eve has no direction. She'll drop every-thing to pursue a new dream and then immediately move on to something else. It's not sustainable, and Mom's trying to make her take responsibility for her actions. There's a point where being flaky isn't fun or cute. She's almost thirty, it's time to grow up."

Bea has criticized Eve in the past, but never so bluntly. It catches me off guard.

"It wouldn't surprise me if that's part of the issue with Mom and Dad," Bea says. "Dad's always defending her. It must be hard when your husband doesn't have your back."

"So, this is Dad's fault?"

Bea sits up straighter in her chair. "No. I'm saying that Mom has always pushed Eve to be better and Dad never backed her up. It would be frustrating."

My skin starts to prickle. Bea has chosen a side now too. Even if she won't admit it.

"I better check on Mom." I stand from the table. "Maybe you should check on Dad? He's living on hot wings, and he doesn't know how to iron any of his work shirts."

———

When I round the corner onto my childhood street, Danny's car is on his parents' driveway. I've been putting off contacting him after talking to Judy, figuring he might need some space.

Apparently that isn't what he needs, because when I enter the house, I find him eating a sandwich at our family dining table.

"What are you doing here?" I hide my grin, but my heart feels lighter seeing him again.

"Nice to see you, too."

"Sorry." I drop my keys on the table. "I mean, hey, what are you doing here?"

"Eating a sandwich." He takes another bite. "Then I'm going to finish patching the hole in Alex's bedroom wall."

"Why are you fixing holes in walls?"

"Because your mom needed help to fix a hole in the wall."

I take a seat in the chair beside him and bump my shoulder against his. "And she called you?"

He raises a brow. "Yeah, why?"

"Do you have the skills for this?"

"Yes."

"Since when?" I poke him in the arm.

"Since always." He pokes me back. "What's with all the questions?"

"I just thought Miles or even Fletcher would have been a more obvious choice." I smirk and he drops the sandwich back onto his plate.

"That's offensive."

I reach over, placing my finger under his chin and gently guide his face toward me. "Did Mom call them?"

"Yes," he mumbles and looks away again. "They were unavailable."

I let out a sharp laugh, and he seems to fight the urge to laugh with me. "Sorry. I'm sure you did a great job."

"I did, and I'll come back tomorrow to paint it." Danny picks up his sandwich and continues enjoying the fruits of his labor.

Since he's here, I grab my laptop from my bag and set it up next to his plate. I've been dying to show him the spreadsheet I created to track my bucket list. Which I definitely did not do to distract myself from the dwindling number of days until Bea leaves for London.

"What am I looking at?" he asks as I turn the screen to face him.

"A spreadsheet?"

"Of what?"

"My bucket list."

"You made a spreadsheet for your bucket list?"

"Yes." I drag the cursor to the top of the page. "I've listed each item, then added a description of the activity and a little section for notes, so I can write a review of how it went."

"What are those numbers?" He points at the last column.

"That's my rating system. I give each completed list item a score out of ten based on several factors."

He wipes a spot of mustard off the side of his mouth. "Do I want to know what the factors are?"

I shake my head. "Probably not. It's a whole different spreadsheet with a lot of formulas that feed data to this one."

I click to the next tab and his eyes glaze over immediately.

"I've only completed three items on the list, but this is making it a lot easier to chart my progress."

"What's this green section?" Danny taps the screen. The first column is entirely green and displays "*10/10*" for each completed activity.

I look him straight in the eye. "That's my activity partner rating. It's a separate metric. Bea scored highly for the dinner party; you also scored well at karaoke and our visit to the observation deck."

A barely-there smile tugs at the side of his mouth and it makes my blood run a touch faster through my veins.

"I don't think the observation deck ended well."

"Circumstances beyond your control don't affect the activity partner rating scale," I assure him.

"Thank God." His relief is mocking. "How's the hand, by the way?"

I've been trying to keep the strapping as clean as possible over the last couple of days, but it's looking slightly tattered.

"It's feeling a lot better. I have a check-up with the doctor next week, but I think the bandage can come off soon."

"You really didn't have to punch him."

The tone of our conversation shifts immediately. Danny drops his eyes and extends his bad knee like the thought of that last game reignites the pain.

"I've seen the video and I'll never forget the sound," I say. "That guy doesn't have the right to heckle you about it just because he supports the other team."

He doesn't look up. "I've never seen the clip."

"Keep it that way," I say forcefully.

"I don't need you to punch people over it, though."

"And upon reflection," I hold up my hand, "that was a mistake on my part."

He reaches over and takes my wrist to inspect my hand. "You're lucky you didn't break it."

"I know, but I couldn't let that ignorant little man say shit about you."

"He was actually an ignorant large man," Danny corrects. "I'm sure he's suffering, though. Imagine having your nose broken by...what are you, five foot six and 115 pounds?"

"Five-seven and 126, but thank you."

"I was close."

I close my laptop and smile wistfully across the dining room. "There was a split second there where it felt good to hit him. Then it was agony."

At that moment, Mom breezes into the room.

"Oh, Katherine. Thank God you're here."

She looks showered and appropriately dressed. It's a shock, because I'm accustomed to seeing her with her lips around the neck of a wine bottle and week-old casserole stains on the lapel of her bathrobe.

"You're looking better," I point out.

"Feeling better too." She beams. "Daniel has helped me clean the grout in the bathrooms and patched that hole in Alex's wall. I'll be calling your brother for an explanation on that tonight."

She continues mumbling to herself as she sifts through the mail that I've been stacking on the end of the dining table every time I visit.

I lean slightly closer to Danny. "Is she high on cleaning chemical fumes?"

"Probably." He shrugs.

"I heard that and no, I am not." She scowls. "Now, I have some things for you to take care of. Starting with sorting the boxes at the bottom of your old closet. Danny can help."

Danny doesn't want to help, but he's finished his sandwich and Mom's wearing that painted-on smile and a look that means neither of us have a choice.

"Mom, can I talk to you for a second?" I glance over at Danny and he gets the hint immediately.

"I've got to check on the wall upstairs," he says as he gets up from the table. Mom reaches over and takes the plate from his hands.

"I'll take care of that for you, Daniel," she says and heads toward the kitchen.

I mouth a thank you to Danny, and when he's safely on the upper level, I hurry into the kitchen to find Mom humming softly.

She doesn't acknowledge me as she retrieves bags of fruit from the fridge, washing them to store in separate, labeled containers. She's been a wreck, but clearly she won't be commenting on it further. Now she'll work overtime to ensure it's erased from our collective memories.

"I found Dad."

The statement hangs in the air for a few seconds before Mom flicks the tap off and her shoulders slump.

"Mom?"

"I heard you." She pats her hands dry on a dish towel. "Where is he?"

"Whiskey Double. In the apartment upstairs."

She turns to face me. "Did you talk to him?"

"Yes."

There's a hint of panic in her eyes as she slumps against the sink. Her fingers twist into the fabric of her dress as she shakes.

"I deserve this," she whispers.

My chest constricts with what her response implies, but I keep my composure and pull her into a hug. Her familiar smell of clean linen and lavender shampoo reminds me how much progress she's made since I saw her last.

"I don't know what you deserve." I hold her a little tighter. "But you need to talk to Dad. And Eve."

Mom agrees as I pull back. The temporary vibrancy she showed in the dining room has evaporated. Now she's a shell in a clean dress.

"I've already lost Eve," she whispers.

"She's stubborn, but you can fix it. With her and with Dad."

"He won't listen." She drops her hands to her sides. "I've tried."

Something flashes in her eyes as she flicks the water on and fiercely scrubs an apple that doesn't deserve such violence. I've got whiplash from the sudden change in her demeanor.

"Mom?"

"Sort out those boxes," she snaps. "I won't ask again."

My nails bite into my palms, and I close my eyes. This isn't about me or the boxes. Mom continues scrubbing, her shoulders bunched and tears streaming down her face.

A wait for a moment, but when she offers no apology or explanation, I head up the stairs and into the hall before stopping. Tears build, so I take a moment to breathe, pressing the back of my head against the wall and closing my eyes.

This isn't about me or the boxes.

When I enter my bedroom, Danny is on the floor, inspecting the baseboard with the bent nail.

"Want me to patch that?" he asks as he yanks off the baseboard.

"No!" I shout and lunge toward him, heart hammering. It's too late though, the board is off and he's spotted the folded paper with the star sticker on the back.

"What is this?" He turns it over to see his name scrawled in my curly, adolescent handwriting.

"It's nothing." I snatch the letter from his grip and tuck it into the pocket of my jeans.

His left eyebrow arches. "Did you write me a letter?"

"Yes, but it was years ago, and it hasn't aged well."

He turns back to the hole in the wall. "Okay. Anything else in there before I seal it up?"

I still have my hand in my pocket, wrapped around my innermost thoughts about this man, and he's staring intently at a hacked-up section of drywall.

"That's it?" I ask. "You don't want to know what it says?"

He stands up and brushes his hands over his thighs. "I do, but you'll tell me when you want to."

With that, he exits my room in search of the tools required to fix my little time capsule.

CHAPTER EIGHTEEN

In the week that follows, Mom takes up an enormous amount of my time and patience. Her mood keeps shifting on a dime and each day I see her, it's anyone's guess what attitude she'll have.

I make the mistake of asking if she's seen Dad and she storms out of the living room halfway through an episode of *Grand Designs* and doesn't resurface for an hour. I'm trying to be understanding, but it has me on edge. So it's a complete shock when she arrives on my doorstep asking if she can stay with us. I call Bea from the bathroom and ask for her thoughts on the matter. She offers to give up her bed and stay with Jamie because clearly Mom needs me.

At first I think it's some kind of trap, until I realize that she genuinely doesn't want to be alone at the house.

So, for the last two days, she's been a model roommate. She keeps the apartment clean, and I like the little Post-it notes she leaves on the bathroom mirror, reminding me to have a good day and achieve my dreams. She's even flexed some advanced cooking skills and hasn't once questioned me about what's going on with Danny. Apparently, in order to get along, all I need to do is not mention Dad. That is until she decides that it's time to venture out of the house.

What started as a gentle knock on the front door has become a hammering in the last thirty seconds. "Dammit, Mom," I groan as I drag myself out of bed.

It's late, and the last time Mom went out, she forgot the code to enter the building and had to call me for it. Still, she shouldn't be out gallivanting around Seattle at this hour.

At least she remembered the building code, I guess.

"Stop the banging!" I call out as I wrangle my boobs back into my tank top on my way to the door. It's three in the morning and between thumps on the door, I can hear my mother giggling.

"What are you doing?" I hiss as I yank open the door.

Mom is on the threshold, phone in hand, and texting frantically. Her pixie cut was immaculate when she left the apartment eight hours ago. Now it's lost all its volume and her makeup has rubbed off her cheeks and chin.

"Mom?"

She looks up, grinning from ear to ear. "Thank you, Kitty. Would you believe I forgot my key?"

"I would, because it's three in the morning and you're banging on the front door." I step aside to let her in. She breezes past me and I smell the mixture of her delicate floral perfume and alcohol on the cocktail dress she borrowed from Bea's closet.

"The night really got away from me."

I'm about to close the door, when footsteps echo at the end of the hall. I hurry to shut it, not wanting to be the target of a passive-aggressive noise complaint letter from the older couple two doors down.

"Kit?" a deep voice calls out, and I peer into the hall to see Danny walking toward me with Mom's coat over one arm and her purse in his hand.

"Where did you find her?" I pull the door open and usher Danny in.

"She's been at the bar for hours." He places Mom's belongings on the kitchen island and we watch as she wobbles over to the couch like a newborn calf. She kicks off her stilettos and drops onto the spread of throw pillows, letting out a sigh of relief.

"Mom, what have you done to yourself?" I take a glass from the cupboard and fill it with water. Mom accepts it with both hands and takes a large gulp.

"Judy and I went to dinner at this nice restaurant on the waterfront."

"And you stayed there till three in the morning?" I ask to test her.

Mom doesn't meet my accusatory stare. "Yes."

"Liar," I hiss. "You were supposed to be home at ten. Danny said you've been at Whiskey for hours."

"Daniel. You traitor." She stares daggers at Danny.

"Don't look at him. Look at me," I scold. "I've been worried about you. Why didn't you come straight home after dinner?"

She taps her nails on the fluted exterior of the glass. "I'm sorry."

"You weren't even with Judy, were you?"

"I was. I swear."

I fold my arms. "But you weren't with her the whole time."

She shakes her head.

"What were you doing at the bar, then?"

She stares at the carpet for a long moment before chugging the last of the water. "Nothing. Just hanging around."

I rub my eye with the heel of my hand. "Did you go to see Dad?"

"I thought about it." Her eyelids droop. "Then I thought better of it."

Please God, let her not have run into Dad in this state. I turn to look at Danny, who must have read my mind because he shakes his head to dispel my concern.

"Miles is a fantastic bartender." She laughs sharply. "Have you ever had a Long Island Iced Tea? Because I had four and they're very good."

"Mom." I snap my fingers in front of her face. "You need to go to bed right now."

She looks at me from under heavy eyelids. "I am quite tired."

"And you can thank Danny for making sure you and your belongings got home safely."

Her smile is serene as she floats into the kitchen and pulls Danny into a hug. "You are a treasure, Daniel."

"Thanks, Mrs. Reilly." He pats her on the arm.

She wobbles back over to me and takes both my hands. I hiss as she squeezes my still tender thumb.

"Oh, I'm sorry, baby. I forgot about your hand." She looks at the more discreet brace the doctor fitted three days ago.

"You really need to be more careful when you close car doors."

"It's fine, and yes, I should be more careful." I force a smile to perpetuate the lie.

Mom shakily leans forward and kisses my cheek before breezing into Bea's room and kicking the door closed.

It takes thirty seconds for Danny and me to burst into laughter.

"She is a mess. I'm so sorry."

"It's fine. I've seen my siblings in worse condition."

He's definitely referring to the time Miles split his head open when he drunkenly tried to do a flip off the treehouse roof.

"Do you want anything to drink?" I ask, realizing that we're both hovering in the kitchen.

"No, I should go."

I reach over and take his hand, knowing full well that I'm overtired and full of false bravado. I try my luck anyway.

"You don't have to go. Fletcher's house is a long drive away."

He looks at my hand in his for a moment before pulling away. "It's not that far."

I flush with embarrassment at the rejection. "Well, thanks again for bringing my mom home. I'll try to keep track of her in the future."

Before he can answer, a high-pitched, jingling ringtone wails from the couch. I hurry over to shut it off, and when I pick up the phone, I see the name on the screen.

Patrick.

I'm certainly not answering it, so I decline the call to stop the noise.

It rings again, and in a panic, I decline the call.

"You alright?" Danny asks. My mouth is hanging open.

"It's someone named Patrick."

"Who?"

"Patrick." I lower my voice. "Who the fuck is Patrick, and why is he calling my mom at three in the morning?"

The phone dings in my hand, and a text message appears on the screen. I shouldn't read it, but it's staring at me.

"What does it say?" Danny crosses the room and peers over my shoulder.

"That he's sorry about tonight, and can she meet him tomorrow?" I drop the phone back onto the couch like it's poisonous.

"I don't think you should get involved in this, Kit."

"I'm not. I just wanted it to stop ringing."

I sit the phone on the coffee table and settle back onto the couch. Danny joins me and we stare at the phone.

"You don't think Mom has something going on with this Patrick person, do you?" I put the idea out into the universe and immediately want to snatch it back.

"I don't know," Danny lies, and he leans over, his shoulder brushing mine.

I stare at the black phone screen. "She wouldn't...you know. Like, you don't think she'd ever have...cheated on Dad?"

I need him to say no. Even though I've had suspicions, someone has to confirm that it's all in my head. These calls and that message are too close to a confirmation for my liking.

Danny looks like he'd rather be sucked into the vacuum of space than answer that question.

"Eve knows," I confirm. "That's why she's so angry with Mom."

I snatch the phone off the coffee table and bury it back in Mom's purse before pacing the entire length of the apartment. I swear the space gets smaller with every step.

"Dad said he never had an affair." I carry on the conversation by myself. "And that was a fucking technicality because *she* did."

I continue pacing, picking up speed.

"Why didn't he tell me the truth? Or Eve? Why would Mom do this in the first place?"

Danny stands up, holding his hands out to halt me. "How about we take a beat and think about this?"

I plant my hands on my hips. "What other explanation could there be? Why else would a strange man be calling her at this hour?"

"I don't know."

"Maybe they met after she and Dad split?" I tap my chin.

"Maybe," Danny responds.

"Still, it's way too soon to be getting involved with someone else." I resume pacing and Danny steps out of the way.

"Sit, would you?" He sighs as I continue muttering rhetorical questions to myself.

I return to the couch and he follows, wedging himself beside me. My heart tries to find a steady rhythm as I lean forward and rest my elbows on my knees.

Mom wouldn't be capable of an affair. She loves Dad too much.

"Take a breath. It could be nothing," Danny says as he slumps back on my couch with his hands behind his head. It exposes the intricate tattoo on the inside of his bicep. From what I can see, it's a dragon figurehead on a Viking longship. He yawns, rolls his head to the side, and closes his eyes.

I study him in my peripheral vision and recall the story behind every feature. The dusting of freckles on the back of his hands from summers spent outdoors. The scar above his left eyebrow from being hit by a puck at practice. Who knew someone's head could bleed that much from a minor cut? It was all over the ice and I could hardly breathe. I thought he was dead. I thought it got him in the temple and…

"You good?"

He has one eye open, and he's watching me.

"What happened to us?" I ask. "You've been back many times over the years, but I only ever saw you at family gatherings. Even then, you barely spoke to me."

He looks away for a second before pulling himself up into a sitting position. For all my sudden boldness, there's a hint of regret, because reconnecting with him has been the best part of these last few weeks.

"Kit." He exhales, and it causes my insides to coil.

"Did I do something wrong?"

"No." His tone is forceful. "God no. You didn't do anything."

"Then what happened?"

He sits forward on the couch, resting his elbows on his

knees and staring at the floor. "You were never going to come with me."

"What do you mean?"

His front teeth dig into his bottom lip. I remember that too. That look of discomfort, when he knows it's time to be real but for some unknown reason he's been conditioned not to show a hint of vulnerability.

"Hockey was everything. I was always going to leave."

"You never asked me to go anywhere."

"Because you didn't want to leave."

"I got accepted to college here and you were going to go anywhere you could get a scholarship." I start picking at my cuticles as I look at him. "College didn't matter for you. It was a means to an end, but I needed it for my future."

"I know that."

"Then why didn't you stay in touch with me? We were both busy, but we promised to make time for each other and as soon as you signed with Philly, I barely heard from you."

"I know." His eyes are fixed on the floor.

I exhale and tuck my hands under my thighs. "I just don't get it. If I didn't do anything, then why did you stop talking to me."

"Because I was homesick even though everything was working out for me," Danny says. "I wanted you in Philly with me, but you were moving on. I saw all the photos Bea posted of you at college parties and you were with all these people I didn't recognize."

"So, you thought ignoring me would make it better?"

He shakes his head. "I knew it wouldn't make it better, but it helped me miss you less."

His shoulder brushes mine again, but I can feel him pulling away. The looming finality of this conversation hangs in the air like static and I know the exact words that will come out of his mouth next.

"I have to go." He stands up, stretches his bad knee and checks that his keys are in his pocket.

"I'll walk you out." I head toward the door and Danny follows.

When we reach the threshold, he doesn't cross; instead, he turns to face me. "I'm really sorry about everything."

"I know you are," I say. "And I'm not trying to make you feel bad about the last few years, but I missed you so much, and all I wanted was to hear your voice again. You couldn't even give me that."

He looks at the floor.

"I get that you were homesick in Philly. It was all new and you were under so much pressure, but what about New York? You loved it there. You told me how happy you were when you brought Alissa back to meet your parents. That was the last real conversation we had."

He looks up and lets out a labored breath. "Yeah, well, there is another reason for that. Alissa hated you."

"What? No, she didn't."

"Yeah, she did. I told her all about you, and then she saw you at that block party and you were wearing this tight green dress and my old leather jacket that you borrowed when we were seventeen and never gave back."

I still have the jacket and I don't intend on giving it back. But Alissa was nice to me that night. We talked about her family, and I told her that she'd have to join us for our next

Larson-Reilly trip to Sterling Lake. She said she wouldn't miss it…she said my dress was pretty.

"Is she part of the reason you stopped returning my calls?"

He's quiet for a moment and it tells me all I need to know.

"She thought it was strange how close we were?" I prompt him and he nods.

"It made her uncomfortable because she thought you were trying to make it into something more than it was," he admits as he steps over the threshold and out into the hall.

When he turns back to face me, I step forward and wrap my arms around his body, and he rests his cheek on the crown of my head. His heart is beating faster than it should.

"Alissa was right," I whisper.

His voice is a deep rumble in his chest. "She was?"

I step back and look him in the eye. "I did want it to be more than it was."

CHAPTER NINETEEN

I wake far too early to find Mom making pancakes. She's sprinkling chocolate chips on the latest batch while listening to Dolly Parton through the tinny speakers of her outdated iPhone.

"Morning." She says, looking and sounding awfully chipper.

"Morning." I yawn as I drop into a dining chair.

Mom swiftly deposits a plate of pancakes in front of me and kisses the top of my head for good measure. How is she not a walking corpse, running on barely any sleep with what I'm sure is enough booze in her bloodstream to make a sailor stumble?

"I have to run an errand." She unties her apron and lays it on the counter. "I'll only be gone an hour or two and when I get back, we could go see a movie and have lunch."

She looks gorgeous. Her hair and makeup are immaculate, and she's wearing her special occasion jewelry: a fine gold chain, diamond stud earrings and no wedding ring.

She got Patrick's message.

"I can come with you?" I offer. "I told Bea I'd get her one of those mini comfort kits for her flight to London."

Mom doesn't miss a beat. "I have to go to the bank, so I won't bore you with that. We'll get Bea's things after lunch."

How can she lie so easily?

"Sure," I concede. "I'll see you later."

She collects her purse and hurries out the door. I leave my pancakes on the table, grab my car keys, and take the stairs two at a time.

———

I'm not skilled at tailing someone, because I lose sight of Mom on five occasions. She weaves her way through the traffic and takes so many turns I end up completely lost.

I'm not even sure what neighborhood we're in, but she pulls into a space on the street and walks into an upscale café.

Her vibrant yellow dress is easy to spot through the large arched windows and she's never looked happier as she approaches a man sitting at a table by the window.

My heart sinks when he stands and leans over to kiss her cheek. He's only a fraction taller than her, with neatly trimmed light-brown hair and an engaging smile.

Mom looks giddy and the rosy blush in her cheeks makes me hate him.

The man, who I can only assume is Patrick, pulls her chair out for her and his hand lingers on her back for a moment too long. She's a different person. Effervescent, younger and genuinely elated to be in the presence of the man opposite her.

My skin heats, and the pounding of my heart reverberates in my ears. I think of Dad. He's made her smile for decades, but I can't remember a time when he made her smile like that.

Mom and Patrick order coffee, but they're so wrapped up in each other they don't acknowledge the server who delivers it to the table. Patrick watches Mom as she tells an animated story based on the hand gestures. He laughs at all the right moments and responds immediately so there's no break in conversation. He's enamored with her, and every giggle and hand touch breaks my heart a little more. They've obviously known each other for a long time.

But how long have they been in love?

I pick up my phone and call Mom's number, watching her as it rings. She declines the call and her expression doesn't fall, even for a second. She looks back up at him and when he kisses the back of her hand I start the car and drive away.

———

"Why was she smiling like that?" I ask as I swirl the dregs of my vodka soda around the bottom of my glass.

Danny stands behind the bar at Whiskey Double. He doesn't know what to say because I've shown up unannounced, am drinking heavily and haven't acknowledged what I said last night before giving him a play-by-play of my morning. Still, he listens as I ask several iterations of the same question without waiting for an answer.

We both know the answer.

"This is the end, isn't it?" I say. "I don't think you can look at someone else like that and not know it's the end of your marriage."

Danny leans across the bar, moves my glass to the side, and takes my hand. "Even if it is the end, it's not on you."

I look into his beautiful eyes and have the most intense onset of self-pity. It feels like my siblings all get to walk away and I'm left to deal with the fallout.

My phone rings and I pull it out of my coat pocket. Mom has already called twice and if I ignore it again, she'll probably call Danny.

"Hey, Mom."

Her voice crackles down the line. "Where are you? I thought we were having lunch."

"I'm at Whiskey with Danny."

"Okay, I can meet you there."

I look up at Danny. I want to stay with him and ignore everything I witnessed this morning, but he gives me a look that says it's time to face this.

I tell Mom I'll meet her at home, and we share a stilted goodbye. She knows something is wrong, but I'd bet money she won't acknowledge it until I do. I slide off the stool and Danny comes around and pulls me into a protective hug. He smells like beer, but his shirt is soft, so I snuggle into his chest.

When we part, he steps back behind the bar, dragging his fingers through his hair and causing it to stick out near his ear.

"Hey, Kit." His voice rattles.

"Yeah?"

"Do you want to stay at Fletcher's tonight?" he asks. "In

case you need a break from your mom. They have a million rooms. You can pick your favorite."

I chuckle as I pick up my coat off the stool. "That would be great."

It takes all my strength not to leave the bar and go straight to Fletcher's. Instead, I repress another wave of nausea and drive home to face my mother.

When I arrive, she's folding laundry like she doesn't have a care in the world. The acidic anxiety building in my body turns to rage in a heartbeat.

"There you are." She beams. "I suppose we can have a late lunch. Or early dinner."

She's foreign to me now. The scared and confused woman from two weeks ago feels so far away. All I can picture is her and Patrick, the way her shoulders shook when she laughed at whatever he said.

And how easily she lied about where she was going today. Did it bother her at all? Did she hold her breath, praying I wouldn't ask any questions? Did she think of Dad while Patrick held her hand, his thumb brushing over the place where her wedding ring used to be.

"I followed you to the café this morning and I saw you with Patrick."

Her eyes widen and she drops a t-shirt back into the laundry basket. "You what?"

"You left your phone on the couch last night and he was calling. I declined the calls, but he sent a message about meeting today."

Her brows draw together. "That's an invasion of my privacy."

"I know."

"Katherine." Her tone is venomous. "I am beyond disappointed with you."

"Why did you lie?"

"I didn't lie."

"You said you were going out, and when I asked if I could tag along, you had that lie about the bank on the tip of your tongue," I say.

Her shoulders drop. "Kit, I—"

"It was so easy for you. Like you're practiced at it."

"What are you saying?"

"I'm saying that maybe you've lied about Patrick before. To Dad."

"I don't have to answer to you." She folds her arms across her chest, her hands trembling.

"You don't think I deserve an explanation? Considering I've supported you this entire time. I've defended you. Now I feel like a fucking idiot."

Mom looks at the floor.

"I helped you with the house. I gave you a place to stay so you wouldn't be lonely. But you're not lonely, are you? You've never been lonely."

Mom moves toward me, and when I back away it brings her to a halt.

"I appreciate everything you have done for me, Katherine. I really, truly do." She holds her hands over her heart. "The only reason I didn't tell you I was meeting Patrick is because I didn't want to make you uncomfortable."

What about Dad? Has she, for even a second, considered what this might do to him?

"Are you seeing Patrick?" I ask.

Mom looks down. "It's complicated."

"It's a yes or no question."

She wraps her arms around herself and lifts her eyes to mine. "Yes."

"Were you seeing Patrick before you and Dad separated?"

"No," she says firmly.

The tension in my muscles loosens slightly. "Is he the reason you and Dad broke up?"

I already know the answer. It was written all over her face at the café.

"Yes." She hangs her head.

I look at my hands. I've been picking my fingernails so much that two of my cuticles are bleeding.

"This divorce isn't something your father and I entered into lightly. We have been struggling for a long time and we tried to make it work. I promise we did."

The surge of anger that has been brewing in my blood suddenly gives way to an ocean of bitter sadness. I thought I wanted to know. I thought that would make it easier to understand what happened, but the truth is worse.

"Don't hurt my dad any more than you already have," I whisper. "The only thing he's guilty of is loving you and giving you everything he thought you wanted."

I pick up my keys and leave the apartment. Mom is already calling my phone when I climb into my car, but I ignore it and cry the entire drive to Magnolia.

———

When I pull up in the driveway, Fletcher is stepping out of the front door, handsome in his jeans and a button-down shirt with his hair styled. Danny had said something about him having dinner with Nolan tonight while Hallie's in Australia.

"Hey, Kit," he calls out as he walks toward me. The exterior lighting on their mini mansion is so effective, he can see my anguish. "Are you okay?"

I've been aimlessly driving around for hours and two blocks ago I thought I'd composed myself. I was wrong. The second his brow wrinkles with concern, I sob uncontrollably.

Fletcher rushes forward, arms outstretched to hold me up. "Hey, hey. It's okay."

"I'm sorry, Fletch," I cry.

"Don't apologize. What happened?" he asks as he gives my shoulders a gentle rub.

"Fletch?" Danny calls from the house. Fletcher steps to the side and at the sight of me, Danny comes running across the lawn toward us. "Is she hurt?"

"I don't know," Fletcher answers.

"Kit." Danny inspects me for damage.

"I talked with Mom."

Fletcher is still confused, but Danny understands. He pulls me into him, tucking my head under his chin and rubbing my back. Danny assures Fletcher that he's got everything under control, and Fletcher gives me a reassuring pat on the arm before reluctantly getting into his car.

Danny walks me across the lawn, and we sit on the step outside the front door. I tell him about Mom's confession and how horrible I feel for Dad. I can't decide if I should tell Bea.

Eve has been shouldering this burden, and now I know how much it hurts, I want to protect Bea from it.

It takes a while, but once I've regained my composure, Danny steers me to the house and into the kitchen. The countertops are an absolute mess with open containers and half-chopped ingredients. A pot of water boils fiercely on the stove.

"What happened here?" I wipe my eyes.

"Trying to make dinner." He shrugs sheepishly.

"Is it successful?"

Danny doesn't get to answer because the pot boils over and water sizzles on the stovetop. He rushes over and grabs the searing handles.

"Fuck!" He drops the pot, upending it and splashing boiling water all over the stove, counter, and floor. He jumps out of the way, avoiding disaster, but he balls up his hands in the front of his t-shirt.

I round the end of the kitchen island and grab his wrists. "Run your fingers under cold water."

Danny does as instructed and visibly relaxes when the cool water hits his skin. We stand there for a moment—me holding his hands under the water like he's incapable of doing it himself.

"I wanted to make you dinner." He sucks in a breath and my heart swells astronomically.

"Oh, really?" I'm on the verge of happy tears. "That's so sweet."

"It's not going well." He looks at the reddening tips of his fingers.

I run a dish towel under the cold water, take his hands in

mine and press the cool cloth against them. "I can take it from here if you'd like."

"Yes, please."

Once the water is cleaned up, I get to work preparing the meal Danny planned. It's spaghetti and meatballs, which come to fruition much faster with me at the helm and Danny watching from a stool on the other side of the kitchen island. It doesn't take long for the sting to go out of his fingers. His pride is a different story, though, and he insists on making the garlic bread.

He burns it, but I eat it and compliment him on a job well done.

"Things didn't go well with your mom, then?" he asks as we pack the last of the dishes in the dishwasher.

"I can't believe how easily she lied to me." I sigh. "It makes me wonder what else she's been lying about?"

"You'll probably never know," Danny says. "I'm not trying to be insensitive, but it is between her and your dad. She wouldn't want to tell you all the details. Especially if she's in the wrong."

"You should have seen them together, though. God, the way she lit up at everything Patrick said." I almost spit the man's name.

Danny takes my hand, his damaged fingers carefully wrapping around my damaged thumb.

"I don't want to talk about her anymore," I say. "The last month has been all about her and I need a break."

"Maybe we can cross something off the bucket list?" Danny offers.

I picture my spreadsheet and mentally scan the list. So

many of them require forward planning, but there is one thing we could do tonight.

"Yeah, there is one thing we could cross off." I don't fight my grin.

Danny raises a thick, blond brow. "What is it?"

"You're going to hate it."

"What is it?"

I tug on his arm. "Follow me."

We only make it a few steps toward the back door before he works it out.

"No way," he groans.

"It's on the list." I slip my arm through his and drag him across the yard.

CHAPTER TWENTY

"This is a bad idea." I wrap my arms around myself.

"The worst," Danny agrees.

"It's cold."

"Yep."

"We might get caught?"

"That would be embarrassing."

I lean over to look at the inky black surface of Fletcher's pool. "You're certain Fletch isn't coming back soon?"

Danny shrugs. "It's his house. He could be home any minute."

Skinny-dipping was a late addition to the list. I remember eighteen-year-old Bea adding it, in the midst of a passionate summer fling. I can't remember the guy's name, but his family was staying in the house next door to the one Mom and Dad had rented out at Sterling Lake. Bea was convinced he was the one and for some reason thought skinny-dipping was romantic. She cut her foot on a sharp rock and the guy panicked from all the blood and left her on the bank.

So far, it seems more stressful than anything else.

"Are we doing this?" Danny asks as he inspects the surface of the water, too.

"Did you turn off the motion detector on the exterior lights?"

"For the tenth time, yes."

"And you locked the side gate?"

"Yes."

I take a deep breath, sucking as much of the night air into my lungs as possible. Thankfully, the cloud cover is thick tonight, so the only light is the ambient glow from neighboring houses. Danny is barely a silhouette on the opposite side of the pool.

"Alright. I'm just going to do it." Danny doesn't sound happy in the slightest, but his belt buckle clunks as it hits the tiles around the pool. I turn around and face the house to give him some privacy.

"And you're one hundred percent sure about the gate?"

"Yes," he groans before the rest of his clothes hit the ground, and he splashes into the water, hissing immediately. "Fuck. It's so fucking cold."

"I told you." I turn back and take a few steps away from the edge. "I don't think I need to do this one. It was a late addition to the list, anyway."

"Katherine," Danny says through gritted teeth. "There is no way in hell you're backing out now."

"But you're clearly not having a good time, so there's no sense in both of us freezing."

He pushes off the pool wall and starts treading water in the middle. I can make out the water rippling in the moonlight. "You just begged me to do this."

"I thought the pool might be heated."

Danny's teeth chatter. "It's almost summer. Fletch doesn't turn on the heating system because it's a waste of electricity."

"Aren't they multimillionaires?"

Danny glides back to the edge of the pool. "I'm not going to freeze my ass off while we discuss my brother's finances. So, either get in and we'll cross this off the list, or I'm getting out."

"Fine, fine," I grumble, and as a sign of good faith, I remove my sweater.

"Faster," Danny urges. "I think hypothermia is setting in."

"You're still not selling it," I say as I kick off my sneakers.

Danny continues to complain until I'm down to my underwear.

"Turn around," I instruct, and even though he can't really see me, he does what he's told.

After silently assuring myself that I can do this, I remove all my clothes and slip into the water.

"Fuck," I grunt in the same manner he did. "This was a stupid idea."

As I sink to my neck and my internal body temperature plummets, Danny turns around to confirm that I've committed.

"Why the hell would Bea want to do this?" I wrap my arms around myself. "It's so uncomfortable."

Danny's eyes widen. "You're uncomfortable? A certain body part of mine has retracted."

I sweep my hand over the surface of the water, splashing him in the face. "It's not a competition."

He splutters, and the water ripples again as he approaches me. "You want to start a fight?"

"No. Please." I back away. "I don't want to get my hair wet."

He's poised to splash me, but my pleading has him reconsidering.

My hair is already falling out of its ponytail and I hate the feeling of the strands sticking to my back.

"Could you do me a favor?" I ask. "If I stand up, can you tie my hair up higher?"

Danny agrees and swims over, stopping behind me. I cover my chest with both hands as I stand up. The night air snap-freezes the water droplets on my skin and I shiver immediately.

"This w-was a terrible idea," I stammer.

"Worst one you've had so far," Danny says, as he pulls the band from my hair. I hug myself tighter as he runs his fingers through the damp strands, trembling when his touch travels across my back and he gathers my hair, wrapping it around his hand.

He holds it for a second before closing his fist. My skin ignites at the gentle sting on my scalp as he tugs on my hair, using his grip to guide my head to the side, exposing my neck.

"Daniel." My voice and body shake even more.

"Katherine," he responds.

He places his other hand on my shoulder, trailing his fingers down my arm like he's tracing the goosebumps. If he isn't himself, we definitely aren't what we used to be. Because we've never been like this.

We've only ever been friends. Sharing secrets, spending every waking moment together and being fiercely protective of each other. Like the time Danny hit Harry Stevenson across the head because he said my hair looked like an oil slick.

My world was collapsed the day he left for college. That was the day I wrote the letter. I wrote down all the thoughts swirling in my head that I never felt capable of speaking. How I thought about him all the time and even a minute spent with him was the highlight of my day. How much I didn't want him to leave and couldn't face being here without him. That he was so lucky he was experiencing a different life while I was left behind. For months, I hated him. I hated him for leaving and I hated that hockey was more important than our friendship. I panicked that I might forget the sound of his voice or the color of his eyes.

It took me too long to realize that it was love.

"I want you to read the letter," I say. "The one I wrote to you."

He leans down and I can feel his breath on the skin where my neck meets my shoulder. "I want to read it."

His mouth lingers there and every muscle in my body tenses. He's going to kiss me. He's finally going to kiss me.

He presses in closer, and as his lips meet my skin, the back-yard lights up.

"Shit." Danny instinctively rushes to the edge of the pool and ducks his head. I'm shielding my face with one hand and my boobs with the other.

"Get down," Danny hisses.

I swim to the edge of the pool as a small silhouette exits the house and runs across the lawn.

"Hey, Kit," Gemma calls out as she approaches. I slink down so my chin rests on the edge of the pool.

"Hey, Gem," I force out. Danny is beside me, trying not to laugh.

"It's too late to be swimming," she says.

"I-It is," I stammer. "It's cold, too, so I'm getting out."

"Okay. Do you want to watch a movie with me?"

"It's probably a bit late for that, Gemma."

She pleads, "It's not a school night and Uncle Fletcher has a big TV."

Danny wraps his hand around my calf, and it makes me jump.

"Are you okay, Kit?" Gemma asks.

"Yeah, why?"

"You're acting weird," she deadpans. "And all your clothes are over there."

She points at the pile of clothes. Danny's are on the other side, but she doesn't appear to have noticed them.

"I forgot my bathing suit."

She frowns and her eyes narrow. "Okay. It's still a bit weird to swim in someone else's pool with no clothes on."

Danny stifles a laugh, and I smack him in the ribs.

"Yeah, it is. So I'm going to get out now and come inside to watch a movie."

"Awesome!" She grins. "Are you coming too, Uncle Danny?"

His head drops back against the wall of the pool before he slowly peers up to look at his niece.

"Yeah, I'll watch a movie with you, Gem."

The color has drained from his cheeks. A combination of icy water, cool night air and embarrassment.

"Gemma, what are you doing out here?" Fletcher makes his way out to the yard, with Nolan following behind.

"Kit and Uncle Danny are swimming."

"Oh God." Nolan recoils.

"You can't see anything," Danny says.

"That's not the point," Nolan hisses. "I know what's happening."

"Nothing is happening," I retort.

Fletcher's mouth pulls down. "Really guys? In my pool?"

"We weren't doing anything," Danny grumbles as Nolan covers Gemma's eyes and steers her back into the house.

We spend the next few minutes being lectured by Fletcher as he paces the fence line. He's not mad, just disappointed that we used his pool for "nefarious purposes", and when he goes back inside, he turns off the exterior light so we can get out.

Danny and I make no eye contact as we scramble out of the pool and tug our dry clothes over our wet skin.

"This one isn't getting a good rating on the spreadsheet, is it?" Danny jokes as we walk back toward the house.

CHAPTER TWENTY-ONE

For the next few days, I don't speak to Mom or Dad. I don't trust myself not to make the situation worse, and when I got back from Fletcher's place, she'd packed her stuff and gone home. I called Bea and when she came home I told her everything that happened. A massive weight lifted off me as I voiced my frustration through tears. Unfortunately, that weight landed on Bea's shoulders, and the hurt in her eyes quickly marred the relief I felt.

Since then, Bea and I have barely been a few feet from each other. She's running work meetings from the apartment and finalizing everything for London. Now and then, as she stuffs something in a suitcase, she stops, turns to me and says, "I just don't get it" or "How could she do this?". I don't have an answer, and I doubt we ever will. That doesn't stop us from talking about it for hours on end.

This cycle continues for days and with still no word from Mom, Bea suggests another bucket list item to distract myself.

I need an activity partner, but aside from a text or two, Danny and I haven't spoken since the pool incident—one hundred percent thanks to shared embarrassment. I push it down though, and ask Danny if he'd like to partake in the next item on the list: *Stay up all night and watch the sunrise.*

With a little cajoling and the promise of a free breakfast, he agrees and we decide to do it the night of the Larson family barbecue.

"Any developments on Patrick?" Danny asks as he hands me a beer and joins me in the treehouse. I'm slightly concerned about both of us spending the night up here. It's only five feet off the ground, but the structural integrity is compromised thanks to decades of inclement weather.

"Nope. I was expecting to face her tonight, but I'm guessing she's out with him." I lift my chin toward the darkened house.

"She might not be with him."

My stomach turns. "But she might be."

Danny looks at his feet dangling over the edge. It's quiet in our corner of the yard and over the fence I can see Judy rushing around, filling glasses with wine and directing Miles while he playfully snaps a pair of tongs by the grill.

I shift slightly, so my thigh presses against Danny's. We haven't talked about him kissing my neck in the pool and I don't care if we do. I just want him to do it again. He doesn't seem to have any such intentions, though, and with all this Patrick stuff hanging over my head like a fog, it's hard to think of much else.

I look over to the Larson home and see Fletcher arrive. His son, Luca, is with him and when he says something to Judy, she pulls him into a tight hug, rubbing his back like a concerned parent would.

"Is Fletch okay?" I ask.

"Not really." Danny follows my line of sight. "You remember Wes? You met him at Fletch and Hal's wedding."

"Yeah, I remember Wes."

How could I forget? He certainly lights up a room, even though I couldn't understand half of what he said.

Danny adjusts his position, drawing his shoulders forward and staring at the damp grass below.

"His wife had a baby a few days ago, but there were some complications. Hallie said something about a hemorrhage. The baby is fine, but Wes's wife didn't make it."

"Are you serious?" I inadvertently press my hand to my heart. "That's devastating."

"Hal is staying in Australia for a while. Fletch didn't want to leave her, but he's got Luca to take care of."

I hang my head. "Yeah, of course."

I can't fathom it. My brain is simply not capable of imagining a situation like the one Wes is in.

Danny and I slip back into silence, watching the evening unfold over the fence, carried off on separate trains of thought. Danny extends his leg now and then, letting out an almost imperceptible wince with the movement.

"We can go somewhere more comfortable."

He shakes his head. "I'm fine. Just a little ache. That's all."

I'll never forget the look on his face after he went down, contorted with pain. As devastating as that was, it was nothing compared to what followed.

He tried to stand on the ice.

That look was worse. Utter horror, because he knew how serious the injury was and he couldn't hide it.

"Can we talk about hockey?" I ask, my voice clear and crisp in the night air.

"What about it?" Danny responds, his tone a low rumble compared to mine.

"What are you going to do now? Look for a coaching job or something?"

"No."

The word is so final and it breaks my heart to hear him say it with such conviction knowing that hockey is the only thing he's ever really loved.

"What about volunteering at the rink? I'm going to be there every Sunday morning and Wednesday night."

"Doing what?" He looks over at me and I realize I've inadvertently steered the conversation from his future to my present.

"Mrs. Schaffer needs help working the front desk and sometimes the concession stand." I shrug. "I've also been helping clean out the equipment room every month."

He curls his fingers over the edge of the decking boards and stares out over my backyard. He's grieving for everything he's lost, but there's still a lot to look forward to. He doesn't have to cut himself off completely.

"I bet you still can't lace your skates properly."

"I sure can't," I say into the darkness. "Not that it matters. I've never skated without you."

I let my head fall on Danny's shoulder. It's an old signal, from a different time when we could read each other perfectly, when I wanted to be held and he'd swing his arm around my shoulders and tell me everything was fine.

He doesn't move, and I pray with all my heart that the years and distance separating us haven't tampered with his memory of our little rituals. It must have, because he doesn't put his arm around me.

"It'll be a long night," Danny says after a while.

I lift my head and reach over to my bag to retrieve my laptop. "Gives me the chance to update my spreadsheet."

Danny lays back with a groan, switching off before I've even opened the document.

Hours later, when the guests have left, Judy noisily jostles her way through the fence and up the treehouse ladder. She's laden with blankets, a plastic container of potato salad and a Thermos.

"If you insist on staying outside till dawn, I can't let you get hypothermia."

Danny and I planned ahead and wore appropriate clothing for the evening, but the warmth and cushioning of the extra furnishings is appreciated.

Judy shows me how the tricky latch on her old Thermos works while Danny builds a nest out of the blankets.

"If it gets too cold, come into the house, please." She rubs her son's cheek before making her way back down the ladder.

By five in the morning, I'm still wondering why on earth I wanted to do this. It's cold and windy, and the cloud cover means we can't even see the stars. The air is syrupy thick, and I can smell the rain.

I close my eyes for a few seconds.

"Kit," Danny says. "Don't you dare fall asleep."

"I'm not asleep. I'm resting my eyes."

"It's the same thing," he scolds. "You're the one who wanted to do this."

"Yeah, when I was a kid. My desires have changed."

Danny rolls onto his side. "Look at me."

I grumble as I open my eyes and roll over to face him. "What?"

"Are we doing this or not? Because the guest bed at Fletcher's place is a lot more comfortable."

"Comfort level is one of my experience enjoyment factors," I explain.

"Then it's a zero."

He rolls onto his back and stretches his arms above his head. The clouds have moved slightly, and a few stars are visible in the sliver of sky between them. I lay back down, stare directly upward and take a calming breath. It *is* peaceful, even with the low hum of traffic from the main street a few blocks over.

"I should have answered when you called after the game," Danny says. "I'm sorry."

The apology catches me off guard, and I take a second to formulate a response. "I was so worried about you."

"I know."

"Did you see my name come up on the screen and make the conscious decision not to talk to me?"

"Yes."

His answer is so decisive it sends a chill through my body. Subconsciously, I was looking for a lie.

"That hurts," I whisper.

Danny sits up beside me, pulling his jacket tighter to fight the wind that sweeps across the yard.

"I was ashamed," he says.

"Ashamed of what?"

His voice shakes. "Because I got laid out seven minutes into the season opener after signing the biggest contract of my career."

"That wasn't your fault."

"It doesn't matter. I've taken hits before. Bigger than that."

The scars on his body and dental implants can attest to that.

He drops his head. "That shouldn't have been the end."

I scoot over, so we're seated side by side. "It doesn't have to be the end. You can still be involved in the game without playing."

"You sound like my mom."

I chuckle. "It's a privilege to be compared to such a wise woman."

"She can't hear you from this far away."

His head rests on my shoulder, and I lift my arm and wrap it around him. At least I wrap it the best I can. My arm is short, and he's still got the shoulders of a professional athlete.

"Hockey wasn't going to be forever and yes, it sucks it ended so early, but this doesn't have to be the end for you. It's the start of something else."

In the moonlight, I can see he's studying my face.

"What are you looking at?"

"It's hard to see in the dark," he muses as he rummages through the blankets for his phone. He taps the screen, and the flashlight comes on.

"What are you doing?"

"Hold still." He holds the light up and leans closer, studying my right cheek. "Yeah, there it is."

I brush my hand over my cheek. "There what is? What are you talking about?"

"That slightly darker freckle an inch from your nose." He sits the phone on the blanket and it diffuses the light. "I just wanted to make sure it's Kit I'm talking to and not Bea."

I touch the spot beside my nose. One of the few, subtle differences between me and my sister.

"Why would you think I'm Bea?"

"Because you're being optimistic as hell and that isn't the Kit I know."

I give his shoulder a gentle push. "Shut up."

He laughs as he falls back into the blankets, dragging me with him. There is so much more to talk about, but for now I'm happy to hear him laugh this way again.

"Kit," Danny whispers, drawing my attention from the side of his face to the expanse above.

The clouds have shifted and the black sky peels away as a glow blooms on the horizon.

"We did it," I say, transfixed by the orange light slowly growing in intensity. Thirteen-year-old me was right to think this was an effort worth making.

"What's the rating out of ten for this one?" Danny asks.

"Ten," I respond without hesitation as I slip my arm under his. "Activity partner is an eleven, though."

CHAPTER TWENTY-TWO

B ea's going-away party turns into an expensive exercise. I tried to keep the cost down but I got outvoted on everything by Jamie and Leah. By the time the party comes around I'm simply a guest on the list. Even Mom threw her hat in the ring and took care of the invitations. She left mine on the coffee table with an RSVP card. Because acknowledging the fallout from the Patrick thing is too much for her. It's a storm cloud that hangs over my enjoyment of the party. That and the fact my sister is leaving Seattle for even worse weather and something called crumpets.

For most of the night, I sit in the back and watch Bea bounce around from group to group. Her smile is so bright and I want to be blindingly happy for her because she deserves it, but an entire year without her feels like too high a price.

Mom reaches over and pats my hand. "Can you smile, Katherine? This is Bea's night, not yours."

I grit my teeth and swallow the combative response that

crawls up my throat. It's the first time all night that she's said something real. Prior to this all she's talked about is the restaurant's wallpaper and whether or not it's peel-and-stick or glued.

I can already feel myself disconnecting. It's easy to block out Mom's opinions on the wine selection, and when Sheryl Hastings saunters over to ply her for information about the divorce, I use the distraction to hide out in the coat closet. It's unmanned, so I slide to the floor, take out my phone and text Eve. She hasn't answered any of my messages, so I don't have high hopes for this one.

KIT

I wish you were here.

I press send on the message as the door swings open. Bea stares down at me for a second before stepping into the closet and closing the door behind her. We're plunged into darkness again and I take her arm to guide her down beside me.

"Talk to me," she says as she reaches over and takes my hand in both of hers.

"Mom is annoying me."

Bea's chuckle cuts through the stillness of the room and her thumb traces the silver ring on my middle finger. It matches the one on her index finger. "What's she doing to annoy you?"

"She's acting like everything is okay. The same way she did when Alex was struggling in LA."

Bea drops her head onto my shoulder. "She does that when she's scared."

"We're all scared. A few weeks ago, everything was

169

normal. Now you're leaving. Eve won't speak to any of us. Dad is hiding out above a bar, and something is going on with Alex. He was acting weird when we spoke last week."

She rubs my arm. "I think it's all bad timing. Everything is happening in quick succession."

I relax back against the wall. There is so much change happening, and it would be easier if Mom acknowledged it. At least then we could talk about it and maybe both of us would feel better.

"Are you at least having a good time?" I ask.

"Is it too early to be homesick?"

"Yes. You haven't left yet."

She sighs. "I'm excited to see London and meet Jamie's family, but I'm going to miss home so much. Especially you."

"I'll miss you too, but I keep reminding myself that it's only a year. By the time you come back, I'll have Mom and Eve talking again, and we'll be renting one of those fancy houses at Sterling Lake for summer vacation."

I look over at Bea, and from the sliver of light under the door, I can see she's frowning. "You're unusually optimistic."

"Why do people keep saying that?" I ask, my shoulders dropping petulantly.

"Maybe all this bucket list stuff has given you a new perspective. I know I felt empowered after I got my tattoo."

"I'm still not sure I'm going to do that."

"It's on the list."

"Yeah, but it'll hurt."

"Yeah. It will hurt like hell."

I shrug dismissively. "I don't even know what to get."

"Get something that means something to you. I got the stars because I wanted a tattoo to represent us."

Bea leans back, lifts her arm and unzips the side of her dress. Inked on her ribcage is a small cluster of stars. Four of them, to be exact. Two are delicate, pointed and identical in every way, one is big, bright and dazzling. The fourth is the most intricate: thick outer lines with a lace-like pattern in the center.

"I love your stars," I say as she zips up her dress.

"And I love having them. It means I get to take my siblings with me everywhere I go. Even when I'm all the way over in London and Alex is God knows where. Or when Eve isn't speaking to us." She stares at me for a long moment and her lips pull up into a smile.

She shouldn't be in the coat closet with me, she should be out enjoying her party.

"Get back out there." I tilt my chin toward the door. "And if you could have Mom latch onto someone else, that would be great."

As the words leave my mouth, the door opens and our mother's eyes fall to the floor. Her mouth pulls into a flat line as she sees her daughters cuddled up on the carpet.

"Here you are, Bea." Her hands are on her hips. "Jamie's looking for you. It's time for the speeches."

Speeches? Is that necessary for a going-away party? Bea turns to me and presses her forehead to my temple. Her perfume is faint under the smell of hairspray and cherry lip gloss.

"Stay here as long as you want and call me if you need some company."

I do want company, but from the look on Mom's face, Bea won't be providing it.

My twin stands and exits the closet, saying something to Mom as she goes. The maternal disappointment is palpable.

"Katherine, this is Beatrice's night. Can you please not spend it on the floor of a coat closet?" It's not an order. The tone of her voice is more pleading.

As selfish as it is, I don't want to leave the closet. The noise and bustle of the party is grating, even from this distance, and the reality that this time tomorrow my sister will be somewhere between Seattle and London is a bit too much for me.

"Mom, it's fine." Bea steps in. "If Kit's happy where she is, I'm happy."

With that, Bea grips Mom's arm and tugs her toward the dining area. The chatter from the party floats back through the open closet door and the guilt of not being overtly happy for Bea weighs heavily on my heart.

I get up and close the door before settling back down with my phone. Eve read my message a minute after she received it. She hasn't responded, and my distress warps into anger. Eve wouldn't even have to talk to Mom. She could spend time with me.

As though through sheer force of will, my phone dings in my hand.

EVE

You're in the coat closet, aren't you?

KIT

Maybe.

EVE

Why?

> KIT
>
> Because Bea is leaving tomorrow and
> you aren't here to say goodbye.

EVE

I'm having breakfast with her in the
morning and going to the airport.

> KIT
>
> ...I was not aware of that.

EVE

I'm not a completely heartless person,
and I'll miss my little sister.

> KIT
>
> I still wish you were here with me. This
> is why I have two sisters. You're
> supposed to step in when Bea's
> unavailable.

EVE

I'm not going to risk running into Mom.

The music in the restaurant picks up again, the speeches are over. It doesn't sound like it's wrapping up, though, and so far nobody has come to pick up their coat. I settle back against the wall and continue texting Eve.

> KIT
>
> I know about Patrick.

The dots dance on the screen for a long time. Starting and stopping over and over until eventually they disappear. I assumed Eve knew about Patrick. That's why she was so angry with Mom. Now I'm worried she didn't know, and I've dropped some pertinent, albeit vague, information that should not have been sent via text.

I drop my phone in my lap, leaning my head against the wall. I'm so tired but I really don't want tomorrow to come.

Fifteen minutes later, footsteps echo outside the closet. I wipe my cheeks in a vain attempt to act like I haven't been sobbing in a cupboard and wait for Sheryl Hastings or whoever it is to collect their coat.

The door swings open, flooding the tiny room with light, and I blink to make out the frame of the person in the doorway.

"I'm here. Are you happy now?" Eve says as she drops her arms to her sides, car keys jangling in one hand and her midnight-black hair falling out of the bun atop her head.

I rush forward and she opens her arms wide, enveloping me in the hug to end all others. I'm sobbing again and she rubs my back as I sniffle into her sweatshirt.

"I am happier now."

"It doesn't seem like it," Eve sighs.

"I am, trust me." I pull back and Eve lifts her hand to wipe my cheek. I'm sure she's smeared my mascara toward my ears.

"I'm sorry I wasn't here," she whispers. "I'm sorry I haven't been here for you."

She holds me again, and it's a warmth I haven't felt in so long. The rage and disappointment coursing through me dissolves, because I understand a little of what Eve has been feeling.

"You knew about Patrick, didn't you?" I ask.

She takes a step back and looks me in the eye. "Yes."

"Why didn't you tell us?"

Her expression softens. "Because Mom needs to be held accountable. And that starts with looking her loved ones in the eye and telling them what she's done."

"She didn't tell me," I admit. "I followed her to the café where she was meeting him."

Eve holds me at arm's length, her eyes sharp. "You saw him?"

I nod, suddenly panicking that I've done something I shouldn't. It's been a long time since I've felt this irresponsible and small.

"I didn't speak to him, though," I splutter. "I saw them through the window and then left."

Eve takes another deep breath and swallows so hard the tendons in her neck protrude. I've made this infinitely worse, and the panic that holds my limbs hostage intensifies as I hear people approaching.

"Eve?" I look at my sister, silently pleading for her to not make a scene here.

"When was this?" She is terrifyingly calm.

"A few days ago."

Her slow blink is the stuff of nightmares. It's the absence of a reaction, and that means she's so livid her body can't physically respond.

"She said it was over." Eve's voice is low, but razor sharp.

"All they did was talk," I say, scrambling; suddenly, being the bearer of bad news feels dangerous.

"Why are you defending her?"

My voice shakes. "I don't know."

Eve pinches the bridge of her nose before she turns and

steps out. A couple of Jamie's friends have come to collect their coats, and I shuffle out of the way, allowing them access to the closet and join Eve by the large potted plant near the door.

"Eve?" Bea's voice is clear and crisp over the soft music that filters out from the dining area. "I thought you weren't coming."

Bea comes into view, immediately pulling our sister into a hug. Eve whispers something in her ear. A second later, Bea bites her bottom lip, nods, and Eve leaves the restaurant without another word.

"What did she say?" I ask.

I've done something wrong. I know it.

"She doesn't want to run into Mom," Bea says. "But everything is going to be okay."

Bea has never been a good liar.

CHAPTER TWENTY-THREE

B ea's departure feels like a lifetime ago. In reality, it's been five days, but our postage stamp apartment feels like an empty museum. I spent the first four days as a complete recluse, relying on Danny to bring me leftovers from the bar after closing and watching Turkish dramas on YouTube without subtitles. I don't know what anyone is saying, but they're all so passionate. It makes me wonder if Danny and I are capable of that.

On day five, Eve told me to cut the bullshit and see Dad.

He's been asking for me, like an eighteenth-century patriarch on his deathbed. At least that's how it sounded when Miles also relayed the message.

I'm not proud of avoiding my father. In fact, I'm not proud of many facets of the mess this family has turned into, but there's something monumentally depressing about visiting my dad in the tiny apartment above Whiskey. He's doing everything he can to make it cozy, but when he sent a photo of his apartment makeover, which was a throw rug, I noticed the dirty dishes on the table and his clothes shoved into the built-in bookcases.

I'd wanted him to go back to Mom, put aside whatever issues they had and see that life together is better than life apart. That was before Patrick came along. Now, Dad's situation seems so much worse. He did nothing wrong, and the only way to free himself was to give up his entire life. The thought sickens me, so I make day six without Bea a bucket list day with Dad as my activity partner.

"Can you tell me which item we're crossing off?" he asks as I get on the I-5. "I've seen some of those list items and I'm too old to stay up all night."

"I've already done that one," I assure him.

"What is it, then?"

"You'll see when we get there."

Dad pesters me for the first fifteen minutes of the drive, throwing out far-fetched suggestions about what our day holds. When he realizes I'm not budging, he stares aimlessly out the window at the gray Washington landscape.

It's not the ideal weather for what I have planned, and when we reach the turnoff for the tiny township of Culver, Dad has some idea what I'm up to.

"We'll have to hire some fishing gear," he says as we drive down Main Street.

"Nope." I shake my head. "I brought the gear from the garage."

He chuckles. "I bet your mother was confused."

"She doesn't know. We haven't spoken in a few days."

The offhand confession sticks in my throat like a ball of

molten metal, because I know there will be follow-up questions.

"You know about Patrick, then," he says in a tone so matter of fact it temporarily stops my breathing.

"What?" I splutter.

"Come on, Kit. I wasn't born yesterday. I thought you'd be the first one to work it out."

I stop the car in the driveway of a small house on the southern edge of Sterling Lake and kill the engine.

"How can you be so blasé about this? She had an affair!"

"It's not that simple."

He looks back at the house we've rented every summer for as long as I can remember. The lake beyond looks ominous as heavy clouds have swallowed every inch of blue sky.

"Dad?"

"It's not that simple," he repeats.

"Then explain it to me, so I don't feel sick every time I look at my mother."

He shrugs. "I don't know how. She was happy, then she wasn't."

We sit in silence for a moment, waiting, but I don't know what for. He's closing up, and the mood shifts exponentially. I don't want our day to boil down to this; all about Mom. It's supposed to be about him. The heavens look poised to open, and if we don't get down to the jetty soon, we won't get to fish.

"Let's get to the lake." I reach over and put my hand on his shoulder. He blinks rapidly, like he's reset himself.

"I can't wait."

We gather the gear from the trunk and I assure Dad we aren't trespassing because I have permission from the owner to park on the driveway. This placates him enough to get him to the jetty, where he groans as he settles on the edge. He complains his bones aren't built for this anymore, but he smiles as he baits his hook with a semi-frozen worm.

"I'm going to miss this the most." He says as he casts a line and hands the fishing rod to me. Alex taught me to cast properly when I was ten, but in Dad's presence I've always pretended it was beyond me so he could help.

"We can still spend summers here."

"Of course we can." He gives me a wink, content to maintain the lie.

We'll never come back here, and the last time we were here, none of us knew it. It breaks my heart. All the other last things we've done as a family come to mind: our last Christmas at home, the last time we stayed up late watching movies on the couch. The last time we had a genuinely happy family dinner.

That one hurts. Family dinners were always our thing and the realization that they haven't been happy for a long time is a tough pill to swallow.

I don't want to fall down this rabbit hole, but there's one question I'm desperate to know the answer to.

"When did you find out about...him?"

"A year ago."

My throat constricts. "What?"

"She told me she wasn't happy, and I ignored it."

A year. Mom was having an affair for a year and we were all blind to it.

"I don't understand." I shake my head to clear the fog.

"You knew about this for a year and you stayed with her? Why not leave before now?"

He studies the gray water at our feet. "Because it wasn't easy to admit that it was over. For either of us."

This revelation brings several things into sharp focus. Their growing distance. All the overtime shifts Dad took, and Mom finding any excuse to have us at the house. She used her children as buffers, so she didn't have to talk to Dad.

"She told Bea and me that she wanted to work on it," I say. "She got scammed by that fake marriage counselor, too."

"I wasn't going to spend hundreds of dollars to talk your mother into loving me again. She'd already decided. The counselor was a way of lessening the guilt."

"She doesn't deserve to feel less guilty. Not after what she did." My tone is acidic.

"She didn't cheat," Dad says firmly. "She fell in love."

"Isn't that the same thing?"

He stares vacantly at the lake. "I would have thought so. But love hurts so much more."

I put my fishing pole down and turn to face him. For such a heavy topic of discussion, he's remarkably composed. His long hair flutters in the icy wind that barrels off the water and his eyes are optimistic and wild.

"I'm not enough for her," he says, with more confidence than I thought possible. "But I need you to do me a favor?"

"Anything."

"Don't hate her for this. We've all made mistakes and we've all got to move on from them." He sighs. "The landscape has changed, but you know the love your mother and I have for you and your siblings hasn't changed at all."

I feel like a child. Helpless and barely able to comprehend what's being spoken. How am I still searching for blame, when the one person who should feel the most betrayed is smiling and casually turning the reel in his hand?

"None of us have been through this before. Your mother and I are navigating it as best we can."

I genuinely don't understand how he can be this calm. Where is the hurt? The anger? Where is that spiteful, all-consuming desire to make her suffer the way he is suffering? Maybe it's because he didn't see her at the café. He didn't see the joy on her face when she saw Patrick or the way she laughed.

Maybe that is a small mercy, because I can't get it out of my head.

"Okay." I shuffle across, loop my arm through Dad's and rest my head on his shoulder as the water laps at our feet. "I trust you."

"What bucket list item is this?" He turns and kisses the top of my head. "I don't remember one about fishing."

I look up at my dad, the wind rustling his hair and his eyes crinkling at the corners as he inhales the fresh air.

"Go somewhere that makes you happy with someone who makes you happy."

He nods and smiles contently as he turns the reel in his hand.

CHAPTER TWENTY-FOUR

My day at the lake with Dad brought a lot of things into perspective. I don't hate Mom for what she did, but brushing it off makes it seem trivial. That's where my anger lies. It's disrespectful, but still, when she asks if I'd like to look at apartments with her, I agree. If only to give her one more chance to be honest.

"I don't know what you're so upset about, Katherine. This place has character."

"This isn't character." I point at the pizza-sized section of plaster missing off the wall above the bed.

It's the fourth studio apartment we've looked at today. Each worse than the one before, but Mom is refusing to admit defeat. According to her, they're charming, or fixer-uppers, or in an unbeatable location for the price. One was a ground-floor studio with a discolored shower curtain separating the toilet from the bed.

"It's Queen Anne, though. I'll be close to you, and there's a Safeway a few blocks down."

"Mom, they've boarded the window shut."

"The landlord said that's temporary. They'll be replacing the AC unit soon." She side-steps a stain on the carpet as she inspects the bathroom. "Oh look, it has penny tiles. Aren't they nice?"

I cross the tiny space and peer over her shoulder. "Yes, fine. The penny tiles are nice."

"See. Character." Mom claps her hands together triumphantly.

Penny tiles aside, the place is still a dive, and as angry as she makes me, I don't want her living here. No matter how close the Safeway is.

"Mom, just move back in with me." I sit on one of the mismatched dining chairs. "Bea will be gone for the next year, so the room is available."

She chews on her bottom lip. "I don't want to be a burden on the only child I have left."

That's a sobering thought. With Bea gone, Eve still ignoring her and Alex in New York, I *am* the only one left. The reality of that is a lead weight on my chest. I'm the youngest by four minutes. This is too much responsibility for the youngest child.

"Mom, you can't live here. Besides, my place isn't that far from the Pacific Grand. You could bike to work like you always wanted to."

She considers the offer for longer than necessary. "I have always wanted to bike to work."

"And now you can." I force an encouraging smile. "You always say it's great exercise."

"It is. There was a fitness expert on the radio, raving about it."

"See, you've already found a new hobby. When you go back to work next week, you'll be a whole new person."

She fiddles with the strap of her purse before joining me at the two-seater dining table wedged between the TV and a set of drawers with two of the fronts missing.

"A whole new person?" She raises an eyebrow and taps her nails on the scratched timber surface of the table. "I figured I'd continue to feel like a wretched piece of garbage every moment of the day."

That's the last thing I expected to come out of her mouth and I'm too shocked to form a response.

"I don't want to be this person, Kit," she says, her tone clear and resolute.

She made herself this person. Inadvertently or not, she made choices, she acted on feelings. She is this person.

I remember the promise I made to Dad on the lake. I don't hate her. I can't, but I can be monumentally disappointed.

"Then why did you do it?" I say. "Why were you with someone else?"

She wipes her eyes before tears have even spilled. "I wasn't."

I let my head fall back and exhale. Why is everyone being so obtuse with the semantics? I'm being spoon-fed morsels of information when all I want is an honest answer.

"I never slept with him," she confirms. "I kissed him, once."

I think of their meeting at the café. What if that laugh and that smile wasn't love? What if it was politeness? It was greeting a friend. It was a mask to hide the sadness.

"It wasn't just a kiss. We fell in love. For months, I met with Patrick. We had countless coffee dates and restaurant dinners. We'd walk around the city for hours. It wasn't a physical relationship, but it was a relationship."

"Mom, I think what you had was a close friendship."

"If it was a friendship, I wouldn't have lied to your father about where I was. I wouldn't have hidden my phone and left the room to take calls. I wanted more. I know I did."

She takes a breath, straightens her back and looks me in the eye as she speaks.

"When I was young, I felt like I was meant to do something big or be someone greater than I was. I loved art and the theater. I studied French cooking and classic literature. Those are the things that interested me. When I met your father, I fell in love with his gentleness and stoic demeanor. He was a closed book, and I was a ball of sunshine. We complemented each other, and I was happy to share my interests with him. He took me to galleries and plays because he knew I loved them. It took me years to realize that we never did anything he wanted because he didn't have any interests. He wanted what he thought he should have wanted. So we got married, bought a house and had children. Suddenly, there was no time for any of the things I loved. It was all financial stress, to-do lists and extracurricular commitments. I became Mom, and he became Dad. We couldn't do the things we used to and that was a loss for me, but not for him. He thought I should have been happy because I had this idyllic suburban life. A loving husband and beautiful children. He gave me a nice house, but I didn't realize it was an exchange. I didn't know all those things meant I would lose myself."

The tears have dried and her shoulders have loosened. She's wanted to say this for a long time.

"Patrick was a guest at the hotel. He works for a tech company and would often have client meetings in the restaurant. We got to talking, and it turned out we have similar interests. Suddenly, there was this person who not only saw that part of me but ignited it. I wasn't just Mom, I was Elaine, again. In his eyes, I was interesting and I wanted to know everything there was to know about him. So, we got drinks, then dinner, then we talked on the phone. I got so wrapped up in who I used to be, I forgot who I am now."

She stares at her hands on the table, picking at her fresh manicure.

"I'm so sorry, Kit. I'm sorry I did this to us."

I don't know what to say. I never thought there could be a justification for an affair. Even an emotional one, but here we are. I feel for her, and it feels like weakness on my part.

"I stopped talking to Patrick last year, thinking that I could focus on my marriage and be happy again. I promise, I tried."

A lot of pieces slot into place. I thought she was miserable because there were issues with Dad, but she was sad because she'd given up Patrick and her old self again.

"Please tell me you've explained all this to Dad?"

"As best I could," she says. "None of this is his fault and I feel terrible that everything he's done for me isn't enough."

He tried so hard. How can it not be enough?

"I didn't mean to fall in love with someone else," she whispers.

All I can think is that Dad was right. Love does hurt so much more.

CHAPTER TWENTY-FIVE

In the days that follow, I adjust to waking every morning and not seeing Bea. I still feel the emptiness in my bones and the silence stretches further with each passing day. It's a sense of longing. The feeling of waiting for something that is nowhere on the horizon. At least I have Danny to cling to. And I do, shamelessly. I know how to change a lightbulb and stop the tap in the shower from dripping, but he docsn't need to know that.

"Are you ready?" Danny asks as I mimic his pose and grip my end of the oversized shipping box. "Lift with your knees. Not your back."

"Should *you* be lifting with your knees?" I raise a brow.

"It's still better than my back."

"If you say so."

I steady myself, bend my knees and on the count of three, we lift the box and maneuver it through the living space and into the small entryway.

When it's in place, Danny uses his shirt to wipe sweat off his forehead. Turns out he has a lot more tattoos than the one on his arm. There's various Viking imagery across his torso, and aside from being momentarily rendered speechless at how insane his body is, I'm thinking how painful that amount of ink would have been to get. Not to mention expensive and time consuming. Getting a tattoo is working its way further and further down the list.

"That's the last of it." I reach over and give Danny a high-five.

I've spent the last two days organizing freight for Bea's things—yet another chore I could rope Danny into. Not that I actively did that this time. He came over to say hi and then felt obligated to help.

He's keeping me calm and on track when it would be so easy to vocalize how much I regret offering my space to Mom. After her confession, a rat scuttled over her foot so she accepted my offer to stay in Bea's room once the house sells. I don't know what the plan is from there, but it's capped at twelve months because my sister will need her room back.

Danny makes a whistling sound; I've been staring at his shoe while my mind's been wandering.

"You okay?" he asks.

I blink rapidly to clear my head. "Yeah, just tired."

"Then let's take a break."

I follow him to the living room and when we sit on the couch, he pulls me to his side.

"This okay?" He lowers his voice, and I nod as he draws little circles on my upper arm with his fingertip.

There is no way I'm reading this wrong.

We aren't strangers to physical contact, but this is tender. This means something.

I press myself closer and let my head rest on his chest. The circle-drawing stops and instead he picks up the end of my hair. It's in a delicate fishtail braid that I spent two hours learning to do from a tutorial online because Bea and I always wanted to learn. This is the first attempt good enough to display. He twists the end between his fingers and his head leans to the side to lie against the top of mine.

"Kit," he says.

"Yeah?"

"I have to ask you something."

I move slightly, settling against him. This is it. I can feel it.

"You can ask me anything."

He's quiet for a moment, then brings his free hand around to gently lift my chin so I'm looking up at him.

"Do you still trust me?" His voice shakes in a way I've never heard before. "Like you did when we were young?"

"Yes," I answer simply.

He's quiet for a second and his body tenses, like he's winding up to something.

"Do you still feel like you did before? About me?"

I nod, slowly. "Yes."

His hand is trembling. "Good, because I think you know what I'm getting at here."

"Say what you're thinking." I look down at his lips, then back to his eyes. Those glorious, gunmetal eyes that look like the sky outside. Blue trying to fight the gray.

"I want to kiss you?" he asks as his hand moves from my chin to my cheek. "But if you're not okay with it, I won't."

"I'm more than okay with it." My answer comes out in a rush and it brings a smile to his face.

"That's good. I didn't want to just kiss you and you not be okay with it, and then it's awkward and our friendship is ruined, even though I already kind of ruined it these past few years. I think we're coming back from that, though. Don't you think? That's how I feel, anyway. I'm sorry if you don't feel the same way. I know I fucked up, but I...I never stopped caring about you. I'm just going through some shit and I don't know what I'm going to do with the rest of my life. I like spending time with you again, though. You make me kind of feel like only one part of my life fell apart, not all of it. I'm not explaining this very well." He sucks in a much-needed breath. "Anyway, I missed you and I like being here with you and I really want to kiss you...obviously not if it's going to make you uncomfortable. I can leave and things can go back to normal. And—what are you doing?"

I slip out from under his arm and throw my leg over his hips so I'm sitting on him. His eyes get wider by the second as I link my fingers at the back of his neck and look directly at his face.

"You're talking a lot," I point out.

He swallows. "Yeah."

"I don't think you've said that many words to me in the entirety of our friendship."

"I don't think I have either." His body relaxes underneath me.

I hope he's serious and this isn't some knee-jerk reaction to such a massive life change, because I'm certain I've always been in love with him. Even when he moved to the other side of the country and got serious with someone else. The hope was always there.

"Can you promise me something?" I ask as I slide my hands down and rest them on his shoulders.

"Anything," he says with conviction in his tone and his gaze.

"There is a lot riding on this kiss," I say. "I've wanted this for a long time, so make our first kiss worth the wait. Okay?"

Danny laughs softly. "That's a lot of pressure."

"It is, but I believe in you."

His fingers press gently into my hips, and it causes my stomach to flip. I've always wondered what his touch would feel like when it meant something more.

I'm suddenly alight with nervous energy. What if it sucks? What if there's no spark? What if this ruins everything?

Every horrible scenario swirls in my head, but when he places his hand on my cheek and brings my face toward his, my stomach flips again and I legitimately don't give a fuck about what happens after.

A heavy knock sounds on the door and Danny and I groan in unison.

"Hold that thought." I place my finger on his lips. There's no way I'm letting the old couple next door complaining about the new planter box in the foyer ruin the first kiss to end all first kisses.

I stand up and rush to the door, swinging it open without looking through the peephole.

"Hey, Kit-Kat." Alex drops his well-worn duffle bag and opens his arms.

"Alex!" I scream as I leap across the threshold and wrap

my big brother in a hug so tight it must shift some of his bones. "What are you doing here?"

"I'm back for the weekend," he wheezes. "Thought I'd drop in and say hi."

I keep squeezing him. "I'm so glad you're back. The whole family has fallen apart."

"It can't be that bad," he says with far too flippant a tone. "Now can I come in, or are we going to talk in the hall?"

I step back and Alex leans down to pick up his bag. He's had it for years and considering how much he earns, I don't understand why he doesn't spring for a new one. The zipper on the top has been re-sewn twice.

"Danny's here, by the way," I tell him as we navigate our way into the apartment around Bea's soon-to-be-shipped luggage.

"Alex?" Danny stands from the couch and attempts to neaten his hair as he makes his way over. "What are you doing back?"

Alex drops his bag on the dining table and shakes Danny's hand. When did we all get so grown up? Last time I saw these two interact, Danny and Miles had stolen Alex's guitar and were holding it for ransom for free tickets to a Nine Acre show at The Palace.

"We're taking a break from recording this weekend, so I thought I'd fly home and check in with everyone."

My heart swells to hear Alex call Seattle home.

"I might go." Danny dips his chin toward the door.

"You don't have to," I protest.

"It's fine. Hallie's flying back in tonight and Fletcher offered to make dinner." He tucks his hand into the pockets of his jeans and as he walks past me, then leans down and whispers in my ear, "Next time."

Every muscle in my body coils and I close my eyes for the briefest moment, hoping it will preserve this feeling: the butterflies in my stomach, my thunderous heartbeat, and my complete and utter inability to stop myself from smiling.

"Good to see you, Dan." Alex gives him a wave as he leaves the apartment.

I'm still giddy from the moment before Alex arrived and, as happy as I am to see him, his timing really sucks.

"You two are thick as thieves again, then," Alex says. "Is something else going on?"

"Nothing yet." I exhale like a love-struck Disney princess.

"But something was about to happen?" Alex screws up his face, showing more disgust than necessary.

"I think so, but it's all very new and confusing, so let's table this discussion for a later date."

"It's fine if we don't have time to circle back. I don't really want to think about the kid next-door hooking up with my little sister."

I laugh at the even more disgusted face he pulls. "It's not something I want to discuss with you either."

I reach over and grab his arm, pulling him into the living room and depositing him on the couch. He kicks off his shoes immediately and sinks into the decorative pillows Bea left behind. It's so good to have him back, even if it is only for a short time.

Like a good hostess, I fetch drinks and snacks from the fridge and place them on the coffee table in front of Alex. He devours several crackers with cheese before chugging an entire can of soda and looking at me like he's ready for the rundown of what he's missed.

I deliver this in record time. I'm practiced at it now.

I tell him about Patrick, and what Mom told me at that roach-infested apartment. I cry when I recount the trip to the lake with Dad and how upset I am that Jamie took Bea away. It's like a floodgate has opened and I can share everything I've been holding onto. For the longest time, I've had to hide something from everyone. I couldn't talk to Mom and Dad about each other without feeling like I was picking sides, I couldn't talk to Eve because she *has* picked a side and I couldn't talk to Bea about how much I wanted her to stay because that would be selfish. I couldn't tell Danny how I felt about him for fear of rejection.

"Hey, hey." Alex rubs my back as I sob into my hands. "We're going to get through this."

"I know. It's just really hard at the moment," I whimper. "And I don't know how to make it better."

"It's not your job to make it better, Kit. You don't have to fix everything. Mom and Dad need to work it out on their own."

"What about Eve?" I wipe my nose with the back of my hand. "She isn't going to get over it."

"That's on Eve." Alex shrugs. "Listen, why don't you come to New York?"

I look up at him as I wipe away more tears. "What?"

"I'm subletting a place in the Village. You can crash there for a bit. See the city, get away from Mom and Dad and you're only a six-hour flight from Bea."

Bea hasn't been gone long, but the thought of seeing her calms me.

"Are you sure I wouldn't bother you?"

"I want you there Kit and you need to get out of here for a while."

I feel like I can breathe again, so it's the easiest decision I've ever made. "I'll come to New York."

CHAPTER TWENTY-SIX

"There are so many things on the list I could cross off on this trip," I explain to a perplexed Danny, who is standing shirtless and bleary-eyed in his brother's kitchen. If I wasn't so excited about this trip to New York and London, I'd be dragging him to his room. He looks like he's made of granite and it's distracting.

I hold up my hand and count. "Leave the country, done. Eat a croissant in Paris. Easy. Bea and I can take a train there. Meet someone famous. Alex hangs out with famous people all the time."

"Eating a croissant in Paris is very specific." Danny scratches the back of his head.

Bea came up with that one and she struck it from the list in our senior year of high school. As a kid she was obsessed with all things Paris, so naturally she joined the French club and convinced Mom and Dad to pay for a class trip to Paris. She was gone for two weeks and it was the longest we'd ever been apart. She sent me several postcards, which all arrived three weeks after she got back. They're safely tucked in a box under my bed.

"I need to make a spreadsheet."

He looks at me through half-closed lids. "Sure. Why not?"

I'm formatting cells in my head when Fletcher walks into the kitchen. He buzzes around making breakfast for Hallie while I give him the rundown of my trip. He offers some sight-seeing suggestions for London. They're all literature-related, and it's clear he doesn't understand his audience. Danny is nodding off, despite sitting upright on a stool. He almost falls forward, but the flat, blaring tone of my phone startles him awake.

"Finally." I look at my sister's name on the screen. She's an hour late for our scheduled video call.

"Sorry I'm late." Bea looks pale in the pixelated image. "What's this news you have for me?"

"I'm coming to London!" I shout, startling Danny again. "I'm stopping in New York on the way, but then I'm heading over to see you."

"Ahhhh!" she squeals. "Are you serious? When? When!"

"I haven't booked anything yet, but I'm planning on flying to New York and spending a week there with Alex before flying to London. I'll send you a copy of the spreadsheet once it's confirmed."

Jamie mutters something in the background, and Bea agrees before returning to our conversation. "Kit, are you going to be okay getting here by yourself?"

"Yeah. I'll research it before I fly out."

Bea doesn't look convinced and as I squint at my sister, she mimics my expression. It's like looking in an exhausted, blonde mirror. Jamie's hand appears from the side of the frame and passes her a glass of water. She gulps it down so fast it looks painful.

"Have you been eating sugar?" I probe. "Or gluten?"

Bea wipes the errant droplets off her chin. "I'm fine. Just thirsty."

"You look sick again?"

"Thanks," she scowls. "How's the new roommate, by the way?"

It's been three days since Alex left and Mom moved back in, but I've hardly seen her.

"I don't know who she is anymore," I explain. "She and Judy are helping host trivia at Whiskey Double tonight and she said something about hiking with Sheryl Hastings on Saturday."

"Wait. What?" Bea tilts her head to the side and closes one eye, like I've spoken in code and she has to decipher it.

"It's nice that she's out doing things. It's taking her mind off the house."

"What's happening with the house?"

Fletcher holds up a packet of bacon and I signal my interest in the offer with a thumbs up. "They got some lowball offer and Dad wants to take it."

Jamie appears in the background and whispers something in Bea's ear.

"Kit, I've got to go to an appointment," she says.

"Okay. I'll text you later."

We say our goodbyes and I hang up the phone, now able to give Danny my full attention.

"Can we talk for a sec?" he asks as he stands from the stool.

"Sure."

"Don't be too long, breakfast is almost ready," Fletcher calls after us as we exit the kitchen.

It's a stupidly long walk to Danny's room, but halfway there, Danny takes my hand, linking his fingers through mine and gently guiding me down the expansive hallway. This act of affection is casual, like we've done it for years. If it wasn't for the sudden increase in my heart rate, I wouldn't think anything of it.

When we get to his room, he releases my hand and closes the door behind us.

"What do we need to talk about?" I wrap my arms around myself at the frigid room temperature. I forgot how Danny likes his habitable spaces to feel arctic. How is he coping without a shirt on? "You're scaring me."

I brace for him to say that what happened in the pool and in my apartment was a mistake and we should forget all about it. I still haven't shown him the letter, and I won't until I know I'm not needlessly carving out my adolescent heart and handing it to him.

"I got a call today." Danny sits on the edge of his bed and reaches out to take my hand, pulling me down beside him. "From Alissa."

"What did she call you for?"

He looks at my hand in his and spins the silver ring on my middle finger. "She found a buyer for our apartment."

Ugh. Hearing him call it "our" apartment makes me irrationally jealous.

"Is that good or bad?"

He shrugs. "I'm not sure. I think it's good. Neither of us want it."

It's a damn shame because that apartment is beautiful. Beautiful enough to be featured in several online lifestyle and interior design publications. Though, when curiosity got the better of me, I combed through the photos, there was nothing of Danny there. No hockey paraphernalia on the walls or jerseys hanging in the his-and-hers closets. Not even a hint of his favorite color, midnight blue, in the color palette. It was like his entire identity had been rolled up and slid under the bed or stuffed in cupboards for the photo shoot. Which is weird, considering how much Alissa mentioned her professional hockey player boyfriend in the interviews.

"Come to New York with me," I suggest. "You can sign the paperwork, we can sightsee and hang out with Alex. Then go to London together."

He thinks about it for a moment before he turns to look at me. "You don't mind me tagging along?"

"Not at all, and Alex won't care, either. He'll be recording most of the time, anyway."

Danny leans forward and rests his forehead against mine— a thank you in our personal language—but he moves closer, because we need to be closer. I close my eyes, waiting for him to tilt my chin up, but too much time passes and when he moves his head away, my disappointment is difficult to hide.

I'm still sitting on the bed when he gets up and throws on a shirt. It's literally the exact opposite of what I want him to do, but I've waited this long and when things finally happen, I want them to be perfect.

"What have you got planned for today?" he asks.

"I have to pick up some dry cleaning and then book my flights."

"Need help?" Danny offers as he slips into the bathroom and picks up his toothbrush.

I don't, really. In fact, when it comes to trip planning, Danny would be more of a hindrance.

"Sure." I grin and, through a mouthful of toothpaste, so does he.

———

Danny and I drag out the morning. We have breakfast with Fletcher and Hallie, pick up the dry cleaning and go for a walk along the pier. We then head to Whiskey Double for lunch and arrive to find a frantic-looking Spencer, who's cornered Miles behind the bar.

"Is everything okay?" I ask her as Danny peels off to get us the booth by the front window. "You look worried."

A curl of chestnut hair falls over Spencer's left eye and she blows it back with a sharp puff. "I'm good."

Miles's eyes widen at her lie.

"What's going on?" I narrow my eyes at both of them and they immediately share a conspiratorial glance.

"I got a lead on a story," Spencer says, and Miles, as if on cue, places a tumbler of amber liquid into her hand. She tosses it back without so much as a twist in her facial expression.

"What's the lead?"

"It's top secret," Miles chimes in. "Strictly a need-to-know thing."

"Then why did she tell *you*?" I smirk and Miles dramatically clutches his chest like I've shot him.

"I have to get back to the office but it was great to see you, Kit." Spencer pats me on the shoulder, then gives Miles a kiss on the cheek and hurries from the bar.

I immediately turn to Miles. "What was that about?"

He shrugs and casually wipes the inside of the glass with a cloth like a cartoon bartender. "Like I said before. It's top secret."

"That's fine. I'll get Danny or Fletcher to get it out of you."

"This thing," he points at his mouth, "is a steel trap."

I lean over the bar. "Steel trap, huh? So it wasn't you that told us all about Donna P's nose job in tenth grade. Or that it was Nolan who peed in Mom's potted fern on New Year's. Or how you and Danny broke your dad's…"

He puts a hand over my mouth and hisses, "You take that to your grave."

I poke my tongue out, and he quickly pulls his hand away and wipes it on his shirt. "Eww."

"Yeah. You're the master of keeping secrets." I laugh.

"Go sit and I'll bring you some food." He sighs.

"Thank you," I say before I stroll over and slide into the booth with Danny.

For the entirety of lunch, we make plans about all the things we can do in New York. Aside from the touristy stuff, Danny suggests some places to eat and some neighborhoods to explore. The deeper we dive into the itinerary, the more he pulls away. His answers get shorter until eventually his suggestions dry up and the conversation becomes entirely one-sided. I change the subject as smoothly as possible, but all the talk about his old stomping ground has done its damage. Before long, I'm making excuses about being tired and wanting to go home.

The car ride is mostly silent, but when Danny pulls up outside my apartment building, he collects the dry cleaning off the back seat and offers to help me take it inside.

"You didn't have to do that," I say as I fish my keys from my purse.

"It's fine," he says, keeping a firm grip on the clothes. "Can we watch a movie or something?"

Since he hasn't been that engaged over the last hour, I figured he wanted to be left alone, so the request takes me by surprise.

"Yeah. Of course."

I slide my key into the lock. As I push open the door, voices echo from my living room. They're hushed, so I can't make out what they're saying.

"Mom," I call out. "Are you here?"

I step into the kitchen, and every fiber of happiness in my body unravels like the seam of a cheap dress.

He's here.

"Katherine." Mom pulls away from the brown-haired man, color draining from her face. "I thought you were out for the day."

For a moment, none of us move. Patrick doesn't even have the decency to wipe the smear of petal pink lipstick off his mouth. Instead, he looks at my mother as if waiting for instructions on what to do next.

"Oh, shit," Danny whispers from behind me.

Suddenly it feels like my tongue is too big for my mouth and all the words that crawl up my throat are in the wrong order and I can't get them out. Why is he in my house?

"Katherine, since you're here, there's someone I'd like you to meet. This is Patrick." She's acting like this is a joyous occasion, but I'm a pot of simmering water, and that smile on her face is the salt that starts the boil.

"Get out of my house," I hiss.

"Katherine," Mom says through tight lips. It's followed by a forced giggle, like this is all a silly misunderstanding.

I take two steps forward and stare at Patrick. "Get out, now!"

Patrick pats his pockets before he leans down and grabs his keys off the coffee table. The coffee table that Dad found for Bea and me at a yard sale. He took it home, sanded and re-varnished it, then carried it all the way up the stairs because our elevator was down for maintenance.

How could she bring him here? How could she let him sit on my couch and drink wine out of my glasses and put his keys on the coffee table Dad gave me?

"Patrick. It's fine," Mom assures him. "Katherine, you're being rude. Can we speak in private for a moment?"

She's unraveling as well. The panic is written on her face in deep lines and red splotches. She looks at Danny, her head tilting apologetically as though he's the outsider and her polite-ness is all it takes to make him feel included.

"I've said what I need to say, and that is get out of my house, both of you."

I'm seeing red, but she and Patrick don't move. Danny's hand rests on my shoulder.

"Fine," I say through gritted teeth. "I'll leave, then."

"Katherine, stop." Mom reaches for me but Danny steps forward, blocking her hand. I grip the back of his jacket, holding myself against his side.

"Daniel?" Mom's brows draw together.

"I'm sorry, Mrs. Reilly," he says. "But Kit has asked you to leave."

Mom looks at me, her confusion growing.

"Having him here is disrespectful to your daughter. She's obviously uncomfortable and you forcing this on her isn't right."

It's the most authoritative I've ever heard Danny sound and I can only imagine how fast his heart is beating right now.

I tug on his sleeve. "Danny. I want to leave."

He looks down at me, his expression stern. "Then let's go."

Mom paces the living room, wiping tears away as Danny walks into my room, takes a duffle from the bottom of my closet and starts throwing clothes into it.

"Get your toothbrush," he tells me as he zips up the bag.

I do as I'm told and as we exit the apartment, he takes my hand and doesn't let go.

CHAPTER TWENTY-SEVEN

For two days, I ignore Mom's calls and stay with Danny. We sleep in the guest bed together, but any heat we had has cooled. On the second night, I expect him to make a move. He doesn't, though. He just holds me until my eyes close, and when I wake up in the morning, he's on the other side of a bed so large you need a passport to cross it. I'm not in the right headspace, and I shouldn't use Danny as a distraction, but I'd do anything to get the image of Patrick in my living room out of my head.

My blood was already boiling when I called Bea to tell her what had happened. She was as livid as me, but short of being available to vent to over video chat, there isn't much she can do from London.

I lay on my back, staring at the decorative wooden beams above, and it takes all my strength not to scream when I receive a scolding text from Mom saying I don't need to speak to her, but I do need to go back to the house and collect the last box of my stuff before the open house this weekend.

I draft and redraft a response in my head as I shower and get dressed. Danny is still asleep, one arm hanging off the side of the bed, so I leave him a note saying we'll catch up later.

Nostalgia hits me hard on the drive over and the reality of the divorce hits me harder. From now on, when I drive these tree-lined streets, a different family will be living in our house. They'll change the furniture, remodel the aging kitchen and have their car parked in the garage. Everything that makes it our house will be stripped away, painted over and replaced. It feels like grief. Losing something that I thought would always be there. With so much change happening already, our home stayed the same. I knew what to expect when I was there. There was comfort in the familiarity of our space.

Not that I recognize it when I arrive.

They've ripped up the carpet in the dining room to expose the hardwood floors, and the furniture is gone. The three-seater couch with the purple nail polish stain on the middle cushion. The dining table where we share our big news. It's all been replaced with high-end rented furniture that's never seen an ounce of love in its life. Our family home, with all our stuff and all our memories, has been restyled with useless trinkets and fake plants.

I walk through the living space and into the kitchen to find a single sealed box on the kitchen counter with my name scrawled on the side. Beside it is a moth-eaten garment bag with Eve's name on it. This box of my old school supplies and my sister's prom dress are all that's left of us.

I instinctively glance up and out the back door to the yard. In an instant, I feel hollow and my breath catches in my throat.

"No!" I shout as I tear open the back door. "No, no, no, no."

The overgrown tree on the fence line is barely recognizable, the twisted, overarching limbs cut away, and all that's left of the treehouse is the damage it did to the trunk of the tree.

It's gone. Torn down and dumped somewhere, leaving the space feeling endless and empty.

I walk down the fence line until I reach the loose palings and press on the aged timber. It doesn't budge. They've nailed it back in place.

"It would have been nice to say goodbye to it."

I turn around to see Eve standing in the middle of the backyard. She looks polished in a dark suit and crisp white button-down. Her inky hair is pulled back into a smooth bun and her fire engine red lips are twisted into a frown.

I run to her, and she wraps her arms around me, squeezing me tight.

"It's gone," I whisper. "All gone."

Eve pats my back.

"Why does she keep disappointing me?" I say. "I'm trying to understand what she's going through, I really am. But then she does these insanely selfish things."

"I'm not going to defend her," Eve says.

"But I have." I start to cry. "And I don't think she deserves it."

It is a terrible thing to lose respect for your parent. I've spent my entire life being guided by this person. Believing that on a fundamental level, she was better than all of us. She knew what was right and what was wrong. But she isn't right, she isn't good. She made a colossal mistake and freely admitted she knew her relationship with Patrick was dangerous, but she did it anyway. She was so vulnerable when she told me her secrets and my heart broke for her. Now I feel like an idiot.

"She had him at my apartment," I say.

Eve pulls away, her hands gripping my shoulders as her crystalline blue eyes narrow.

"She what?"

"It was bad enough knowing he existed, but now he's real and I keep seeing this image of him standing in my living room."

Eve's hands drop to her sides. "I can't believe she did that."

A sudden sense of betrayal builds, even though I shouldn't feel bad about ratting on Mom. Eve is my sister. She has a right to know.

Eve walks over to the gardening shed and yanks open the door. The sound of scraping metal pierces the quiet as she reaches inside and feels around for something above her head. She withdraws when she finds what she's looking for and kicks the door closed with a bang.

"They're still good," Eve confirms. "Want one?"

She holds out a filthy pack of cigarettes that looks older than me.

"I'm good. Thanks." I shake my head.

She takes out a cigarette and pinches it between her lips as she upends the package and a faded green lighter falls into her palm. It takes several clicks, but she lights the cigarette and inhales deeply. Her eyes close and a pleasurable sigh escapes her as she exhales.

"Fuck, I needed this," she says. "Come and sit."

I follow my sister over to the tree, and we sit on the grass beneath.

"I think it's time we talked. Like, really talked." She blows out a plume of smoke and I try not to inhale it. "And I'm going to start by telling you I'm sorry."

Eve looks me in the eye and a crease appears on her forehead. She looks like Mom. They have the same long lashes and a slightly upturned nose. She'd be so angry to hear that.

"I needed you. I still need you," I say.

"I'm here now." She drives the dregs of her cigarette into the soft earth and scoots over, lifting her arm high and pulling me to her side.

My heart can't find its rhythm and all the hurt and anger that's been building seems to gather at the base of my skull. I didn't get to go to London with my boyfriend or fly to the other side of the country. And I certainly didn't get to cut myself off from everyone.

"I know you're angry that Dad got hurt, and Mom shouldn't have done what she did. But I also saw her lying on the couch for days on end, unable to shower or change her clothes. I noticed she wasn't eating, and she started drinking because it was the only thing that made her feel a little better. You have every right to be mad at her. I'm furious, but I didn't know how to fix it and I needed help."

Eve is silent as she stares at her lap.

"Bea and I wanted our sister," I whisper. "But you hate Mom more than you love us."

She pulls me in close, tucking my head beneath her chin

and rubbing my shoulder. "Kit. I am so sorry I made you feel that way. It isn't true."

Her body heaves and her voice shakes as she cries with me. We stay like this for some time. Letting everything drain from us in equal measure. She keeps telling me she's sorry and I believe it. Eve might be stubborn, impulsive, and, at times, selfish. But she's not a liar.

"Darren's cheating on me," she whispers. "He has been for months."

I pull back and look up at her. "Are you serious?"

"Her name is Steph, and she works in the accounting department at his company."

I sit up with my back against the tree and Eve's hand in mine.

She looks down. "When I first suspected it, I told Mom. She said she knew I'd find some excuse to bail on getting married. That this was just another thing I wasn't going to see through to the end."

"I'm sorry." I squeeze Eve's hand and she closes her eyes.

"I shouldn't have cut everyone off, but I'm so angry. I hate Darren for what he's doing, and to know she did the same and judged me for wanting to leave him…I don't understand any of it."

"She didn't sleep with Patrick," I say. "They kissed once."

"Is that how you define an affair?"

"I don't know how to define an affair. That would be up to Mom and Dad."

Eve thinks on this for a moment as she picks at her fingernails.

"I would have said an affair is physical infidelity, but when

I found out about Darren, it wasn't the sex that killed me. It's that she makes him happy. They talk all the time. They have inside jokes and meaningful conversations. I've overheard him on the phone, consoling her after she's had a bad day, and I've seen his face light up when she texts him. That hurts so much more than knowing they fucked in my bed."

Eve closes her eyes, tears salting her cheeks.

"Evie. I'm so sorry. Why didn't you say something?"

She tilts her head back and gently wipes the smudged mascara from under her eye. "I just didn't want this to be another thing I failed at."

"Eve, no." I wrap my whole body around her, and she sinks into me, heaving as she sobs into my shirt. "This is not a reflection on you. This is him being a gutless piece of shit who was too scared to do what's right."

I hold my sister and she cries for longer than she will ever admit. When the tears stop, she tells me about the plan she and Spencer have devised to get her out of the engagement with her life and finances intact. I want to ask for the intricate details, comb through them for faults so I can develop contingencies, but I stop myself.

Eve closes her eyes and leans into my side in the shadow of the tree that once held our favorite place in the entire world.

She doesn't need my logic. She needs my support, so I'll dish it out in spades.

CHAPTER TWENTY-EIGHT

E ven though I assure Alex several times that Danny and I can make it from JFK airport to Manhattan on our own, he's still standing in the arrivals hall with sunglasses and a baseball cap on. Sometimes I forget he's a celebrity, mostly because I vividly remember every bout of food poisoning he's ever had and the time he put a spoon in the microwave to see what would happen. Now Danny and I have to stand off to the side while he signs autographs for a gaggle of young women who insist they've signed up for the pre-sale VIP tickets for his tour next year.

Danny leans against a wall and yawns as it takes a few minutes for the last of the fans to clear off. He was quiet on the flight over. Quieter than usual. When I tried to spark some conversation about his time in New York, he shut it down faster than an underage party with a noise complaint.

Danny is silent on the lengthy cab ride to Alex's apartment, but squeezes my hand as we cross the Manhattan Bridge. It isn't tender, though. More like he's bracing for something painful that's waiting on the other side. He relaxes as we drive through Midtown, but my heart still breaks knowing he doesn't want to be back here. He had to come back anyway to sort out the apartment, but I'm still laden with guilt for pushing him to join me and pretending it would solve his problems.

"This is it." Alex pushes open the door to the third-floor walk-up and props it open with his old duffle.

I step inside and my thoughts immediately shift to the eye-watering sum Alex must pay to rent an apartment this size in the West Village. The living area is at least double the size of mine and three arched windows make up the entire front wall, letting in all that natural light I keep hearing about on renovation shows.

It screams Alex, though. From the guitar left on the couch like something else caught his eye to the clothes scattered across the floor in one of the bedroom doorways.

"It's gorgeous." I move further into the space. "How many bedrooms is it?"

"Two," Alex says as he points to the door with the clothes on the floor. "That's the master, and the second bedroom is over there."

Danny and I follow Alex across the apartment to the second bedroom and peer inside.

"Are you kidding?" I frown at my brother, who is sporting an irritating grin.

"My house. My rules," he says as he steps away, allowing Danny to get a better look inside the room.

The spacious guest bedroom contains a queen-sized bed, a large dresser and a long bench seat, which I'm guessing is supposed to be at the end of the bed. Alex, however, has rearranged the furniture so the queen bed is pushed up against the far wall and the dresser and bench stand end-to-end in the center of the room to create a low wall. On the opposite side of the room, under another large window, is an air mattress.

"I don't care who sleeps where." Alex drops onto the couch. "But one of you is on that mattress and the other is in the bed."

I try not to laugh and Danny's cheeks go pink as he drops his bag at the foot of the air bed.

"I'll take the floor."

"Good man," Alex calls back from the living room.

"You don't have to," I assure Danny.

"Yeah, he does," Alex interjects.

I scowl at my brother, who continues to grin as he picks up the guitar and gently drags his fingers across the strings. "My house, my rules."

"I'm twenty-six."

"Then you understand how rules work."

I fold my arms and huff, which renders my argument useless. "Why are you like this?"

"Because I don't know what's going on with you two and I don't want it being explored under my roof."

Danny shrinks behind me and when his phone rings, he scrambles to get it out of his pocket.

"Oh, thank God," he mutters and answers the call.

I join Alex on the couch to give Danny some privacy in the bedroom.

"You're overreacting." I elbow him in the ribs. "Nothing has happened."

He continues to strum the guitar. "I take my job as your big brother seriously. I've been keeping Reuben away from you for years."

I raise an eyebrow. "Your guitarist?"

"Yep." He confirms. "He's been crazy about you since you visited me in LA four years ago."

I had a feeling he liked me when he tagged along on an all-day bus tour in the California heat, even though he's lived there all his life. I didn't know the crush extended beyond my departure three days later.

"Well, I appreciate you looking out for me, but I can take care of myself," I assure him. "And really, it's Danny's safety you should be worried about. He lifted his shirt up the other day and…"

"Yuck. Stop it." Alex screws up his face and slaps his hands over his ears. "I don't want to hear that."

I give him a shove and when he laughs, it feels like everything is back to normal for a second. Bea isn't gone, Alex never drank himself into oblivion and almost lost his career. Eve is in a state of euphoric love and Mom and Dad are planning the next phase of their lives together. If I close my eyes hard enough, could I hang onto that false reality?

"Kit." Danny steps out of the bedroom and returns his phone to his pocket. "Alissa said the papers are at the apartment when I'm ready to sign."

His mouth hardens into a line, and he looks at the polished timber floor beneath his feet. We need to get this done; the sooner the better. It's a big deal, but maybe it's best if we don't act like it's the final nail in the coffin of Danny's life in New York.

"Great." I stand up and clap my hands together. "We can head over there now, sign the papers, and meet up with Alex for dinner."

Alex agrees to this plan as he collects a set of keys off the coffee table and slaps them into my palm.

"Let's go." I head toward the door with Danny meandering behind.

———

Our subway ride uptown is silent and for the first time in a long time, I don't know what to say. I hate that he's hurting and I hate that I can't fully understand this pain. The last two months, I've felt so lost and he's been my anchor, but I don't think I'm his. I'm not sure how to change that.

"It's a nice building," I say to break the tension as we step into the opulent foyer of his former apartment building. He says nothing but forces a smile for the doorman before he takes my hand and leads me to the bank of elevators.

When we're inside the elevator, he pulls my hand up and kisses the back of it once.

"Don't let go, okay?"

"Okay," I whisper, and I'm not sure if he's trembling because we're in an elevator again or because this is the end of an era. Maybe he does need me.

I keep my promise as we step out onto parquet floors that only add to the hallway's opulence. The gold wall sconces and deep emerald wallpaper make me feel like I'm in a billionaire's library.

"This hallway is too dark," I huff when we stop outside a dark timber door. "I don't like it."

One side of his mouth lifts. "Liar."

He draws the key from his pocket and slides it into the brass lock. With no resistance, he pushes open the door and afternoon light floods the hallway.

I'm speechless. The lifestyle magazine spreads and Alissa's social media feeds didn't do this place justice.

"Holy shit." I'm still gripping his hand and I pull him into the apartment. "It's fucking massive."

I wander around, mouth agape as I study every detail of the empty space and try to calculate what his mortgage payments have been. It's a one bedroom, but the walk-in closet is huge, the bathroom has twin sinks, and the shower takes up an entire wall.

I step back into the main living area and see Danny leaning against the kitchen counter. The heaviness of his heart is palpable, and I have the stark realization that I can't fix this for him. There is nothing I can do right now to ease this pain.

"It's a lot to clean," I grumble as I rejoin Danny in the kitchen. "All those stainless-steel appliances will show fingerprints."

He doesn't smile. He's too busy watching the stack of documents on the marble counter like they might sprout legs and fling themselves from the bay window in the breakfast nook.

"Are you okay?" I ask, keeping a respectful distance.

He swallows hard, the tendons in his neck straining, and his eyes close for a second. My heart is in my throat and every one of our uneven breaths is amplified in this wasted space.

"I'm fine." His tone couldn't be more contradictory to his words as he stares at the papers. I feel like I'm intruding on an incredibly private moment.

Danny picks up the silver pen and scribbles his name on every dotted line. He doesn't read any of it.

When he's done, Danny leans back against the counter and holds out his hand. I walk over, and when I'm close enough, he pulls me into him, pressing me against his chest as his hand tangles in my hair.

"You don't have to be okay about this," I whisper into the lapel of his jacket. "This is hard."

He takes a breath, sharp and sudden.

"What's all this been for, though? I worked so hard for years. I put hockey above everything. I put it above my friends and my family and any kind of life, and it was a fucking waste." He grips me tighter. "What am I going to do now?"

"Anything you want."

"I don't know what I want. I didn't have a plan B."

"That's okay, too," I say. "Most people don't know what they really want."

"I did, though. I had everything and now it's gone."

I step out of his embrace and he roughly wipes his eyes. He can't look at me, so I turn and inspect the documents on the counter.

Alissa's signature is beautiful and perfect, swept across the bottom of the page like it's something to be framed.

"Why did it end?" I ask.

Danny keeps his head down, dragging the back of his hand across his nose and clearing his throat.

"She said we grew apart."

"Did you?"

"I think it was more about the change of circumstance."

How delightfully diplomatic. Now I really dislike her.

"Like I said before, hockey doesn't have to be over completely." I try to tread lightly but I can't entirely stop the pragmatic side of me getting involved. "You can still work for a team or coach or do something."

"It's not the same."

"But it's better than nothing."

He turns around to face me again. "You don't get it."

"No, but I know how important it was to you, and giving it up completely will never be an option. We both know that."

He folds his arms, matching my stance. Suddenly, this escape from reality is crumbling around us. The air feels thick.

"I'm not myself anymore, Kit," he whispers.

Maybe he isn't, and I only know the kid that left for college. Suddenly everything feels fragile. We're together again, but there's still distance and we've made promises to each other before. Then they became too hard to keep.

Now, we've created a false reality. One where we have my bucket list to keep us entertained while we both navigate all these life changes. It's not forever. It's a vacation from real life and soon I'll have to go back to my job and he'll have to find a new one.

"You need time." My voice echoes off the eggshell walls. "I don't want to be a distraction while you work out how to cope with what you've lost."

I love him and I don't want us to fall apart like we did before.

"You're not a distraction."

"Yes, I am. I've taken your mind off hockey for a while. Which is something I've never been able to do," I point out. "You're looking for something familiar to hold on to."

His arms fall to his sides. "Why would you say that?"

"Because that's what I've done to you." My stomach turns over itself. "You said you don't feel like yourself anymore and maybe I've pushed too hard, trying to get us back to where we were because I needed it. I've rushed you."

The hurt in his expression is a knife to my belly, but we're so close to letting this get infinitely more complicated.

"Take some time to think," I say, trying to appear like my heart is in this decision. "Because I can't replace what you lost and I don't want to push you into thinking I can."

CHAPTER TWENTY-NINE

D anny decides to forgo dinner with Alex, so I hand over the key to the apartment and promise to give him space. I don't want to, though, and I realize that the moment I step out of his old apartment building. But he was right when he said I don't understand. I really don't and I feel useless. So, the best thing I can do is give him time to process all of this and not worry about what we're doing.

"Best steak in the city," Alex says as he comes to a stop before a recessed doorway somewhere near Delancey Street station.

"Are you sure about that?" I look up at the neon sign overhead. When fully operational, it would say *Sal's Bar and Grill*, but five of the letters are out and two are blinking.

"It doesn't look like much, but it's great," Alex assures me as he opens the door and I follow him inside.

The interior is about what I expected. Dark timber paneled walls, torn carpet and apparently no one in the place can change a light bulb. Alex steps around the low table by the door with a stack of food-stained plastic menus. There isn't a hostess in sight. Not that we need one, because Alex has spotted Reuben at a table in the back and is already making his way over.

"Ru, you remember my little sister, Kit?"

Reuben stands up and holds his hand out. I shake it as he jerks his head to get the unruly mass of dark curls out of his eyes. "Hey, Kit."

"This is Alfie and Ash." Alex inclines his head toward the two people on the other side of the table. I follow both of them on Instagram so I recognize that Ash's hair is teal green this week, as opposed to the pink of the week before, and Alfie looks much younger in real life thanks to the smattering of freckles across his cheeks and his boyish grin.

"Nice to meet you." I smile as I sit between Reuben and my brother.

Before the steaks arrive, Alex and his band discuss the upcoming album, and Ash fills me in on what life has been like in the studio. Alfie and Ash only joined the band last year, but Reuben was one of the first people Alex met when he moved to LA. I've often wondered if Reuben is the reason Alex went so severely off the rails. He was always in the paparazzi shots with Alex, leaving various nightclubs and bars.

"How long are you in the city for?" Reuben asks, as an impressive-looking steak is placed in front of him.

"Only a week. Then I'm flying over to London to see my sister."

"Oh, nice." He says as he cuts his food with a knife that

belongs in the machete category rather than silverware. "Have you been to London before?"

I shake my head. "First time."

"You're gonna love it. The food is great and there's so much history." His brown eyes light up. I don't remember him being this engaging when we met years ago. I was desperate for Alex to hate LA and move home, so I didn't warm to any part of his LA life. Including his new industry friend.

"Can you give me some sightseeing tips, then?" I ask, before scooping some mashed potato into my mouth.

Reuben spends the rest of the dinner periodically adding landmarks to the notes app on my phone. Each time he thinks of something, often completely unrelated to the present topic of conversation, he has this sharp intake of breath and takes my phone out of my hand. The sixth time he does it, my phone rings.

"Danny is calling you," Reuben says as he hands my phone back. I take it, pressing the answer button and failing to excuse myself before dashing outside.

"Hey, is everything alright?"

"Yeah," he says. "Where are you?"

My body floods with relief at the sound of his voice.

"At some restaurant on the Lower East Side with Alex and his band. Where are you?"

"Madison Square Park."

There's shouting in the background; drunken revelers passing too close to where Danny is sitting.

"Do you want me to meet you there? Or are you coming back to the apartment?"

"No. I'm going to get a hotel."

My heart sinks again. "Do you want to be alone tonight?"

He's quiet for far longer than polite conversation allows. "Yeah."

"Okay." I nod, already feeling the emptiness. "Can you let me know when you're checked in? So I know you're safe."

"Yeah," he whispers as more people pass him by. "I'll see you tomorrow."

We say goodnight and I lean back against the rough brick wall of the restaurant. He needs this, and I need to let him have it.

———

It's late when Alex and I get back to the apartment. Reuben decides to crash on the now unoccupied air mattress and Alex, with all the subtlety of a sledgehammer, takes the guest bed, leaving me with the master bedroom.

I shower, say goodnight to my brother and slip into bed, intending to add Reuben's list of sights to my London itinerary. When my phone dings in the early hours of the morning, I open my eyes to the violent glow of my discarded laptop.

DANNY

Do you still have the letter?

Since I can't hide it behind the baseboard anymore, I've been searching for a new hiding spot. The best I could come up with was the zippered section of my purse and it's still safely in there.

KIT

Yeah. I have it with me. Why?

DANNY

Can you read it to me?

KIT

Right now?

DANNY

Yeah

I'm not sure if this is a good idea, but that night in the pool, I told him I was ready to share it. A knot forms in my belly. Every second of that night is sharp in my memory. My hair wrapped around his hand and the longing in his voice. Goosebumps form on my skin and I close my eyes, take a deep breath, and pick up my phone.

DANNY

Please, Kit.

I take a moment before I respond. My whole heart is in that letter and after what he went through today, is this what he needs?

DANNY

Katherine.

KIT

Okay. Give me a second.

I fetch the letter, and when I'm back in bed I turn on the bedside lamp and unfold the paper, smoothing it out as best I can.

Danny answers on the first ring.

"Here goes nothing."

I'm already rethinking this, so I take my time.

"What's wrong?" he says, after waiting too long.

My voice is a trembling whisper. "I'm scared."

"Why are you scared?" he asks. "If it's what you wanted to say to me, then say it to me."

I stare at my handwriting. It's an angry mess. "It's not a happy letter."

"I still want to hear it."

"I wasn't in the best place when I wrote it." I hold the phone between my ear and shoulder. "You'd just left for Minnesota and I was upset."

"Please. Read it," he says softly.

I take a deep breath and look at the paper again.

"You're in the air now. I waited until you took off before I left the airport. I thought there was a chance you'd get off the plane and there was no way I wasn't going to be there if you did. I hate the little part of myself that thought it was a possibility because I know better. Hockey comes first, and if going to college in Minnesota gets you even a tiny step closer to your dream, then it's worth it.

I guess I just don't understand how a city the size of Seattle can feel empty now. I still have Bea and I'm excited about college, but it doesn't feel right without you here.

I don't think we can be this far apart. Our souls aren't built for it. At least mine isn't, and it's going to be a long time before we see each other again."

I take another deep breath and wipe the tears off my cheek.

"The first thing I did when I came home was scream into my pillow. It smells like you, by the way. That made it hurt more. You shouldn't have

stayed here last night because I realized that everything you said was a lie, so I wouldn't cry so much. I want to be okay with you leaving—I don't want to be this desperate and I don't want to resent you for following your dreams—but I do and I'm angry and jealous of the people who get to see you every day. It's so unfair that I'm not one of them anymore."

I turn the letter over and through the phone I can hear soft music and the rustle of clothing. I'm too far in it now. I have to read the last part.

"I'm sorry I told you that I love you. It was selfish and only for my benefit. You said you love me too, but you don't love me the same way. You probably never will, but I still want you to know that I'll never get over you. I love you with every fiber of my heart and soul. I love you in a way that so painful it makes me wonder if there is something wrong with me. When you climbed up my treehouse ladder and asked me to be your friend, I didn't know it would turn into this. I didn't know it would hurt so much to say goodbye. I don't regret shaking your hand though. It was the start of something big. I just wish you felt that too."

I fold the paper and drop it onto the crumpled sheets. I had no right to think those things, let alone put them in a letter. I'm stuck in a moment that passed a long time ago, but I feel lighter knowing that I did recover and I'm glad he left and got to do what he loved for as long as he did. He deserved every happiness because he made me happy for the time I had him.

The phone is still against my ear and a car door slams in the background, followed by Danny's hushed voice.

"Come downstairs," he says.

I climb off the bed, throw on my coat and take the stairs to the ground level two at a time. My habitual five-mile runs are paying off, but when I push open the door and see Danny standing on the sidewalk, my heart beats so hard I briefly worry about possible cardiac arrest.

He doesn't say a word, he just stands there, hands hanging loosely at his sides, waiting for me. I wish I could bottle this moment. Save some of the anticipation for later when the inevitable disappointment catches up with me. For now, though, I savor what I can as I descend the steps to stop in front of him.

He holds out his hand. "More than friends?"

I shake his hand and he pulls me to him, sliding his other hand into my hair and gripping the back of my neck.

"You're wrong," he whispers. "I do love you the same way."

He pulls my mouth to his and I know, without a shadow of doubt that this kiss is the one. It's worth the wait because it's so perfect it will ruin me for all other kisses. Nothing will ever compare, and I will remember every second of this for as long as I live. Even when we're old and shout at each other from different rooms or when he takes a wrong turn because he thinks he knows better even though I'm the one looking at the map. I will remember the softness of his lips and the milk and honey smell of the shampoo he bought at the airport because he forgot to pack his own. I will remember the way he holds me. Like I'm made of glass, and he's terrified that I will slip from his grasp and shatter. I will remember the sound of the city fading away and the crisp night air brushing my cheeks. I will remember how good it feels to have him.

CHAPTER THIRTY

Danny holds my hand for the entire walk to his hotel, like he's terrified I'm going to run away. When we step into the elevator, he waits for the doors to close before he wraps his arm around my neck and pulls me into him, burying his face in my hair as he pushes the button for the top floor.

He's too fiscally responsible to book the penthouse, so I'm curious about where we're headed.

"What are we doing?" I ask as we step out of the elevator.

"It's about to rain."

Danny holds my hand, guiding me through the hallways until we reach the door to the roof. He pushes it open and holds it there with a semi-crumbled concrete block.

"Bucket list item six," I say.

"Except I can't dance," he says. "Sorry about that."

I look up at the band of heavy clouds that stretch out above us. It's so dense the city lights are reflected in its swirling, gray mass.

Danny walks toward the center of the rooftop. "We'll definitely get in trouble if someone catches us up here."

"Better make it quick then." I hurry over and wrap my arms around his neck as the first droplets of rain land on our heads.

"I never wanted to do this one," I explain. "Bea added it to the list because she thought it would be romantic."

"Did you come up with anything on that list?" Danny raises a brow. "Because it's all things Bea saw in a romantic comedy."

I contemplate it for a second. "I was more in charge of formatting than content. I came up with the dinner party one, though."

"And how was that?"

"Horrible," I admit. "Never again."

He wraps his body around mine and kisses me as the rain splashes my cheeks. When we break apart, I blink away the water droplets gathered on my eyelashes and sway us from side to side so I can cross *"dance in the rain"* off the list with a clear conscience.

"Can we go inside?" I ask as the rain gets heavier.

Danny takes my hand and we rush back to the corridor as a crack of thunder rattles the night. We're both soaked and every nerve ending in my body is firing as he kicks the block out of the way and closes the door.

He's breathing heavily, and his cheeks are flushed. Droplets fall from the ends of his hair, and when he turns to look at me, my heart flutters in my chest.

It's Danny.

My prom date.

The guy who taught me how to ice skate and fish and climb the trellis outside my bedroom window so I could sneak out to see him. He's the one who stood up for me at school when I let Bea cut my hair, and he's the one who walked me home all the time, even though I only lived next door.

He's the one who learned basic morse code so we could communicate by flashlight late at night through our respective windows.

He's the one who held me every time I cried.

He's the one who told me that everything was going to be okay.

He's the one.

"Kiss me again," I say. "Please."

He places his hands on my waist as he presses my back against the wall of the corridor. Is this the moment I should bottle? It's charged with even sweeter anticipation. I know what to expect this time, and I can't live without it.

Danny leans into me and a few water droplets fall from his hair and land on my cheeks as he kisses me, tender and unhurried. Like he's exploring.

"Back to the room?" His voice shakes as he presses his forehead against mine.

"Immediately." I say and he takes my hand, leading me back to the elevator. The entire ride down to his floor, Danny fidgets with the ring on my middle finger and taps his foot. I lift his arm and wrap it around my shoulder so I can rest my head against his chest.

His heart is beating impossibly fast. It makes mine flutter.

The room is small, and the queen-sized bed in the center has barely enough space to walk around it. As a result,

Danny's suitcase is standing upright in the corner under the wall-mounted TV. He hasn't been here at all today, judging by the perfectly made bed and the glassware still sporting those little paper hats.

"Oh no. There's no air mattress," I joke.

"That's a shame." Danny forces a laugh, but my joke isn't enough to dissipate the tension that pulls his shoulders tight.

"I'm going to take a shower." He steps past me and disappears into the bathroom. I'm glad, because we both need a second to regroup.

I don't know what to do, so I linger by the door and suddenly feel unsure about what to do with my hands. I put them on my hips. That feels standoffish. I hang them at my sides. Awkward. Clasped behind my back? No, that's a middle-aged father of three waiting for his wife to finish talking to an old acquaintance they've run into at the grocery store.

It's not just my hands that I don't know what to do with. It's my whole body. Should I lean against the wall? Would that hide the nerves building inside me again? Maybe I should get my phone out and do the daily crossword on that news app? I haven't done it today and Spencer and I are getting pretty competitive with it.

"Are you coming with me or not?" Danny's head appears around the bathroom door. I've half pressed myself against the wall with a hand in my pocket; it definitely looks like I'm trying to listen to whatever he was doing in the bathroom.

I rip my hand from my pocket as Danny steps out into full view. He's naked, except for a standard-issue hotel towel around his waist.

I'm speechless, and he's acting like being naked in front of me is an everyday occurrence. His eyes are fixed on my face.

I'm quite certain this is delayed shock. I've seen him without a shirt a few times, but I always look away because I don't want to make things awkward. Now that I can have a decent look, I realize he has muscles I didn't know existed. They're all toned from hockey and shiny from the rain. I want to touch them more than I've ever wanted anything. I want to trace all the tattoos with my fingertip and then kiss him until he's as certain as I am that we can't live without each other.

"Kit?" Danny lifts a brow and waves his hand in front of my face.

"We're doing this, aren't we?" My body is tingling all over.

He squares his shoulders before he removes the towel from his waist and drops it on the floor.

"Holy fuck." I slap my hand over my mouth.

He picks up the towel and covers himself again. "What? I thought we were doing this."

"No, sorry. I didn't mean to …" I try to catch my breath. "I really do want this. It's just I've never seen you naked before and I'm…I'm in shock. That's all."

There is a definite stain on his cheeks, and he grips the towel tighter.

Fuck. I'm ruining this. Not that I thought having sex with Danny for the first time would be seamless. I just thought I'd have a touch more composure.

"I'm going to need a second here. Can you go into the shower and I'll meet you there in a minute?" I instruct him as I wipe my sweaty palms on my jeans.

Danny does as instructed and slips back into the bathroom,

ensuring he remains covered. I stay in the entryway and take a couple of breaths before I peel off each item of damp clothing. I hang my sweater and shirt on hangers, spaced out in the open closet, and place my jeans over the chair. No sense in leaving them in a clump on the floor. I do want to wear dry clothing when I inevitably return to Alex's apartment for the interrogation over where I've been all night.

I step into the bathroom, hands covering my boobs, even though Danny is facing away and has his head under the surprisingly well-pressured stream of water. He has to duck a little because at his full height the spray would hit his chin.

"Okay. I'm here," I say as I open the glass door and step into the cubicle. There's barely enough room for both of us and if he turns around too quickly, I'm getting an elbow to the head. "Don't turn around yet."

"Couldn't if I wanted to." He laughs as I step up behind him, press my forehead into the space between his shoulder blades, and wrap my arms around him. He threads his fingers through mine and holds both my hands against his chest. I can feel his heart beating, but it isn't as rapid as before. It's a steady rhythm in comparison to mine.

I've wanted him for as long as I can remember, but I'm glad it's taken this long to come to fruition. I didn't understand my feelings for him all those years ago. I knew it was love, but I didn't comprehend the gravity of it. Now it feels earned and important.

"You're worth the wait," I say into his back and he slowly turns around.

He leans down and kisses me with one hand on my cheek and the other on my waist. We ease back and I run my hands over him, finally getting to trace the tattoos, starting from his shoulder and following the pattern down his bicep.

"Are you going to get one?" he asks.

"I don't know if there's anything special enough to have on my skin forever," I admit. "I also don't know where I'd get it."

He runs a hand over my shoulder blade. "Here?"

I shake my head. "Too painful."

He then runs his hand down my arm and turns my wrist upward. "Here?"

I shake my head again. "Too visible."

He agrees before lifting my arm over my head and turning me around. I'm pinned to him as he runs his finger down the left side of my body to my hip before coming back up to my ribs. "Here?"

I let my head drop back onto his chest as the water falls between us. "Maybe."

His hand comes back to my face, and he runs his thumb over my cheek as he kisses me again. It's passionate now. There's less gentle and languid exploration. Every touch has a purpose and inside I'm screaming for it.

That is until I turn too fast and crack my elbow on the wall-mounted soap dish.

"Fuck!" I shout as I rub the spot where a bruise is already forming. "That hurt."

His brow furrows, and he lifts my elbow, inspects it for a second, then gives it a gentle kiss. "Better?"

Not really, but he looks concerned.

There's no room in this shower for any of the activities I want, so I lean past him and turn the water off.

He reaches over my shoulder, pushes the shower door

open and holds my hand as I climb out so I don't slip. The process isn't graceful considering there's little room to move, and we both try to dry ourselves facing away from each other to preserve some of the mystery. To add insult to injury, we try to exit at the same time and become wedged in the door frame.

"This isn't going well," I say as he steps back and lets me out of the bathroom first.

"How did you want it to go?" He secures the towel around his waist and runs his hand through his damp hair. Several strands fall forward on his forehead and my heart skips a beat at what a privilege it is to look at him.

"I don't know, but I thought we'd be more coordinated than this."

"I'm nervous."

"Me too." The flush travels from my neck to my cheeks.

He takes my hand and places it on his heart. "I want it to be good for you and I don't want you to regret it."

I can't guarantee tonight will be faultless, but I hope we can look back and laugh at all the things that weren't perfect. What I *can* guarantee is that I won't regret this.

"I want you," I say. "I've always wanted you. Why would I regret this?"

He hooks an arm around my waist and pulls me to him. His mouth finds mine and I reach for the towel at his waist, yanking it off and dropping it on the floor in one swift movement.

"Now?" He smiles against my lips.

"Now."

He rips my towel off, grips the back of my legs and hoists

me up, pinning me against the wall as he trails kisses down my neck.

"Why haven't we done this before now?" My voice is a breathy mess.

"To preserve the friendship."

I drag my fingers through his hair, tugging on the damp strands. "Idiots."

My legs are jelly, and if he takes even one step back, I'm going to fall to the floor.

His mouth moves back up my neck, but I pull on his hair until we're eye to eye. "Put me on the bed."

He immediately turns around and lowers me onto the bed. With the lights off, the glow of the city streams in through the sheer curtains, and as I move toward the headboard, I take a moment to watch as he slides up beside me. I'm still in shock that any of this is happening, and I can't stop the ridiculous grin that splits my face.

He lifts his arm to pull me against him, but we both miscalculate and his forearm smacks me in the nose.

"Oh shit. I'm so sorry," he panics and I laugh even though my nose is tingling.

"It's fine. It's fine," I assure him as he wraps his arms around me and kisses the tip of my nose.

"Katherine," he says.

"Daniel," I respond.

He takes a breath. "You mean everything to me."

It carries so much weight, but I am lighter than air.

"You mean everything to me."

We both roll onto our sides to face each other, and he trails his finger from the middle of my thigh, up over my hip and into the dip of my waist. I move in closer until our bodies are flush against each other and take a moment to compose myself.

I barely get the chance because his hands are on me, caressing every inch of my skin. It's euphoric, and I can't concentrate on anything other than where he's touching me. It feels like the number of nerve endings in my body has tripled, and when he slides his hand between my legs, I can't control my breathing.

A fluttering sensation spreads from my toes to the tips of my fingers and it sends all my thoughts scattering. We need to be closer than this, and as his lips move from my mouth, across my cheek and down my neck, I reach down between our bodies. His breath hitches and the groaning sound he makes has my pulse racing even more. I've never heard him make such a noise and I smile as his head falls back against the pillow.

We continue this long-awaited exploration of each other and quickly lose track of time. I thought I knew everything about him. Every freckle. Every scar. But now everything feels new and different in the best possible way.

"Danny," I whisper, and he shifts to lie on top of me, pushing my thighs apart with his knee. His weight is heavenly and when I take a shuddering breath, he pulls back and looks at me.

"Are you sure about this?"

I stare into his eyes and place my hands on his stubbled cheeks. I take in the scars on his face, his stunningly long lashes and the small dent on the bridge of his nose. It's Danny and he still is and always has been the love of my life.

I shift my hips. "I've never been more certain of anything."

It's surreal and I drink in every sensation. The clean smell of the sheets, the smooth texture of his skin and the warmth of being held by him.

That's when the tension unravels, the joking stops and there's a fire in his eyes. I breathe in, press my forehead to his and switch off my brain from everything else in my life because I've decided this is the moment I want to bottle. This is what I want to remember forever.

He whispers my name, and I close my eyes. It's a connection I can't describe. Like the final pieces of a complicated puzzle have aligned.

His lips brush mine and his hand slides down the side of my body. I gasp when he adjusts my hips, changing the angle. It's too much, but at the same time, not enough. We can't get any closer.

I arch my back, dig my nails into his skin and close my eyes. I'm going to see stars.

And I do.

CHAPTER THIRTY-ONE

"*A*re you freaking out?" Danny asks as we lay on opposite sides of the bed.

"No," I lie. I've been freaking out since the sun came up. It didn't stop me from having sex with Danny again, and we were more coordinated the second time.

We spent the entire night dozing in each other's arms, then waking up and doing more things we've never done before. Admittedly, I was the one who initiated most of it, because he's a professional athlete. His body is ridiculous, and he was lying right beside me. I also thoroughly enjoy the little sounds he makes in my ear every time I get him riled up.

Enjoyable and long-awaited evening aside, the reality of the day has all my muscles in knots, because we need to have a conversation about where to go from here.

"You're freaking out." Danny rolls onto his back and shields his face from the morning sun with his arm. He looks incredible in the daylight, with his bare chest and tattooed biceps. Not to mention his glorious golden hair. I hope he keeps it at its current chin length, because I'm not done running my fingers through it.

I'm about to do that when my phone dings with a text.

"Shit. Alex is wondering where I am."

Danny peers at me with one eye. "He's going to be mad, isn't he?"

"I am not telling him about this. I'd get a better reaction if I told him I spent the entire night roaming alleyways looking for someone to buy heroin from."

He frowns. "I'm not a bad guy."

"No, you're not. You're the best guy. But I'm his little sister, and even if you were a pediatric oncologist with a cabinet full of humanitarian awards who works at a homeless shelter every Thursday, you still wouldn't be good enough."

"But I've known him since we were kids."

"Doesn't matter."

Danny yawns and stretches his arms over his head. "Let's get back to the apartment and face him, then."

We definitely should, but if we leave this bed decisions have to be made, and I want to put that off as long as possible. He shifts under the sheets, pulling his leg up and exposing his knee. I've never seen the surgery scars and when he notices me looking, he covers his leg with the sheet again.

"You're perfect," I whisper.

He leans down and brushes his lips against mine. It's delicate at first, but then I press myself into him, my fingers drawing circles on his chest. He deepens the kiss, his hand sliding over my hip before I drag my leg up, throw it over his body and lift myself up to straddle his hips.

"We're not going back to the apartment yet, are we?" he says as he sits up on his elbows.

I lean down to kiss him again and he gets carried away for a moment before pulling back. I recognize the look in his eyes and know he doesn't truly share this idea that the real world doesn't exist while we're in bed. Which is a shame.

"What are we doing here, Kit?"

"I'm kissing you."

"I see that." He sighs. "But we should talk about this."

"Yeah, we will."

That crease forms between his eyebrows. "Are you okay with what happened?"

"Okay? I'm over the moon," I say. "But I decided that while we're in this bed, we don't have to worry about anything else. Not my parents, or Alex murdering you, or what you're going to do with the rest of your life."

He contemplates this for far too long before he grins.

"Yep." He lifts his hips and I gasp.

"Oh, we are never leaving the bed." I lean down and kiss him again, tangling my fingers in his hair. He sits up more and wraps his arms around my body, one hand pressing on the center of my back to hold me against him. I've never felt so loved.

"No, we aren't," he says against my mouth.

I grind against him and his eyelids flutter. It's short-lived because his phone vibrates across the nightstand and he frowns. He ignores the call, though, and continues to kiss me.

"You can answer it," I assure him. "Say goodbye to your loved ones before you face my brother."

He laughs as he reaches over to collect his phone. I can't

see the caller's name, but his brows draw together immediately.

"Yeah, I better take this."

I slide off, expecting him to step into the bathroom for some privacy, but he stays in bed, grabs my hand, linking our fingers and holding it against his chest.

"Hey, man. It's been a while," he says into the phone as I snuggle up beside him and close my eyes while he carries on his conversation. The deep cadence of his voice is melodic. I could listen to it for the rest of my life.

"Text me the address and I'll be there," Danny says before hanging up the phone and placing it back on the nightstand. He lifts his arm and tucks me into the nook against his side.

"Is everything okay?" I ask.

"Yeah. Well, I don't know," he says. "I have some bad news."

A spike of panic radiates through my whole body. We're still in the bed. Nothing can get us here. "What is it?"

"That was my old assistant coach. He wants to meet up while I'm in town."

I audibly exhale. "That doesn't sound bad."

"He's in Toronto at the moment, but he'll be back next week for a night before he heads to Miami."

I tap my fingers on his stomach in a gentle drumbeat. He won't be coming to London with me, then. But he doesn't want to say it.

"I can make it over to Bea on my own," I assure him. "You can drop me off on this side and she can pick me up. There's no room for error."

He laughs softly, then kisses the top of my head. "I'll meet you over there as soon as I can."

I trust Danny; he wouldn't interfere with this trip unless it was necessary. I also don't want to draw any conclusions, but an important meeting with his former coach seems like an opportunity.

"Don't worry about me. I'll be fine." I lift my head up to kiss his cheek.

He goes quiet for a long time and I can hear my heart beating in my ears. I think of the crowded airport, the immigration line at Heathrow and making small talk with a cab driver. The plane is definitely a different model to the one we flew over here on, so what if my carry-on doesn't fit in the overhead bin and the flight attendant asks me to check it in front of all the other passengers? What if I don't eat the plane food and can't swap with anyone, or the airline loses my bag? What if Jamie gave me the wrong address and I can't find Bea?

"Kit." Danny brings me back to reality. "I'll cancel the meeting."

"Don't you dare." My tone is more threatening than intended, but at least he agrees.

———

My week in New York passes quickly and Alex spends most of that time staring at a blank notebook, growing increasingly frustrated with himself. He even snaps at Alfie when he offers feedback on the one song they do have. I can tell he's itching for a drink. His leg keeps bouncing, and he's tapping his fingers on his knee.

When it gets too much, I take Reuben aside and tell him I'm worried. He promises everything is okay, but I'm not sure I believe him. Especially when an unopened bottle of bourbon appears in the cupboard beside the fridge. When Alex goes to get pizza, I pour it down the sink and drop the empty bottle down the garbage chute. At 2am this morning I heard him rifling through the kitchen. He slammed the cupboard door and swore before going back to bed. This morning, when I woke up, his notebook had two new songs in it. One about love and one about regret.

"Are you sure you're okay?" I ask my brother as we hurry through breakfast before I have to get to the airport.

"I'm fine, Kit. Stop worrying."

"Are you having trouble writing?"

His eyes snap up from his half-eaten breakfast. "I can write."

"I know you can. You're amazing. But I heard you and Reuben talking yesterday. Something about the label being pissed off."

"It's fine, Kit. You didn't hear anything." He doesn't look at me and he slices his pancake so forcefully the knife makes a horrible scraping sound against the plate.

"If you want to talk about it, I'm here," I say and Alex pauses the disgruntled massacring of his breakfast. His shoulders drop and the tension in his body appears to release all at once.

"Thank you," he says. "I love you, Kit. You know that right."

"I do and I love you too."

We don't talk about music for the rest of breakfast, but when we go back to the apartment to collect my bags, he takes a call behind the closed bedroom door. I can't hear what is said, but Alex begs whoever is on the line to give him more time.

I ask no questions, but give him an extra tight hug when he drops me off at the check-in counter at JFK.

The flight to London is seamless. Alex assured me that my arrival and subsequent passage through immigration at Heathrow would be easy, and even though he was right, I'm still exhausted when the cab drops me off at my final destination.

Jamie's apartment is in a narrow building on a street lined with willowy trees that rustle in the cool afternoon breeze. A group of young women stroll down the sidewalk, arms linked and chatting excitedly about what the night has in store for them. It's more peaceful than I imagined. I assumed London would be loud and dirty, but the building in front of me is welcoming with its white stone facade and bright blue door. It feels like a home.

"You're here!" Bea squeals as she throws open the door and hugs me so tight I worry my in-flight meal of tomato-flavored chicken with rice might make a reappearance.

"I've missed you." I lay my cheek on her shoulder for a few seconds before she pushes me back, holding me at arm's length to study my features. I had my eyebrows done by a new lady at the salon, so they're a touch darker than I like, but aside from that, I'm exactly the same. I can't say the same for Bea, though. Her cheeks are drawn and her skin has lost its rosy glow. It's chalky, and her hair is flat. Even her roots are showing.

"How's London?" I ask in place of stating the obvious change in her appearance.

"So good. I love it here. Jamie's really enjoying working with his family again and we've been spending weekends at their country estate. How ridiculous is that? A country estate." She laughs to herself as she ushers me inside.

"It does sound like you're enjoying yourself."

"So much." She grins.

Jamie's apartment is considerably smaller than its US counterpart. The sofa isn't as far back from the flatscreen TV as it should be for comfortable viewing and the washer is under the bench in the postage-stamp kitchen. Bea gives me a quick tour, which can be done without moving if you choose the exact right spot to stand. It has one bedroom plus a study, which has been furnished with a single bed for my arrival. It's cozy, though, and Bea is definitely responsible for the frosty-blue bed coverings and little trinkets that decorate the timber desk and compact bookshelf. I assumed that with Jamie's family's money, he'd live somewhere more opulent. From my research, the neighborhood is fairly upscale, so I guess space was the trade-off.

"It's not the Four Seasons, but at least we're together." Bea's grin is infectious and she clasps her hands together, eyes lit with pride.

"It's perfect." I match that energy as I wrap my arm around her shoulder.

By the time I settle in, Jamie's back from work and I've filled Bea in on everything from home, including my talk with

Eve and all the Danny developments. She's thrilled, but I don't miss the trepidation in her expression when I tell her about his meeting with the assistant coach.

"I bet it's a job," I say. "Which is fantastic. It's the best possible outcome."

"The best possible outcome would be a west coast team, though."

I swallow and ignore the tingle in my nose. "I mean, that would be good, but he really loved living in New York."

Bea reaches over and takes my hand. "Whatever happens, you two will work it out."

All I can hope is that he doesn't let my letter influence his decision. We're older now and he needs this.

It isn't long before Jamie and Bea finally decide on dinner at a French restaurant down the street. I'm happy that we won't have to walk far because we need an early night so Bea and I can be up to catch the Paris train.

"How are things going at home?" Jamie asks as he settles on the couch while Bea finishes getting ready. I've taken the wingback chair, which is more comfortable than it looks.

"Fine, I guess. I've sorted things out with Eve, and I called Dad to check in last night. He said he's taken up cross-stitch to help with fine motor skills in his old age."

Jamie laughs, which is the exact reaction I had when Dad sent through a picture of what I'm guessing was supposed to be a bouquet of flowers.

"Not missing Bea too much, then," Jamie says.

"I do miss her but it's okay. I'm going back to work at the bank after this trip. That will keep me busy until Bea comes home."

Jamie clears his throat and his jaw goes rigid. "Yeah, of course."

Have I missed something? Because Jamie looks like he's about to run out for apology donuts.

"Are you okay?" I ask.

He nods with forced enthusiasm. "Of course. You know me…I'm just…British."

"That makes no sense."

"Yes, it does," he stands up and brushes invisible fluff from his jeans. "We best get moving or we'll miss our reservation."

I raise a brow. "We don't have a reservation."

Jamie averts his eyes and calls out, "Beatrice. Sweetheart. We're going to be late."

Bea steps out of the bedroom, purse in hand. Though she's still fastening her earring as Jamie sweeps us out the door.

On the walk to the restaurant, Bea points out several of the businesses they frequent. Outside their dry cleaner, I ask Bea if Jamie is okay only for her to brush off the question and pull me toward their local supermarket and the café where they often have breakfast.

"Is Jamie having issues at work?" I whisper, holding Bea to my side.

"No. Work is fine. We're both doing great."

We deviate from the more direct route to the restaurant so Bea can show me the small park she passes through on her morning walk and the movie theater she's been to three times with some of Jamie's friends. Bea's smile is constant as she gives me this tour and while her eyes are shining, a large pit forms in my stomach. I think I know what's happening.

After dinner, which was not as delicious as Jamie led me

to believe, we walk home a different way, giving my sister the opportunity to point out her local bookstore, bakery and a clothing boutique, all of which look cramped and unwelcoming. The pit in my stomach grows larger, and by the time we arrive back at the apartment, I can't hold my tongue.

"You're not coming home, are you?" I say as Bea sits on the couch beside me.

She studies her hands, pinching the skin of her palm.

"I don't know what to say."

"Just tell me the truth."

She inhales. "I really love it here."

"Okay." My voice shakes.

Her eyes shoot up to mine. "Okay?"

"Okay," I confirm.

"What does that mean?"

I shrug. "I can see you love it here, but what about your business?"

"Leah bought me out. They've appointed a new co-director."

"Oh. I see." I say. "You knew you weren't coming back?"

"I didn't know how to tell you."

I start picking at my cuticles.

"You could have just told me," I utter as Jamie appears from the bedroom and leans on the door frame with his hands in his pockets.

Bea scrambles over to me, taking my hands in hers to stop my nail-picking.

"I also thought you'd come here, see how much I love it, and understand why I want to stay."

"I understand why you want to stay," I say. "I don't understand why you lied about it."

I look at my sister. There are tears in her eyes and my heart breaks a little more.

"Who else knows?"

Bea and Jamie share a look that makes my heart sink even further.

"A few people. Mom and Dad and Alex. I told Eve before I left and Leah...and most of the Larsons know," Bea mumbles.

So almost everyone in my life knows and they've been pretending that she'll be back in a year? That hurts more than the actual news.

"Kit, do you reckon we could have a pow-wow outside?" Jamie approaches.

I let go of Bea's hand. "Okay."

I follow Jamie outside and onto the sidewalk. The night air whips around us as he looks down and rubs his hand on the back of his neck. He has no idea what he wants to say and I'm not sure there is anything he could say to make me feel less stupid.

"Jamie, it's fine," I say as I uncross my arms.

He looks up at me. "Is it though? I'm taking her away."

"She wants to be here."

He nods. "She loves it."

"I know and I'm happy for her."

Jamie's shoulders fall and he lets out a sigh of relief.

"Oh Kit, you have no idea how hard this has been. We've been stewing over it for months. Neither of us knew what to say or how you were going to handle it."

Bea has enough to worry about, she doesn't need the stress of this hanging over her.

"I am upset, Jamie," I say. "But if this is what she wants, then I'm happy for her."

I wipe tears off my cheek with the back of my hand.

"I'm so sorry. Honestly, neither of us wanted to hurt you."

I pull back. "Then lying about it wasn't the best idea."

"We just…we didn't," he stumbles over his words.

"I want her to be happy. If that means relocating, then it's fine but I'm not okay with being lied to. Especially when everyone else in our lives knows. It's embarrassing and I feel like an idiot."

Jamie holds his hands up. "You're right. We should not have lied."

I shake my head. "It's not just you. It's everyone. Mom and Dad lied about the affair. I think something bad is going on with Alex but he's brushing me off. Eve is leaving Darren because he's sleeping with Steph from accounts and if all the Larsons know about Bea moving then Danny probably does too and he didn't say anything."

I suck in a much-needed breath as the tears really start to flow. Jamie pulls me into a hug, tucking my head under his chin and patting me on the back.

"I'm so sorry you have to deal with all of this Kit."

I sniffle. "I'll be fine but promise me you won't hide anything else."

Jamie pulls back, holding me at arm's length. His mouth pulls down at the corner and he looks right past me to the front door of their apartment.

I turn my head to see Bea standing here.

"What?" I say slowly.

"Ummm, well that's the thing." Jamie scratches his temple. "I have this big dinner tomorrow night. It's with a potential investor and my brother is trying to take the lead but you see, now that I'm back this is a chance to show that I'm a chap worth his salt."

Jamie steps slightly further back as Bea stands beside me.

"You're rambling, Jamie," I say.

"Yes, right. Well, the thing is, this dinner is very important and I would dearly love my beautiful girlfriend to accompany me."

I let out an exhausted breath. "So I'm going to Paris on my own?"

"Just for the first day. Then I'll meet up with you there." Bea links her arm with mine.

I'm running over the logistics of getting to Paris. I've got it all pre-booked and ready, but I wasn't expecting to have to do it on my own. That wasn't part of the bucket list.

"I guess that's okay," I mumble. "Is that all you have to tell me?"

Bea and Jamie share a look and I'm certain that neither of them is going to keep their promise.

CHAPTER THIRTY-TWO

I don't realize the gravity of what I'm doing until I'm in the Eurostar departure lounge at St Pancras Station. All morning I've been going over maps of Paris, trying to work out the most direct route from Gare du Nord to my hotel. The driver I booked will know where he's going, but I want to make sure it's the most direct route.

I miss Bea and the comfort that comes from being with her but she convinced me that doing this on my own has added an extra layer of complexity to my bucket list.

I twist my earbuds into my ears and start playing Danny's songs again. He sent me a playlist for the train journey before I left New York, and when I close my eyes and listen, my nerves settle and I squash the fear of not knowing what to expect when I step off at the other end.

I'm three songs in when a tall figure invades my peripheral vision. Out of politeness, I keep to myself and pray this person understands basic public transport boundaries.

"Traffic was a nightmare," a familiar voice says. "I almost didn't make it."

My eyes snap up, and I take in Danny's half smile. He leans forward and drops his bag beside mine. I stay in my seat, still a little shell-shocked at his sudden arrival.

"Are you going to kiss me or what?"

I really want to, but a thundercloud hangs over our reunion.

"Did you know that Bea's moving here permanently?"

He looks confused. "What?"

"I know you heard me."

"Yeah, I heard you. But as far as I knew, it was just a year." He looks me in the eye. "Shit, though, are you okay?"

I close my eyes tight. He didn't know. Of course he didn't know. Why did I doubt it?

I stand up and throw myself against him. "I'm so glad you're here."

He runs his fingers through my hair and kisses the top of my head. "It's okay. Tell me what's going on."

There's a little time before boarding, and I fill Danny in on what happened with Bea. The more I think about it, the more frustrated I get. Keeping it from Danny as well feels calculated. If he knew, he would've tell me, so he understands why I'm upset.

I'm feeling better as we board the train and take our seats. Danny is starving and exhausted, so after scarfing all the snacks I purchased for the trip, he promptly falls asleep against the window. I'm so glad he made it. I've been stress-sweating just thinking about my arrival in Paris. I don't speak any French, so the plan was to show the hotel address to my driver and lock myself in the room until I had the courage to explore.

With Danny sleeping soundly, I pull out my phone and see a barrage of notifications. My heart breaks when I read the original message from Mom.

> MOM
>
> **House has sold.**

It's gone. Just like that?

I open our sibling chat and see Bea, Eve and Alex have all exchanged messages about the house sale. Since I added nothing to the chat, there are now three private messages checking I'm okay. I respond to each in quick succession. I tell Bea I'm on the train and to enjoy her dinner with Jamie. I ask Eve to check on Dad and I make one more attempt to see what's going on with Alex. He doesn't respond.

I settle back in my seat as Danny's head rolls to the side and he huddles into himself. His eyelashes are impossibly long —one of the universe's greatest injustices. I study the multiple scars that have appeared on his hands over the years. They're still his hands, though, right down to the chewed nails and the silver wristwatch his parents gave him when he signed his first A-league contract.

"Everything alright?"

I was too busy looking at Danny's hands, I didn't realize he was awake.

"The house sold," I say as he sits up, places his hand on my cheek and kisses the tip of my nose.

"I'm sorry."

I frown. "We aren't neighbors anymore."

"We haven't been neighbors for a long time."

"We've always been neighbors. Because you always came home to that house. Now I won't be on the other side of the fence."

He pulls me close, and I cuddle him as we stare out the window at the picturesque countryside that sails by. "Mom tore down the treehouse and nailed the fence shut."

Danny rubs my upper arm. "Damn. The treehouse was the best thing about that place."

"It was."

I say little else for most of the journey, though Bea messages me again to apologize for keeping London a secret. I tell her it's fine but it makes me wonder when I became a person in need of such coddling. I'm the most responsible of all of us. Stable job, impressive savings account and I always read the terms and conditions on everything I sign. I even took care of Mom when Dad moved out.

I could have handled this. I think.

Our arrival in Paris isn't the euphoric experience I was expecting. Danny does his best to shield me as we're jostled through the overcrowded station. When we make it outside, I get a last-minute notification from the car service informing me they've had to cancel.

"Not sure I'm sold on Paris," Danny grunts as he finds himself in the flight path of an angry pigeon who decided his jacket needed a little something extra to make it pop.

I do the best I can with baby wipes in the cab while we weave through Paris traffic in what I'm quite certain is not a licensed taxi.

"Look at that." Danny points out the window to the Eiffel

Tower coming into view. I don't know if it's the architecture or the carnival ride through Paris traffic, but for someone who got shit on, he's surprisingly upbeat.

We make it to the hotel and pile out of the car with our luggage. Danny helps with my suitcase, expertly navigating a cobbled street and somehow squeezing himself and the luggage through a door frame built for someone half his size. I'm thinking I should have sprung for pricier accommodation, especially when we're checked in and ushered to a door three steps from the end of the check-in counter.

"It's snug," Danny says as he hoists the suitcases onto the bed so I can enter the room.

"The location is great, though," I say, folding myself over the rear-projection TV so we're able to close the door. The photos on the website definitely made the rooms look bigger. There's a foot of space around the double bed and only one of us has the luxury of the nightstand/wooden stool. The TV dwarfs the small writing desk it's perched on, and an office chair was apparently a necessary addition to the workspace. Even if guests did want their nose to touch the television while sitting at the desk, I can't get my head around the ornate armoire in the corner. It takes up so much space, and since the key appears to be rusted in the lock, it isn't even useful.

"At least we've got a private bathroom," Danny points out. "That's luxury."

He sticks his head through the sliding pocket door. "Oh cool. The shower is over the toilet. That'll cut my morning routine in half."

I don't know whether it's the house sale, the underwhelming accommodation, the Bea situation or everything my parents have going on, but I promptly burst into tears.

"No, no, no." Danny kicks the foot of the bed and lets out a grunt as he steps the two feet across the room to console me.

"We can stay somewhere else," I cry. "I'll find somewhere better."

"No. This place is great. All we need is a bed to sleep in."

At that moment, the clerk clicks on the TV in the reception area and the muffled sounds of a French sitcom vibrate through the walls.

"I'm sure they'll turn that off at some point," he assures me.

"Reception is manned twenty-four hours a day." I'm a red-eyed, sniveling mess. "I thought that was a selling point."

"It is! It absolutely is." Danny rubs my shoulders before he shuffles past me, to the only window in the room. The frosted glass is covered in fingerprints and when he pushes it open, the metal track at the bottom makes an alarming scraping noise. "Look at this view, though."

I lean around him to peer out into the impractically narrow courtyard. There's a small bench along the wall where an older couple is having a heated argument while blowing cigarette smoke directly through our window.

"I don't know what they're saying but that fine mesh tank top really shows off that elderly man's nipple piercing." Danny stares at me, eyes wide, bracing for a meltdown. Instead, I laugh.

He's momentarily shocked, but then he kisses my forehead and holds me as my laughter once again turns to tears.

We spend twenty minutes trying to get our window to

close again before settling in. When we do, we realize our suitcases can't be accessed unless they're open on the bed, and
Danny gets too close to the armoire and informs me it's emit-
ting a strange smell. That does it, so Danny stuffs the oversized key tag into the pocket of his jacket and we head out to
see the sights of Paris. The first stop is a bakery on Rue Cler,
so I can cross "eat a croissant in Paris" off the list. I take notes
on my phone to add to the spreadsheet before we continue our
stroll to the Eiffel Tower. I attempt to push everything out of
my head and enjoy the fact that I'm in Paris and I'm with
Danny.

Which is a tad difficult when Danny is paranoid about
getting pickpocketed and three different people offer to sell us
either wine or roses. We take a few pictures and relax on the
grass until I'm sick of being accosted as part of a scam.

Late in the afternoon, we make our way back and stop in
at a small, yet opulent restaurant three doors down from the
hotel.

"Are you going to tell me how the meeting went?" I ask as I
hand the menu back to the waiter, secretly hoping I didn't
order something adventurous by mistake.

Danny shifts in his seat and takes a sudden interest in his
empty glass. The dim tungsten light turns his hair a beautiful
golden color, but that little crease above his eyebrow has me
worried.

"Danny?"

His eyes finally lift. "It was about a job."

I smile through the looming dread. "That's fantastic.
What's the job?"

"It's the assistant coaching position. Nelson is retiring, so

Ed is stepping up next season. They've offered me his job, and I accepted."

Whatever little piece of my heart that's left cracks in two, but my smile holds fast.

"This is incredible. I'm so happy for you."

The corner of his mouth lifts for a second before he catches himself and goes back to staring at the table.

I raise a brow. "Are you happy for you?"

He shifts his weight again as he plays with the intricate silver handle of a butter knife.

"I'll have to leave again," he says. "I don't want to do that to you. Especially with Bea staying in London."

I can already feel the emptiness of home creeping in. Having Bea was what got me through not having Danny last time.

"Please don't worry about that." I blink hard to stop the tears that threaten to hold our evening hostage. "This is going to be so good for you."

I take a steadying breath and signal to our waiter.

The thin man with an expertly groomed mustache walks over, smile wide and eyes beaming. I open the wine list and choose the most expensive champagne they have. The price is eye-watering, but it's okay because I've maintained a robust savings plan since I was a teenager and I saved a bundle on the hotel. If it can be called that.

"We're celebrating," I explain to the waiter, who I'm pretty sure thinks we're getting engaged, judging by the giddy expression on his face.

"Kit, you don't have to do that."

"I want to, because this is a big deal."

Our champagne arrives, and we clink our glasses together in a toast.

"I'm proud of you, Danny." I take a sip, and the champagne is like sweet stars coming to life on my tongue.

"Thank you, but you can say it without an expensive bottle of champagne."

I take another sip. "One of my bucket list items is to buy something expensive that won't last."

He finally smiles. A full smile, one that shows his teeth and is reflected in his eyes. "Practical." He laughs as he takes another sip as well.

"What made you change your mind?" I ask once the food is delivered to our table. "About getting back into hockey, I mean."

He rests his fork on the side of his plate and takes a swig of champagne. "I figured Ed wanted to meet about a job, and I thought it would be better to turn him down in person. But we got to talking about the team and everything I've missed since I left and it didn't hurt as much as I thought it would."

His eyes sparkle and it dulls the devastation I'm feeling at losing him again.

"Everything got taken away so suddenly and I thought if I gave it up completely, then it would have been my choice."

"But it's so much of you, leaving it behind was never an option."

"I don't think it was either," he says.

I reach over and take his hand. There is so much we'll have to work out, but we're in Paris and this opportunity is a great thing.

I lift my glass. "Congratulations on getting back in the game, number twenty-eight."

CHAPTER THIRTY-THREE

The few days we have in Paris are filled with tours and attractions as we religiously follow the *Best of Paris* blog published in the online magazine Spencer works for.

We cover so much ground, by the time we get back to the hotel each night my feet are cramping, and Danny has taken to finding some kind of takeout so I don't have to put shoes on.

"What have you got planned for us today?" Danny asks as we squeeze into the bathroom to brush our teeth. My back is pressed against his front, and I'm terrified that toothpaste will drip from his mouth onto my freshly washed hair.

"The Louvre," I say. "It's the last touristy thing we have to do."

Danny gently shuffles me to the side so he can spit in the sink. We both rinse our mouths out and he plants a kiss on my lips like we've been at this for years.

"Alright. Let's get moving then."

On the mean streets of Paris, Danny and I haven't shaken

our roles as clueless travelers. We line up outside the Louvre for almost an hour before overhearing an English couple talking about entering through a mall entrance. Danny and I follow them, inconspicuously of course, and gain entry almost immediately. We walk around using my precise method of structured enjoyment: I follow the map through each part of the museum in the most logical way. Danny doesn't seem overly interested, but to his credit, appears to listen when I read the information panels and tell him the most interesting parts.

"This is the big one," Danny says as we stand amongst a sea of people.

"I finally get to meet someone famous," I say. "That isn't you, Alex or Fletcher."

"You know a surprising number of famous people."

"Yes, but I've known all of you since we were kids, so I remember all the embarrassing shit you've done. It makes your status less intimidating."

"Alright. Consider me humbled." He says as we shuffle into the gallery along with every other tourist in Paris.

Danny is at my back, keeping his hand firmly on my waist as we move forward slowly. It takes a while, but eventually we make it to the front.

"I thought it would be bigger," Danny says.

"Not what I said when you dropped that towel for the first time." I giggle and Danny pinches my butt.

"Shut up. We're in public," he scolds as I hold up my phone and snap some pictures.

I don't know what I was expecting of the Mona Lisa. Danny is right, though, I was expecting something a little more grand. I wish I had time to take it all in. Instead, my space is invaded by several languages talking over each other, elbows being wielded like weapons and the acrid smell of other people's bodies all pushing together.

I can't stand it, so I turn around and Danny and I weave back through the crowd. It isn't until we've left the museum, I realize I didn't really look at the painting itself. I only saw it through my phone's camera. The experience leaves me rather deflated, but it does mean I've crossed something else off the list.

I text Bea when we're boarding the Eurostar and she says she can't wait to see me. The morning after Jamie's big dinner, she called to say she was staying in London and to enjoy my time in Paris. There was no way we could squeeze another person into that hotel room and it was nice to spend time alone with Danny.

"Do you think you'll ever leave Seattle?" Danny asks as we split a box of crackers I bought at the terminal.

The thought has crossed my mind. "I'm not sure. It's my home. I have a job and most of my family is there."

It's the wrong answer because his jaw tightens. He was hoping for something more resolute.

"We can still make this work," I say, as more of an assurance to myself than to him.

"Yeah." He exhales and hands the cracker box back to me before twisting headphones into his ears and plugging them into his phone.

I lean over to pull out one of his headphones, but notice he's watching a hockey game from last season. It thrills me until he rips out a headphone and turns to face me.

"Why are you so upset about Bea moving to London, but you're buying expensive champagne to celebrate me going back to New York?"

"Danny…" I stammer.

"Is there any point in asking you to come with me?"

I figured this question was coming but I'm only now realizing how scared I am for him to ask it.

"Are you asking me to come with you?"

"Yes. Will you move to New York with me?" His tone is sharp.

I feel like a deer in the headlights. I want to be with him and I'm so happy that he's taken this job, but Seattle is home. I'm not sure this is a decision I can make on a train ride through the French countryside.

"Can I think about it?" I ask as Danny slouches back in his seat. "There are a lot of things to consider, Danny. I'd be packing up my whole life and starting over again."

The wind has noticeably gone out of his sails as he takes my hand. "I know. I'm sorry to drop it on you like this."

"I need some time," I say. "Everything between us changed in New York and with Bea deciding to stay in London, my head is all over the place."

"I understand." His head drops and he stares at our clasped hands.

"It's not a no, Danny," I assure him. "But everything is moving for me at the moment and I just want to stand still for a second."

He's quiet for a long time as he runs his fingertips over my knuckles.

"Leaving you was the hardest thing I've ever done, even

when everything I'd worked for was right in front of me," he says as the tendons in his neck stretch, and his breathing becomes heavy and uneven.

I take his face in my hands, kiss him gently and then press his forehead to mine until he relaxes.

"We've missed each other before and as hard as it was, we can survive it. I just need some time."

He leans back in his seat. "I get it."

I wipe away tears with the back of my free hand as Danny pulls me into him and kisses the side of my head.

———

A few hours later, we arrive at Bea's apartment.

"Are you okay? You look sick," I say as I take in her appearance. Dark circles ring her eyes and she's pale.

"Gee. Thanks." Her eyes soften and her mouth lifts in a half smile.

"Do you need to see a doctor?" I ask. "You've definitely got Mom's gluten allergy. Too much dairy takes its toll on her, too. Doesn't stop her from rolling the dice on mozzarella sticks everywhere we go, though."

Bea laughs as she pulls me into a hug. "I missed you."

"I missed you too." I continue to hold her close and ignore Jamie's throat clearing. We're blocking the doorway, but Bea doesn't seem to care either.

"Right," Jamie says. "We might head to the pub then, hey Dan?"

"Sure," Danny agrees, which is followed by suitcase wheels clunking as they're pushed over the threshold.

"We'll see you later." Jamie hovers beside Bea and me for a second. When he realizes we aren't letting go of each other, he pats us both on the shoulder and shuffles us out of the way so he can close the front door.

"How was Paris?" Bea says into my hair. "Did you love it?"

"It was fine."

She rubs my back. "Paris syndrome?"

I pull away to look her in the eye. "Yes! I didn't know that was real."

She chuckles. "I thought the same thing. I didn't want to say anything. Did you eat a croissant?"

I nod. "On the first day."

"Efficient as ever." She takes my hand and we sit on the couch. She genuinely doesn't look good.

"I'm sorry this trip has been a bit of a mess," Bea says. "And I am genuinely sorry that I didn't tell you the truth."

A strand of unwashed hair falls across her forehead.

"I am happy for you. Please don't think I'm not. But all this stuff with Mom and that man…" I can't bring myself to say his name. "Nothing is the same anymore."

She shuffles closer and takes my hand. "You're right and I know I made it worse by keeping London a secret. We really didn't want to upset you. Not to mention that I was trying to work it all out in my own head. How much I'd be giving up and if it was worth it. I love Jamie with all my heart, but I had no idea what life would be like here. It was a complete leap of faith but circumstances changed. London is the best option now."

"Circumstances have changed?" I raise a brow.

She swallows hard. "I'm not sick, Kit. Well, I am, but it's kind of normal."

"Oh." I put my hand over my mouth as a heavy realization dawns on me. "Bea?"

The last remnants of color have drained from her face and when she opens her mouth, her eyes light with panic.

"Bea?"

In a flash, she's off the couch and painting the kitchen sink with every morsel of food she's had today.

"Oh my God!" I hurry to her, pulling her hair from around her face and rubbing her back. She hangs there for a minute, and when she finally brings her head up, I swoop in, flushing her stomach contents down the sink and getting her a glass of water. Which she slurps down in a second.

I inhale and take my hands off my hips because I know I look like Mom. "How far along are you?"

"Fifteen weeks."

"Is that too early to tell people? When do you start telling people?"

"I'm not telling people. I'm telling you."

I pace the kitchen. "This is irresponsible, Beatrice. You're so young."

"I'm twenty-six and in a stable, long-term relationship."

"Yeah, but it's with Jamie," I huff.

"You like Jamie."

"I love Jamie," I refill the glass of water and hand it to her. "But he always forgets to unplug the toaster."

Bea's mouth presses into a line. "He just forgets."

"And what if he forgets and leaves the apartment then it

burns down with your baby inside." I take my sister by the arm and walk her back to the living space.

Bea's face pinches. "Why would the baby be alone in the house?"

"You're missing the point."

"I don't think there is one."

We settle on the couch again, and Bea lifts her arm to tuck me against her side. Her skin smells like vanilla body wash and her fleecy sweater is like a cloud beneath my cheek.

"I can't believe something is growing inside you." I place my hand on her stomach.

"I know. It's kinda gross when you think about it."

We sit together for a long time talking about baby names and how Jamie is already convinced it's a girl. I can't wrap my head around it. My sister is going to be responsible for a whole human being. She can barely make cereal.

"Do you think everything is going to work out?" I ask, not entirely sure what I'm referring to.

"Everything is going to be great."

Her voice shakes, so I hold her a little tighter.

CHAPTER THIRTY-FOUR

My first day back at the bank is a backslide into what used to be a perfectly acceptable reality.

On the upside, nothing has changed. On the downside, nothing has changed.

The offices are still too small and the smell of photocopied paper and lemon cleaning spray is still a little too thick in the air. Apparently, when my colleagues realized I'd be back soon, they decided several tasks could wait for me, so I spend the morning getting through the backlog of work on my desk. Brian seems to have let this behavior slide because the front windows being re-frosted and delegating every task is enough to fill his plate.

The highlight of my painfully average day is Danny meeting me for lunch. He tells me all about the morning, which started with breaking the news to Gemma that the next phase of Uncle Danny's career means he'll be moving to New York. She's handling it as well as expected, and I think it's because she had grand designs on her former pro uncle being involved in her blossoming hockey career.

By the end of the day, I'm ready to scream at any customer that walks through the door. They all move at a snail's pace, incapable of a succinct request. It makes my brain itch and the urge to leave is overwhelming. When the clock hits five, I've already gathered my things and I'm waiting at the end of the block for Danny to pick me up. Two hours ago, he said he'd made plans for us tonight and since he isn't great at organizing things, I'm rightfully concerned.

"Kit-Kat," Eve sings my name as she jumps from the passenger seat of Danny's car and climbs into the back.

My expectation of a romantic evening with Danny is slashed to ribbons.

"Evie?" I say slowly as I climb into the car. "What are you doing here?"

"I didn't want to miss this one." She smiles as she undoes the top button on her collared shirt. She still looks like a real estate agent, even though she's off the clock.

"Miss what one?" I look back to Danny, who smirks.

"The next bucket list item!" Eve squeals.

I mentally scan the list and my heart sinks.

"How much is this going to hurt?"

"A lot," Danny says.

Eve chimes in from the back seat, "It depends on where you get it."

Danny reaches over to take my hand. This is an ambush. I'm Bea-less and I don't have a clear head. I've been dealing with stupid people all day, so my mental energy is tapped.

"What if I get a flesh-eating disease from the needle?"

"Is that a thing?" Eve raises a brow.

"I don't think so," Danny attempts to assure me. It's entirely unconvincing because he won't look me in the eye.

"I haven't decided what to get," I protest.

"You can decide when we get there. But you should totally get something badass. Like a pair of smoking magnums crossed over your chest."

Both Danny and I turn to Eve with matching looks of disapproval.

"Alright. It was a suggestion. Get a butterfly then."

Danny is aware of my unease on the ride to the tattoo shop and when he opens the door to help me out, he pulls me close and leans down to whisper in my ear, "You can back out."

"It's on the list, though." I dig my teeth into my bottom lip. "And I said I'd do everything on the list."

"Yeah, but this is big…"

"Come on, or we'll miss the appointment," Eve interrupts as she undoes another button and pulls her hair out of its tight bun.

The tattoo shop is small, but tidy. It smells of disinfectant, which I appreciate, but I can hear the buzz of a tattoo gun and it makes the space much less welcoming.

"Hi." Eve steps up to the small reception counter. "This is my sister, Kit. She has an appointment for five-thirty."

The cheery receptionist smiles at me, but I'm busy studying her intricate sleeve tattoo: a medieval tower with roses wrapped around it, and above, over the cap of her shoulder, is a hand holding a crown that drips with blood. I'm a *Blood of Gold* fan as much as the next person, but I doubt even Fletcher or Hallie would get that tattoo.

Eve helps me with the forms and when we're done, we take a seat on the black leather couch in the waiting area. Through a narrow archway, I can see a woman lying on a table as a large fire-breathing dragon is tattooed on her ass and upper thigh.

I nudge Eve. "I'm not getting anything like that."

"That's fine. Get something little like I did."

Eve has two tattoos. The constellation of her zodiac sign on her ankle, and a feather at the top of her spine. The constellation matches the one she got with Spencer, and the feather was a drunk bet she made with Miles. He's a former musician who now owns a bar—there was no way she was going to win a drinking game against him, so her "feather-weight" tattoo is justified.

"How about this one?" Eve angles the portfolio toward me and taps her finger on a picture of a bluebird.

"What does that mean?"

She shrugs. "Nothing, but it's pretty."

Danny, who was talking to my tattoo artist, comes over to check on my progress. Eve points out the bluebird.

"Don't get that," Danny says. "It doesn't mean anything to you."

"Like all yours means something to you." Eve rolls her eyes.

Danny opens his mouth to retort, but the tattoo artist comes over to introduce himself.

"Hey, Kit. I'm Dex. Are you ready?"

"No," I say.

"Great," he deadpans. "Let's get this done."

I follow Dex out the back and settle into a chair. The girl with the ass tattoo is almost in tears. Her eyes shut tight as the artist drags the gun over her reddened skin. I will hear the sound of that gun in my nightmares.

"What are we doin' today?" Dex asks as he pushes a stool over for Eve to sit on. I look at Danny for help.

"It's your body," he says. "Get something you want to look at forever. Or nothing at all. It's your choice."

He holds my hand but releases it when his phone rings. Ed's name flashes on the caller ID. "Sorry, I have to take this."

"I'll step in, then." Eve shuffles over and takes my hand.

"It's about his new job." I feel the need to explain that the call is worth leaving me here, on the cusp of having ink needled into my skin.

"What new job?" Eve asks. "I thought he was just living off his hockey money."

"That's not a long-term plan. He could probably retire and call it a day, but that's not the life he wants."

"God." Eve sighs. "Why not? It sounds amazing."

"He got offered a coaching job in New York. He's moving back before the season starts."

Her eyes soften. "Oh shit. For real?"

"Yeah," I say. "It's okay, though. It's a big opportunity for him, so I'm happy."

"Bullshit," Eve scoffs as she looks at me and does that thing where she narrows her eyes and presses her mouth into a hard line. It's visual truth serum.

"Of course I'm not completely happy. He's asked me to move with him, but we've just started exploring this new relationship and it's a big commitment. What if I'm not happy there? I would be moving there for him and even though we love each other, what if it doesn't work out? It feels irresponsible."

"Let it out, honey." She pats my hand. "Dex, be a dear and grab us some whiskey."

"We don't have any whiskey."

"That's nice. Thank you." Eve ignores him completely, and he grunts before wandering to the front of the shop.

"I don't regret how things have changed. What happened on our trip was amazing."

"Yeah, Alex told me you disappeared for a night. How was it?" Eve's grin is wicked. "And, like how…you know…was his?"

"I'm not getting into that."

She holds up her hands, palm against palm, and separates them slowly. "Tell me when to stop."

I slap her hands away. "Stop it! I'm not sharing any details with you."

She shrugs. "Bea would. That's all I'm saying."

"No, she would not."

"Umm, she told me everything when she slept with that guy from Miles's bar. The one with the neck tattoo that works weekends."

My eyes are screaming. "She what?"

"It was right before she started dating Jamie. Apparently, he was good. Into some interesting stuff, too."

We both stare off into space for a second. Wyatt, the owner of the neck tattoo with eyes like shards of polished jade and biceps that indicate he tears phone books in half recreationally, is someone all three of us Reilly girls have lusted over at some point.

I can't believe Bea did it, though. I can't believe she didn't tell me.

"His hands are so big." Eve is glassy-eyed. "I reckon he could pin you—"

"Bourbon is all I got," Dex grunts as he hands us each a mug with a thimble of amber liquid in the bottom.

"Good enough," Eve says, and she bumps her mug with mine. "Cheers! To Wyatt the bartender and his enormous hands."

"I heard he's getting his PhD, too," I say as I throw back my drink.

"In what?"

"Either aeronautical or astronautical engineering."

"Wow." Eve's eyes widen. "What's the difference?"

"One is planes and one is rockets." Dex, sporting a scowl, folds his arms across his broad chest. "Can we start, please?"

From the look on Eve's face, she finds Dex more appealing than the bourbon.

"So, Dex…how long have you worked here?" She flutters her lashes.

"Just pick a tattoo," he deadpans and Eve, being the ideal wing woman, pesters him with inane questions to buy me some time to decide. Either that or she's making it a personal challenge to piss off the man who is about to needle me.

I block them out and crane my neck to see Danny pacing outside the shop window. He says something into the phone before his face splits into a smile—one I haven't seen in a while.

It's his game-winning smile.

At the final buzzer, he would grin like that as he took off his helmet, pulled his arm around and kissed the number twenty-eight on his sleeve. To this day, seeing him that happy is my favorite sight.

"I've got it." I sit up and look at Dex. "I know what I want."

It's small and takes Dex no time to draw up. He doesn't ask any confirmation questions, presumably out of fear I'll change my mind.

"It's kind of boring." Eve wrinkles her forehead as she looks at the stencil marks on my skin. "What about a peacock or something? I saw this one where the tail fans out across this woman's whole back."

"That takes hours across multiple sessions." Dex glares at her.

"Would give us a chance to get to know each other. Wouldn't it?"

I wave my hand in front of Eve's face. "I'm never coming back here. No offense, Dex. You seem nice, but no more tattoos after this one."

"It was just a suggestion," Eve huffs.

"I've made my choice. Can we get it done?" I say as Dex lifts the gun to my ribs.

Overall, it's not that bad. It only takes a few minutes and once I relax, the pain is much more tolerable. Danny finishes his call halfway through and I tell him to stay in the reception area to keep it a surprise. He keeps sticking his head into the back room and Eve tells him if he keeps interrupting, she'll make him wait in the car.

"He's stupidly in love with you, Kit. I think moving to New York is worth the risk," she says as Dex finishes and starts wrapping up my tattoo.

"It's not that simple, Evie."

"You should go to New York," Dex chimes in as he cleans up the table beside him.

"Thanks for your insight, Dex." Eve's grin is devilish. "But now is not the time for your opinion. Even though you're on my side."

"I'm not on your side. I want you out of my shop and figured if she went to New York, you'd go with her."

Eve throws her head back and laughs. "I swear to God. If you keep being this mean to me, I'm going to marry you."

Dex scowls as he packs up his equipment.

I look out at Danny. He's pacing the reception area and chewing his thumbnail to the cuticle. Anyone would think I'm giving birth, not having two words tattooed on my rib cage. My heart swells though, and when he looks up and forces a smile through all that painful concern, a thought crosses my mind. One I've never had before.

Eve might be right.

CHAPTER THIRTY-FIVE

Growing up as one of four kids, I rarely got my own space or time to breathe. When I moved out of home and in with Bea, I found some independence. She was there when I wanted to talk, but was happy to leave me alone when she knew I needed it. Unfortunately, Mom is not as attuned to my needs as Bea, and whenever I arrive home, she's in my face.

I blame it on her sudden decision to quit her job. Which was completely irresponsible and only highlights her increasing lack of judgment.

She's also reverted to her old ways: ignoring past confrontations and going overboard with the mothering. Right after my trip, this manifested as unpacking my suitcase and doing all my laundry. It also includes her joining Danny and me as we catch up on season three of *Blood of Gold*. She doesn't know what's happening, so she sits in the occasional chair and asks questions about every plot line.

Danny has spent the last two hours tensed on the couch, trying not to touch me and watch the show. Every time Mom opens her mouth, his muscles somehow stiffen even more. I'm worried he's going to snap.

"Mom!" I interrupt her inane questions about where she's seen the main actress before. "Do you want to go to your room and read for a while?"

She looks over at me and then at Danny, who's staring straight ahead. I'm traumatized by the sly smile that creeps across her face.

"Yes Katherine, I would love to. Judy lent me this book on that serial killer from Colorado. The one that chopped off all the victim's hands and kept them in his freezer. They think he ate some fingers."

"Oh wow. That sounds great." I open my eyes so wide they almost dry out and she waves off my discomfort before disappearing to Bea's room.

"Sorry," I say as I lean into Danny, who lifts his arm to cuddle me. "I don't know how much longer I can do this. She wasn't this taxing for the first twenty years I lived with her, and she's acting like we never fought before I went away."

His voice is a low rumble. "We can go to Fletcher's."

"As great as that would be, I'm meeting Dad for breakfast tomorrow, so I've got to be up early."

I arranged this meet-up while boarding the flight home. When I said goodbye to Bea, she asked me to check in on Dad for her. She'd spoken to him the night before and said he didn't sound like himself. I'm sure Eve told him that Mom is living with me and I'm worried he thinks this plants my flag firmly in Mom's camp. If only he knew the truth, he wouldn't feel that way. I'm tolerating Mom. I'm still angry about Patrick, but apparently the statute of limitations has passed on the offense, so no apology is required on her part.

Mom doesn't surface for the rest of the evening and after another two episodes of *Blood of Gold*, Danny and I head to my room. He doesn't have any stuff at my place and since my door doesn't lock, he sleeps in a pair of pajama pants Jamie left behind. They're too tight on his thighs, and cut into his hips, but he says he'd rather be uncomfortable in those pants than wear nothing with my mother in the next room.

"I'm an adult and it's my house." I run my hand over his lower stomach. "She knows better than to come into my room unannounced."

"I don't care," he hisses. "Stop touching me and go over to that side of the bed."

I take my hands off him and stifle a laugh. "If that's what you want."

"She's already going to think something's going on when I'm here in the morning."

"Again. It's my house."

"Did you even tell her about us?"

I reach for his hand. "No, because it's none of her business."

His voice softens as he threads his fingers through mine. "Really? I thought you would have told people."

"Well, obviously Bea knows, and Eve. But aside from that, no." I shuffle closer to him again. "Why? Have you told people?"

He breaks eye contact. "Yeah. I've told people."

I pull up onto my knees to face him. "Who'd you tell?"

"Fletcher and Hal." He swallows. "They asked how the trip was and how you were doing."

I press my hand to my heart. "That's sweet."

"I told Mom and Dad, too, but it's because they were over for dinner. And Leah was there. Nolan was late, so he found out later."

"What about Miles?" I poke him in the ribs.

"He was at the bar." Danny looks away again. "So I texted him."

The color in his cheeks deepens and I poke him a little harder. "That is even sweeter. You couldn't wait to tell all your siblings."

He swats my hand away. "Yeah, okay, that's enough. Now get on your side of the bed."

I shake my head. "No, no, no. You can't say and do cute things and then send me away. Kiss me."

"I don't have to do shit." He purposely deepens his voice. "Now, take your lips and all your other bits to the other side of the bed. No touching with parents in the house."

"Fine," I groan as I slide under the covers and face the other way.

A moment later, the mattress moves and I feel him scoot up behind me, laying his hand on my waist but avoiding my tattoo.

"You said no touching." I grin.

"I know what I said." He kisses the back of my neck. "This is all you get."

———

The next morning, with perfect eyeliner and a new knee-length knitted dress that hugs her curves, Mom bids me good-bye. She gives me no background on where she's going. It certainly isn't work, but she says she'll be home after lunch. My gut tells me she'll send an apology text and I won't see her till tonight.

I push whatever she might be doing out of my mind because I'm already running late to meet Dad, thanks to how long it took to sneak Danny out of the apartment.

"I'm late, I know. I'm sorry." I kiss Dad on the cheek, then slide into the booth opposite him.

"It's no problem, Kit-Kat."

The diner is an old favorite of his. It's a long, narrow space with red walls, black booths, and checkerboard floors. Dad used to take Bea and me here as kids. He likes the hash browns, and we liked looking at all the stickers that cover the lampshades over the counter. The nostalgia is tangible, and after everything that's happened lately, eating here feels more like a punishment than anything else.

"How was your trip?" Dad asks as he waves down our server.

I toy with the idea of telling him about my concern for Alex and asking why he kept Bea's secret about staying in London. Though, I don't think he needs that right now.

"It was great. Bea told me about the baby too."

"She's certainly putting down roots in England," Dad says as the server arrives at our table. While he places our usual order, I notice the lines around his eyes and how shaggy his hair has gotten. He looks older than his fifty-six years and it's a stark contrast to how perfectly put together Mom was this morning.

"Won't be long," the kind-eyed young woman with a septum ring says as she takes our plastic menus.

Dad doesn't acknowledge her because he's now taken a keen interest in the table's surface.

"Dad?" I lower my voice. "What's the plan here? You can't stay at Whiskey forever."

He looks over my shoulder toward the kitchen. There's no chance our food is arriving soon to save him from a tough conversation.

"I'll look for a place." His tone is non-committal.

"Why are you putting it off?"

"I'm not. The rent is cheap and I'm settled there. Why should I move?"

I fold my hands in my lap. "For starters, it's a longer commute to the office."

"It's close to downtown."

"You hate going downtown."

"It's a good place. The bar has entertainment and Miles gives me a discount on food," he mumbles.

"You hate noise and deep-fried food."

He leans back, shoulders slumping. He won't look at me.

"Dad, please tell me what's going on."

I think of Mom again and the new highlights in her hair, the absence of a wedding ring, and the smile she was wearing when she left the house this morning. None of it seems fair.

He looks down at the table and stumbles over his words. "I made a mistake."

"What do you mean?" I say, way too loudly for the size of the café.

I instinctively glance at Dad's left hand. The thin gold band is still in place.

"It's really hard," he whispers. "Harder than I thought it would be."

My stomach drops. "What are you saying, Dad?"

He drags his hands down his face and the muscles in his jaw tighten when he finally looks me in the eye. "I want it all back. I want my house and my wife and my family."

"Dad, I don't…" I mumble, my mouth going dry.

"We're married and have children together. I've devoted almost forty years of my life to her and I threw it away." He sounds exhausted.

"You didn't throw it away. She did."

He holds his hands up. "It was nothing. I blew it out of proportion."

"No, you didn't." I look directly into his eyes, at a loss for what else to say. I want to tell him she's seeing Patrick, but it's not my responsibility to break his heart even more. She needs to be the one to look him in the eye and tell him what's happening. Eve is right about that.

Dad looks at his hands again. "Is she happy?"

I deflect the question. "Why do you want her back?"

"Because she's not the only one who lost everything."

At that moment the server appears with our food. She reads out the order and places our plates on the table. Dad is silent for a moment before digging into his hash browns. I can't imagine what he's going through, but I honestly believe that going back to Mom isn't the right thing to do. I push my plate away.

"I'm sorry, Dad. But this is giving me whiplash. I thought you were moving on. You said you were okay and just needed time."

He stops eating and stares at his food.

"I don't need any more time."

My empty stomach folds over itself. How do I tell him that it's too late?

"Are you sure you're not just a little lonely?" I ask. "Because you have so much to look forward to."

It sounds hollow even to my own ears. The house is gone, Mom is with Patrick, and he'll be a long-distance grandparent.

"I'm going to talk to her," he says. "It might not be too late."

CHAPTER THIRTY-SIX

For the rest of breakfast, our conversation is superficial. Eve must have told him about me and Danny, and aside from an offhand comment about him thinking we were just friends, he doesn't ask for any more detail. I'm thankful because I don't want to talk about New York right now.

"How long is your mom staying?" Dad asks as he pulls the car into a space at the end of my block.

I shrug. "No idea. I'm not sure she's even looking for a place."

I curse my honesty and pray it doesn't give him false hope.

"It's nice that you're keeping each other company," he says as he climbs out and comes around to open my door. When I step out, he gives me a hug.

He holds me for a long time, like we may never do it again. It breaks my heart because I know he's thinking about all the times we had breakfast at that café as a family and that when he goes back to Whiskey, reality will set in.

His body suddenly goes slack and when I step back, he's looking right past me. "Dad?"

The color drains from his face and when I turn to follow his line of sight, my stomach hits the sidewalk.

Mom and Patrick are on the opposite side of the street, standing outside my apartment building, and she's staring at his face like it's the only sight she ever wants to see.

"Dad." I reach for his arm, but he steps around me to get a better view.

"Is that him?" he whispers.

"Yes," I say as I stand beside him. "Dad, I'm sorry."

I look over at Mom again. She keeps playing with her hair and laughing.

Dad isn't an angry man. The only time I've ever seen him mad was when Bea used his first pressing of *Piano Man* as a frisbee to send notes over the fence to Leah. But as Mom touches Patrick's cheek, a deadly storm swirls in Dad's eyes. If he wants to walk over and give them a piece of his mind, I won't stop him.

His anger quickly turns to disappointment when Mom presses her body against Patrick's. The passion in their kiss is devastating.

"I'm so sorry," I whisper, and Dad turns to face me.

"Thank you for breakfast, Kit." He claps me on the shoulder and without another word, he gets into his car and drives away.

The roar of the engine is enough to alert Mom, and as Dad rounds the end of the block, she's looking directly at me with worry pinching her features. She says something to

Patrick, who turns briefly to look at me before he walks off down the street.

"Katherine." Mom twists her hands nervously as I approach. "Can you stop for a second?"

I walk straight past her and say through gritted teeth, "We're not doing this here."

She follows me but remains silent until we're in the apartment, and when I turn to face her she's waiting, hands by her sides and her head high. This alone makes my blood boil.

"He wants to meet you properly. Without you telling him to get out."

"I don't want to meet him. I want nothing to do with him."

How can she ask that of me? And what about Dad? She knows he saw her. She can't deny it, or brush it off.

"He's a kind man, and he makes me happy. I just want to have him in my life without shame or judgment." Her voice shakes.

"Maybe you deserve the shame and judgment!" I bark. "You're killing Dad. You know that, right?"

"I'm not trying to hurt him."

"Why are you doing it, then? Why are you in such a hurry to be done with your old life? The rest of us aren't ready yet."

There are tears in her eyes, but I'm numb to her pain. This all feels like a rollercoaster and I'd very much like to get off.

"Patrick has asked me to move in with him," she admits.

"What?"

"I can't stay here." Her mouth pulls into a line. "He's separated from his wife and has an apartment downtown. He's asked if I'd like to stay with him instead."

"His wife?" I balk. "He's married too?"

"Not anymore."

"You never said he was married."

"You never asked," she counters.

"That is such a cop-out."

I think of Dad again. He deserves so much more than this, and it feels like Mom and Patrick are getting rewarded for how long they've waited to be together.

"I want to live my life, Kit. I want to move on."

"You can't just do whatever you want with no conse-quences."

Her expression turns hard, her mouth flat and her eyes piercing. "Why not? Eve does. She's been doing whatever she wants since she took her first steps. Alex got to pursue music, Bea got to move to London to be with the man she loves. Even your father got the thirty-plus years of hum-drum suburban life he always wanted. When is it my turn?"

Her eyes are bright and hopeful now, but I can't reward her for what she's done. She doesn't deserve the peace of mind and validation.

"What you did is not okay. I won't pretend that it is." I scrunch my eyes shut for a second, trying to clear my head. "What makes it worse is that you don't seem to care what it's doing to all of us."

Her head falls back, and she sighs with exasperation. "All I've ever done is worry about my family. I've spent my life caring for everyone but myself. I've fed you, clothed you, dropped you off at every extracurricular activity you've ever done. I kept a nice house, entertained neighbors, hosted every major holiday and spent my life making sure that my husband

and my children didn't know how much it wore me down. I had to pretend that I had everything I wanted. I had to suppress the urge to tell you and your siblings to leave me the hell alone because at some point every single day I thought about what I could do with my life if it didn't revolve around you."

She pats her wet cheeks with trembling hands.

"That's what having children is. Putting others above yourself for the rest of your life and sometimes it's not a gift. Sometimes I think about all the ways you destroyed my body, but it's nothing compared to the countless times you crushed my spirit. I am a shell of the woman your father married because from the moment Alex was born, I became a mother and nothing else. To make it worse, everyone around me told me I was complete now. I had everything I could want out of life and I feel like a monster to admit that it isn't enough for me."

Tears fall from my eyes as I stare at my mother. She looks like a weight has been lifted.

"I love you, Bea, Alex and Eve more than anything in the world. But I still have to love myself and I didn't love the woman I was becoming."

Mom's trembling hands fall to her sides and she closes her eyes. This is the most human I've ever seen her. It's raw and real and I'm so glad we aren't sweeping anything under the rug this time. It's what I wanted all along.

"I don't think you're a monster," I whisper.

"That doesn't mean I don't feel like one all the time," she says as she collects her purse and leaves my apartment.

CHAPTER THIRTY-SEVEN

My second week at work is worse than the first. I'm back to tearing people's dreams to shreds on a daily basis, and after my time off and the perspective I gained, it's clear the job isn't for me anymore. I used to love the structure of my day, but the meticulous data entry and application assessment has lost its appeal.

It doesn't help that I haven't heard from Mom since she left my apartment. When I told Danny about it, he decided lunch at this new restaurant in Belltown with a perfect beurre blanc would cheer me up. He's right, of course, because it takes my mind off things for a moment. However, it does allow my mind to wander back to the New York decision.

"Thank you for this." I take his hand as his phone buzzes across the table and his eyebrows raise when he reads the number.

"Is it Ed?"

"Yeah, sorry. I won't be long." He stands from the table as he puts the phone to his ear. "Hello?"

I hear Ed's chipper voice come through before Danny steps out of the restaurant to take the call. Through the window I see his brow crease, and I can't tell if it's confusion or disappointment from this distance. Either way, Danny's job is the last thing on my mind when I see who's walked into the restaurant.

I recognize his light-brown hair, athletic build, and the smile he unleashes on the unsuspecting hostess.

Patrick.

My gaze follows as they show him to a table for two in the back. I continue watching as the server takes away the second set of silverware. Of course he dines at upscale restaurants alone. He's secure.

I guess that comes with a full head of hair and a budding new relationship.

Against my better judgment, I stand and walk across the restaurant to his table, silken beurre blanc forgotten.

My hands tremble as I approach, and when I'm only a foot from the vacant chair at his table, he looks up. His eyes are green. With a little ring of brown around the iris and creases at the corner of his eyelids. Like he's spent too much of his life smiling and now it's catching up with him.

"Patrick," I say.

He smiles politely. "Hello."

I reach out and grip the chair, pressing my fingers into the metal frame at the top. "I'm Katherine Reilly."

He holsters that dazzling smile for a moment.

"I know, Kit," he says. "Please, sit down."

My skin prickles when he calls me Kit. I don't know him.

Danny is still on the phone, so I pull out the chair and perch on the edge.

"I don't know why I came over here," I admit.

"I'm glad you did." His brow creases, and it's too much like pity for my liking. He doesn't have the upper hand here, so why do I feel I need to impress him?

"I have to say something." I take a breath so deep the smell of grilled meat lodges itself in my throat.

"I'm here to listen."

Fuck. Why does he have to be so amiable? Alex is going to hate him and Eve will eat him alive. That thought makes me happy, but it's short-lived because I don't understand why my brain is picturing a scenario where Patrick is part of our lives and my siblings have to meet him. So far, I'm the only one who's been unlucky enough to experience that.

"I really hate you," I whisper.

"I know," he says. "And I don't blame you."

"You destroyed my family and you hurt my dad. He deserves so much better than what you and Mom did to him." My voice shakes. "I'll never forgive you for that."

He doesn't defend himself, even though I probably would if our roles were reversed and someone expressed their hatred for me over lunch.

"What makes you so special?" I ask. "What makes you worth all of this?"

"I don't know," he responds. "I ask myself that every time I'm lucky enough to be with her."

He sits back in his chair and rests his hands on the table. He isn't wearing a wedding ring, but there is a tan line where it used to be. I'm reminded that our family wasn't the only one torn apart by this whole mess.

"Then what makes her so special?"

There is a softness in his expression as he looks me in the eye.

"She's the most incredible person I've ever met. I could listen to her talk for hours about art and history and how much she loves to cook. Hearing her voice, even for a second, is the best part of my day." He leans forward. "When I met her, something clicked, and suddenly the whole world felt so much smaller because I needed nothing else. As long as she existed, I had everything I'd ever need."

There's that stupid, giddy smile again.

"Fuck." I wipe my eye. "That's actually nice."

He laughs, and it's a deep, sobering sound.

"She's married, though, and you had to know what you were doing was wrong."

"That's what we talked about most. At first, she confided in me about how isolated she felt in her home life. I encouraged her to get back into the theater. I even introduced her to a friend who runs a community playhouse. She's starting rehearsals for *My Fair Lady* in the fall."

I definitely heard that wrong.

"I'm sorry, what?"

"It's her passion. She dreamed of being on Broadway one day, but obviously she met your dad and her life went another way."

I feel empty as I listen to this stranger tell me things I never knew about my mother. Is this really who she is? Because I've known her a lot longer than Patrick and he's describing an entirely different person.

"She loves you and your siblings so much, and I know she'll always love your dad," Patrick says.

"Then why throw it all away?"

"She didn't throw it away," he says. "She wanted something else."

"Something better?"

He shrugs. "I can't answer that. But all of this has a lot more to do with what your mother wants for herself than who she wants to be with."

"She's already made that decision, hasn't she?"

Patrick shakes his head. "No. I've told her I'm all in and she said she needs time to herself. I just want her to be happy, so whatever she decides, I'll respect it."

His expression changes and his confident posture sinks slightly.

"For what it's worth, Kit, I am truly sorry for everything that's happened. I never meant to fall in love with a married woman, and I know she didn't intend to find such common ground with me. What we have began as an innocent friendship. Neither of us intended for it to be anything more."

I believe him and what's worse is that he seems like a genuine person.

I stand up and fruitlessly press the wrinkles from my linen dress. The sincerity in his eyes makes this a much harder pill to swallow. "Thank you for talking to me."

"It was a pleasure to finally meet you under better circumstances." His infectious smile is back, but I don't linger on it before I walk back to my table.

CHAPTER THIRTY-EIGHT

A week after the irritatingly pleasant run-in with Patrick, I'm still in two minds about the experience. We left the restaurant as soon as Danny finished his call and he held my hand on the silent car ride home. I've never been more thankful to have him in my life, and to show my appreciation, I take him on our first official date.

"Where are we going?" Danny asks as he climbs into the passenger seat of my car.

"It's a surprise," I say. "But you've done it a million times before."

That has him guessing, so for the entire drive from Fletcher's house to the ice rink, he throws out ideas. All of which are wrong and some border on stupid.

As I pull into the parking lot, he stares at the building he used to spend more time in than his own house. "Hockey?"

"You can teach me to skate."

"You know how to skate."

"Re-learn, then. I haven't done it in years." I unbuckle my seatbelt, but he doesn't do the same. With his new job and renewed passion, I thought it would be fun to come back to where it started. The place he was made.

Now I'm worried that I'm completely off base.

"Shit. I'm sorry." I reach over and take his hands in mine. "I just thought you might like to get back on the ice again in a low-stakes environment before you head back to New York."

He says nothing.

"Danny, I'm really sorry. We'll go get dinner or something."

He clicks the button on his seatbelt, and it slides back across his body.

"No, it's not..." He takes a deep breath. "I just need a second."

We spend a few moments in silence while he gathers his thoughts. I didn't realize how much the rink has changed since the last time I was here with him. There are more paint chips on the brickwork and the sign above the door has faded to where some letters aren't readable.

"I'm ready," Danny says and exits the car.

We enter the building, hand in hand, but Danny is half a step behind me.

"Hi, Mrs. Schaffer." I wave at the older woman manning the front desk. "Thank you again for letting us use the rink."

Especially considering my volunteer hours have dwindled over the last month or so.

Her eyes light up when she sees Danny, and she rounds the

desk, arms out, and pulls us both into a disjointed hug. Danny kindly takes the brunt of it, and I'm able to slip out easily.

"Daniel." She grins. "It is so good to see you again."

Danny's cheeks flush. "It's good to see you, too."

When we spoke on the phone, I told her not to mention his injury and when she inadvertently glances at his knee, I shake my head.

"Right, yes." She composes herself. "The ice is all yours. Just lock up when you're done. Did you bring your own equipment?"

"No, but all we need is skates."

"Not a problem. You know where to find them."

Danny is silent and slow-moving as we make our way to the skate room. There's a vast difference between going back to his old team and going back to his roots; I didn't realize it would be this hard.

"Sit there." He points at the wooden bench in the center of the room. I do as instructed and take off my sneakers. Danny scans the racks of skates before selecting my size and crouching in front of me. I hold my foot up and say nothing as he slides one skate on and begins lacing.

"How does that feel?" he asks as he finishes lacing the second skate.

"Good."

"Not too tight?"

"It's perfect," I say as he helps me to my feet. With the skates on, I'm closer to his height.

"Are you going to skate?"

"No. I'll watch you."

I was hoping he'd say yes, but I won't push him any further. He's here, that's all I can ask for.

He holds my arm as we walk out to the rink and when I smell the clean, cold scent of the ice, a wave of memories hit me. All the time I spent here with Danny comes back in a flood. Late night practices, Saturday morning games. The cardboard signs Bea helped me make that had Danny's number on them. Unfortunately, it also brings back the pain of saying goodbye and all the days I spent here praying that he'd walk back through those doors at any moment and assure me this rink was enough for him.

"Here." Danny holds out his hand. I take it and he helps me to the boards.

It takes a few moments to get in the zone, but when I step onto the ice, it's like riding a bike. I do a few laps with Danny watching from the sideline. Now and then, he throws out a supportive comment.

"Are you sure you don't want to join me?" I ask as I come to a stop in front of him. "I'm scared to go to center ice."

"No, you're not." He almost smiles.

"No, I'm not, but I would like to do it with you. For old times' sake."

He looks out over the rink for a second and his expression softens. There is still time before he leaves for New York, and he's doing exactly what he did before he left for college. He's distancing himself from what's coming, so he doesn't think too much about it. It's a terrible tactic, especially now, because he's about to face the harsh realization that his career has pivoted. Even though he's still involved in the game he loves, it's not in the same capacity, and that'll be much harder to process once he's back in New York.

"You don't know how much I've missed this."

I reach over and take his hand. "You're right. I don't know. But if you want to teach me a slapshot, I'm pretty confident I could master it in the next forty minutes."

His laugh echoes around the rink. "You have no chance of that. It took me years to get it."

"How about you throw on some skates and show me how it's done?"

He looks at me for a long moment. The lights overhead are reflected in his eyes and his cheeks are pink from the cold. "Wait here."

"Couldn't leave if I tried," I joke. "My skates are too tight."

"They're meant to be," he calls back as he jogs to the equipment room.

I do a few more laps while I wait. With confidence building, I move further and further out from the boards until I'm circling the middle. I close my eyes and listen to the slicing of the blades; it's the soundtrack of the years when I had nothing to worry about. When I open my eyes, Danny is skating toward me with a stick in his hand. His movements are careful as he comes to a perfectly graceful stop in front of me.

"Thought you couldn't make it to center ice?"

"I may have lied." I wink as he drops a puck.

"I know." He smiles, and it's big this time. He's in his element again, skating a few circles around me and moving the puck with absolute precision. The nets aren't out, so he settles for driving the puck around the ice over and over as I watch from the middle. After a while, he seems to forget I'm here, but I don't care because he's happy again.

"Thank you for this," he says eventually as he skates back to me. "I needed it."

"You're welcome," I say. "I thought I'd pushed you too far for a second there."

"I needed the push," he whispers as I wrap my arms around him and follow his line of sight up to the mass of metal beams under the roof. Where his number hangs.

"Lucky number twenty-eight," I say.

"Is it still lucky?"

"It will always be lucky," I assure him as he slides his arms around my waist.

"I still can't believe you got assigned my birthday." I exhale a visible breath

"I didn't get assigned it." He holds me a little tighter. "I picked it."

My heart thumps hard, and despite the expanse of ice beneath my feet, warmth floods my body.

"You picked it?"

"Yeah. I wanted your birthday as my number."

I'm in this now, I can feel it in every muscle and bone in my body. I'm in this so deep I don't want to let him go.

I hold him tight and my whole body almost melts into him as my fingers grip the lapel of his jacket. "It might be time to show you something."

That little line appears between his eyebrows as I lift my sweater and show him the tattoo on my ribs. In simple cursive script are the words twenty-eight.

"You got my number?" He grins as he holds my waist to inspect it.

"I figured it's the only thing special enough to have on my skin forever," I explain. "And if we don't work out, I'll say I got it so I don't forget my sister's birthday."

He throws his head back and laughs before he takes my face in his hands and kisses me.

It's another memory to bottle.

CHAPTER THIRTY-NINE

For the next two days, I lose Danny to the ice rink. After our date, something shifted, and now he can't get enough of the place. He's been taking Gemma there every day, and this afternoon when he called to ask if I could pick Bea up from the airport myself because he wanted to stay, there was a heartwarming level of excitement in his voice.

I love this shift in his attitude and it made booking his flights to New York a happy affair. I still haven't decided what to do, but he's giving me the space I need to think it through.

I've also been busy making sure Dad is still functioning.

He's been avoiding everyone since our ill-fated breakfast and I'm tired of my parents being unable to confront their issues. I'm planning to tell him that but when I arrive at Whiskey Double, I'm not prepared for what I find.

My dad, fifty-six-year-old Doug Reilly, transport and logistics coordinator for Pacific North Freight, lover of survival shows and early nights, is standing behind the bar, swinging a bottle of vodka from hand to hand like he's in *Cocktail*.

"Dad?" I crane my head over the gaggle of young women at the bar who are desperately trying to communicate their drink orders.

"Kit-Kat!" he calls out. "I'll be with you in a sec."

He swings the bottle again with Miles encouraging him from the other end of the bar. The girls in front of me cheer as he fills each of their glasses before doubling back and adding cherries and a straw. When he's done, he claps his hands over his head before taking a bow. My mouth hangs open as he rounds the end of the bar and comes over.

"What are you doing here?" he asks, like this situation is perfectly natural.

"I came to see you…" I stammer. "In your apartment upstairs."

"I'm down here most nights now. Miles is keeping me busy."

I look over at Miles, who gives me a thumbs up.

I blink hard, trying to clear the haze of confusion. "Can we talk?"

"Sure. Let's go outside."

I follow Dad through the crowded bar, which takes longer because he stops to high-five an entire table of men my age. They call him Dougie, and they share several inside jokes in only a few seconds.

What is happening?

"It's good to be off my feet for a minute. My back is killing me." Dad sighs as we sit at one of the outdoor tables.

I raise a brow. "Because you're a bartender now?"

"Just from seven till close, Tuesday to Sunday."

"When do you sleep?"

He waves off my concern. "Haven't slept in months."

It's been two weeks since he cried in the diner and told me he wanted Mom back. Now he's fallen into this carefree bachelor lifestyle where he bartends six nights a week and garners the interest of women in their twenties. The red flags are flying with abandon.

"What about wanting Mom back?" I lean forward in my seat to rest my elbows on the table.

He leans in, too, and the night air mixes with a scent I don't recognize: wood-smoke cologne. For the last twenty-six years, I've only known him to smell like musk shower gel and mint toothpaste.

"I've spent months sitting around upstairs, just waiting. I don't know what I was waiting for. Maybe for it to stop hurting. It didn't. Seeing her with that man was the wake-up call I needed." He shrugs. "She's not waiting for me. So why am I waiting for her?"

There's no malice or pain in his voice. It's acceptance, and I feel slightly better about what I've orchestrated tonight.

"You're going to be fine, Dad."

He nods. "I will. It just hurt to find out that what made me happy made her miserable."

"That's why you need to talk to her, because I can't tell you how she feels and you shouldn't guess for yourself."

He lifts his head and his upper body relaxes.

"Dad, I …" I start, but he looks past my shoulder.

"Elaine?"

I turn to see Mom coming toward us. She looks beautiful

in a pleated red dress and strappy heels. A kind smile lights her expression.

"I asked her to meet us here," I explain to Dad. "I think you need to talk."

"We do." Dad stands up and wipes his palms on his thighs.

"Hey, Mom." I stand from the table and she pats my arm. "I'll be inside."

I step away, allowing Mom to take my chair. When I reach the door, I turn, and see Dad's knee is bouncing under the table and sweat is beading on his brow.

———

I sit at the bar for two painfully sober hours.

Forty minutes into their talk, Mom and Dad went upstairs to the apartment. I wanted to follow because I couldn't spy on them from here, but at one point the discussion got heated, so they needed privacy.

"Do you think you've made a mistake with this *Parent Trap* thing you're doing?" Miles asks as he sits beside me in the booth.

"Parent-trapping is trying to get them back together."

"And you're not doing that?" He raises a dark eyebrow.

"No. I'm tired of being on the receiving end of all the things they should say to each other. It's bad for my mental health, and if they actually spoke to each other, they'd get some closure on the situation."

"Right. A reverse parent trap." Miles leans back and looks through the front window of the bar. "Heads up, here comes your mom."

I slide out of the booth and race to the door, pushing it open and stepping out before she makes it across the outdoor dining space.

"Are you okay?" The question comes out in a rush.

My stomach knots as I look at her. She lifts her head, and even though tears glisten on her cheeks, she looks relieved.

"I'm good, but I'd like to go now."

"Yeah, of course. Do you need me to drive you?"

"No." She says. "My car is down the block."

"I'll walk you." I link my arm through hers, and we walk in silence to her car.

When we approach, she unlocks the sedan, but before she climbs in, she turns to face me.

"I'm not moving in with him," she says. "I just want you to know that."

I never asked if she did, but after our heated conversation I assumed that's where she went. I wasn't thrilled about it, but it seemed logical if she wants to see where things go with Patrick.

"Why not?" I ask.

She looks away, brushing the short strands of hair off her forehead. "I'm not ready for it."

"Where are you living, then?"

"I got a place in Queen Anne. No roaches, but the windows are painted shut. I really love it, though."

I try not to tear up, unsuccessfully. "That's great, Mom."

"I'm not seeing him either," she whispers.

Once again, I'm confused. What was all this for if she wasn't going to be with him?

"My marriage didn't end so I could be with someone else.

It ended because I wasn't happy with myself. So I'm going to work on that."

"That's really mature, Mom," I say. "I'm proud of you."

She inhales deeply, her shoulders loosening. "You don't know how good it feels to hear you say that."

When Mom drives off, I get into my car and head over to the rink. On my way, I make a quick stop at the apartment to change my shirt, so I'm more suitably dressed.

When I arrive, Danny is on the ice with a line of pucks, firing them one by one into the back of the net. I climb the stands to the second row and sit down, my hands tucked in the pockets of my coat. The rink must have cleared out hours ago, and with no one around the music that pumps through the speakers reverberates off the walls. It feels like no time has passed since I sat here as a teenager.

"Hey! Twenty-eight!" I cup my hands around my mouth and shout over the music. Danny spins in one fluid movement and his eyes light up when he sees me. "You're looking good out there."

He skates over to the boards, and I hurry down to meet him, grabbing his jersey and kissing him as soon as he's close enough.

"What's that for?" Danny says, his breathing heavy. I'm still gripping his jersey and holding his face to mine.

"I love you," I say. "I've loved you since I figured out what love was and I'm going to love you until I forget what love is. You are everything to me and I don't want to spend a second without you."

I step back, untie my coat and drop it to the floor. Danny throws his head back as he laughs.

"You still have that?" he says.

"Of course I still have it. It's the finest piece of clothing I own."

I do a twirl to show off my handiwork. When writing the bucket list, I went through a regretful crafting era. The result was a thrifted blue hockey jersey that I stripped of its badges and replaced with the number twenty-eight in puffy paint. Danny's name on the back is written in glitter glue, though the passing years have stripped it of most of the glitter.

"I can't believe you wore that in public." Danny laughs.

"I can't believe you let me."

He reaches for me, and I lift myself up, swinging my legs over the boards. He steadies me, wraps my legs around him and holds my hips.

"So, tell me why you're here this late, wearing that old thing?"

"Because I wanted to talk to you."

His gaze is fixed on mine, his attention unwavering. "I'm listening."

I drag my hands up his chest, my fingers twisting the laces at his neck. I know what I want to say, but once the words leave my mouth, it's a promise. A big one.

"I want to come to New York with you," I say.

I expect a cheer or at the very least, a smile. Instead, he stares at me, eyes softening and his shoulders falling.

"Kit." He runs a hand through my hair. "I don't think you do."

"No, I do. I promise. I'm just going to need some time to sort out the lease on the apartment and finish up at the bank. I'll only be a few weeks behind. I swear."

His hand is on my neck, and he tilts my head forward to kiss my nose.

"I think you should stay."

"No. I love you and I want to be with you. I can do this. I can come to New York, and I'll get a job at another bank, and we can hang out with Alex, go to nice restaurants, and spend Saturday mornings in the park. It will be great."

"It sounds like you're trying to convince yourself," he says.

I went in too hard, and he saw right through me. I might not be one hundred percent ready to move but I am ready for us.

"But you love hockey." I let go of his jersey laces. "So, I can do this for hockey and for you."

He takes my face in his hands, kissing me like he's making up for every day we spent apart.

But we won't be apart anymore and that's what matters.

CHAPTER FORTY

On Bea's first night back, we talk at length about our parents. I've had time to ruminate on everything, so the discussion is part rational conversation, part incoherent sobbing. Mostly incoherent sobbing from Bea thanks to her hormones.

Mom made mistakes, but if I put myself in her position, I don't know what I would have done. I think about Danny, too, and what I would do for him. What I would give up for him. Would I settle for something that makes me unhappy just because it's been the norm for so long? It's a topic I need Bea to help me unpack because the closer we get to his departure, the more certain I am that I want to go with him.

"Being pregnant sucks," Bea says as she stretches out on the couch. "Every second of the day I'm either tired, sick, hungry or gassy."

"Alright, Snow White. What are the names of the other three dwarves?"

"I believe they're emotional, aching and homicidal."

I laugh. "Lucky Jamie."

Bea tells me all about the nightmare her body has been lately, and honestly, I'm not built for it. It's like the ultimate invasion of personal space, and it doesn't seem to get better when the kid is on the outside. I don't think Bea has thought that far ahead, but I'm proud of how much research she's done on the pregnancy side of things.

After a horrifying discussion about mucus plugs, I leave my achy twin on the couch to spend another eight-hour day crushing people's dreams at the bank. This only heightens my desire for a career change, and I curse the stupid amount of perspective the bucket list gave me. I was happy and now my safe and structured life feels lacking.

On my way back to the apartment, I pick up a pizza with anchovies and pineapple at Bea's request and decide that it's time for a Danny and New York debrief.

"Bea," I call out as I let myself in. "I got the pizza."

"What toppings?" a familiar male voice responds as I kick off my shoes.

"Alex!" I scream, dropping the pizza on the counter and running to my brother. He springs up off the couch and pulls me into a hug.

"Hey, kiddo." He holds me tight as Bea strolls out of her room.

"Oh yeah, Alex is here."

"I see that," I say as I sit on the couch.

Bea inhales the pizza while I fill Alex in on everything he missed. He feels guilty about not spending more time with me in New York, but I'm happy that he's more himself than the last time I saw him.

"Have Mom and Dad spoken to each other since your intervention?" he asks.

"Yeah, Miles told Eve, and she said that Mom's been to visit Dad a few times," I explain.

"What about Eve? How's she handling it." Alex asks.

"She still wants to rip out Mom and Patrick's throats," Bea says through a mouthful of anchovies and pineapple.

"Patrick?" Alex muses. "That's the guy's name?"

"Yes," I confirm and Bea looks at me and it immediately becomes apparent that it's an apology before she's even committed the crime.

"Kit had lunch with him the other day."

Alex's expression darkens. "Why would you do that?"

"I didn't have lunch with him. I was at lunch with Danny and he was there, so I spoke with him."

"Why would you do that?" He drags his hand down his face.

I don't know why I'm compelled to defend the man who came between my parents but I do it anyway.

"To be honest, he seems nice, and he clearly cares about Mom," I explain. "But that doesn't excuse what he and Mom did. Dad deserved better."

Alex contemplates what I've said for a moment. Knowing full well that if I've decided Patrick isn't the worst human on the planet then maybe there might be some truth to it.

Alex takes one of Bea's discarded pizza crusts and chews on it. "I guess it's going to take time for everyone to adjust. But we'll get there eventually."

His statement sounds so resolute and it brings with it a sense of relief. It feels like I've been treading water, waiting for someone to pull me out and tell me exactly what I'm supposed to do to set everything right. There is no sense in that because things aren't going to go back to the way they were and maybe that's okay. Like Alex said, we all need time and if, at the end of it all, we're all happy then that's the best any of us can hope for.

"How much longer are you staying in New York?" I ask.

"Not sure yet, but I like it out there. I'm thinking of making it permanent."

"Well, that's even more of a reason for me to move," I say. "Danny is flying out next month to start that coaching job."

Bea frowns. "I thought he turned it down."

"No, he didn't. We've been talking about it constantly." I assure her.

"Yeah, he did. Leah told me. He had a flight booked, and she argued with the airline to get him a refund."

There is no way that's right.

"Why would he do that?" My heart is hammering. That job is a great opportunity, he can't possibly have thrown it away.

"Umm, because your relationship has changed. Didn't you talk about this?" She's looking more confused by the second. "And I'm the one that has baby brain."

Alex chimes in, "What's happening here?"

I ignore him. "He didn't tell me anything."

"You know honest communication is the foundation of any relationship, right?" She takes another slice of pizza.

I raise a brow. "Have you been talking to Gem?"

"No, Fletcher says it all the time. Which is hilarious because Leah said he's got serious writer's block and he's hiding it from Hallie."

"Can someone tell me what's going on with Danny Larson?" Alex interjects.

"They slept together," Bea says.

"I knew it!" Alex shouts. "You were so cagey when you got back after disappearing for an entire night."

"Yes, okay, thank you for sharing, Bea." I turn to Alex. "Danny and I are a thing now."

"Great." Alex stands up and clasps his hands together. "Do either of you have a shovel?"

———

I leave Alex to stew over Danny's punishment and head to Fletcher's house. Traffic is a nightmare and when I finally make it to Magnolia, I'm greeted by Hallie, who, judging by the dark circles under her eyes, has just flown in from her latest trip to Australia.

"It's great to see you." She gives me a gentle hug.

"You too. I need to talk to Danny." My tone is sharp and it leaves Hallie wide eyed.

"He's in the kitchen." She closes the door behind me. "Is everything okay?"

I take off toward the kitchen and find Fletcher sitting on a barstool, sipping a beer, while Danny crunches on an apple beside him. His eyes light up when he sees me, but my expression quickly extinguishes that.

"Kit?"

"Why did you turn down the job?"

He sits the apple core on the counter and stands up. "Because I didn't want it."

"That's bullshit." I step up to him, dwarfed by the six-two wall of muscle. "Why did you really turn it down?"

"I didn't want to move back to New York."

"Yes, you do," I scold. "You love it there and you got handed the opportunity of a lifetime."

"What do you want me to say?" His voice shakes a little.

"I want you to say that you didn't turn that job down because of me."

"That's part of the reason."

"No!" I shout and push on his chest. "Don't make me the reason you don't do this."

He holds his ground and wraps his fingers gently around my wrists, holding my hands to his heart. "I know you don't really want to move, and I don't want to leave you."

"What about hockey?"

"I still love it. But it's time I put you first."

My shoulders drop. Is he being serious right now?

"This is the right thing for both of us," he says. "Besides. I got a better opportunity."

"There is no way you got a better offer than coaching your old team! And you're being flippant about all of this. It's concerning."

He nods and clearly can't contain his amusement at how worked up I'm getting.

"Don't smirk," I hiss. "Explain yourself."

I step back and put my hands on my hips, effectively giving him the floor.

"After you took me to the rink, I called Mrs. Schaffer to thank her. We got to talking, and she said she was putting the rink up for sale. I told her I'd buy it. The next day she accepted my offer. I take it over next month."

My eyes go wide. "You did what?"

"I bought the rink, and I think you should hand in your notice so we can run it together. I want to turn it into a hockey training academy."

My legs are like wet noodles, so I'm forced to lean on him.

"I can't believe you did that."

"In a good way or a bad way?" He raises a brow.

"I don't know." I stammer. "Did you do a cost-benefit analysis? Or look over the books to see if it's profitable?"

That's a no, judging by how tight his lips are.

"You don't know how to run a sporting complex, also it needs renovating and you can't even use a spreadsheet."

"Yeah, I can."

"No, you can't. I know you played around in my bucket list spreadsheet. It took me hours to fix the formulas."

He huffs. "I was trying to add your notes and scores after the Mona Lisa visit."

"Yeah, and you're supposed to enter the data in the high-lighted columns. There's literally no need to manually add anything to the other section. That's why they have formulas."

Fletcher clears his throat. "I think we've gone off on a tangent here."

"Obviously!" Danny and I say in unison as we look at his brother.

"Just making sure we're on the same page." Fletcher holds

up his hands defensively and Hallie laughs. Danny ignores them both and leans down to kiss me.

"I still feel the need to point out that honest communication is the foundation of any successful relationship," Fletcher interrupts.

I pull my mouth away from Danny's. "Really? Why don't you tell Hallie about your writer's block, then?"

Hallie stares at her husband. "You have writer's block?"

Fletcher picks at the label on his beer bottle. All these Larson boys look the same when they fret. Hooded eyes and pouty lips.

"I'm stuck on act three."

Hallie rounds the kitchen island and pulls Fletcher against her body. "Oh, baby. Why didn't you tell me? I have a million ideas for how I want act three to go."

Fletcher's shoulders sag in relief as he stares at his wife with adoration.

"Can we work on it now?" he asks.

"I'll get my notebook," she says as he drapes his arm over her shoulder and they exit the kitchen.

"Fletcher is right about the communication thing." I turn back to Danny.

"Fletcher is rarely right about anything," Danny says. "But yes, I should have told you what I was doing, so from now on, no more secrets. Especially about big life decisions."

I hold my hand up between us, extending my pinkie finger. He holds up his as well, linking it with mine and giving it a firm shake.

"Deal."

I roll onto my toes and kiss him before resting my forehead

against his. "Do you even have a laptop? I've never seen you with one, but I want to start a renovation budget spreadsheet. I've got some ideas for how we can upgrade the booking system. Mrs. Schaffer writes session times on one of those yellow legal pads and it's absolute madness—Wait, what are you doing?"

He scoops me up, throws me over his shoulder and carries me toward his room. "Can I be honest for a sec?"

"Yes, we said we would be."

"Shut up," he says. "I don't want to hear about spreadsheets or budgets or a cost whatever analysis."

"Cost-benefit analysis," I correct him. "You're not off to a strong start if you can't remember the name of it."

He pinches my butt. "You're not shutting up."

"Why don't you make me." I giggle as he pinches me again.

"That's the plan." He lowers his voice as he opens the door to his room and sets me on my feet.

"Let's go then." I tease and he pulls off his shirt and kicks the door closed.

He starts kissing my neck and I press my hands against his chest to halt him for a second. "By the way, Bea told Alex about us and now he wants to talk to you."

"Oh, no." Danny frowns.

CHAPTER FORTY-ONE

I'm exhausted after going over the expenses for the rink. Danny isn't taking over for another three weeks, but we want to start strong. He's been coming up with session schedules and doing equipment stock takes, while I'm trying to get my head around the accounting software and renovation budgets. Though his playing career wasn't as long as expected, Danny was smart with his money and it's because I drilled the importance of saving into him when we worked weekends at the snack counter. With his finances organized, I go through mine to work out how much I can invest as his business partner and draft a resignation letter for Brian.

"Are you sure about tomorrow?" Danny says as he rolls over and pulls me against him.

"No, but even if I could get them all in the one room, I'm not sure if they would talk."

He buries his nose in my hair. "Because Eve is a loose cannon?"

"That's why I'm going to tell her the plan. She'll shut down if she's blindsided. This way, the ball is in her court."

"It's a good plan," he says. "You're full of good plans."

Historically speaking, he's right. Little Kit Reilly had a plan for everything. Big Kit Reilly has been feeling less in control these days, but in a good way. Trying to control everything is exhausting, and constantly worrying about everyone moving on has taken its toll. Dealing with all this change is like assembling a puzzle. I know what it's going to look like at the end but for now I'm working on the corners.

After way too much cuddling with Danny, I drive over to Eve's apartment and find her packing her clothes to take to Spencer's.

"Have you left him?" I ask as I refold all the clothes she's stuffed into a suitcase.

"As soon as he gets back from his business trip. I'll have this suitcase packed and ready so when I hand back the ring I can make a quick exit." She smiles, and it's alarmingly serene. "Spence and I have everything arranged so I can walk away."

I wouldn't describe Eve as vindictive, but we have known her to exact revenge on those who wrong her. She once cut the bristles off Alex's toothbrush because he took too long in the bathroom and made her late for a concert. So this new level of maturity is surprising, and it gives me high hopes for my plan tonight.

"Speaking of walking away." It's not a great segue, but I'm rolling with it. "Bea is flying back to London tomorrow, so I figured it would be nice if we all hung out tonight."

Eve throws another sweater on the pile of clothes. "Sure. Where?"

"The house has finally settled and the keys are being given to the new owners tomorrow, so I thought take-out on the floor of the old dining room would be a nice farewell."

"Count me in," she says, and I hate that I'm about to ruin her vision of the evening.

"Eve, there's something else." I lower my voice and when she looks up at me, a wave of her raven hair falls over her eye. She tucks it behind her ear.

"What is it?"

"Mom and Dad are going to be there."

She drops a pair of wedge-heeled boots on the bed. "I knew there'd be an ulterior motive."

"It's not an ulterior motive. They're in a good place and it would be nice to have dinner in the house before it isn't ours anymore."

"I don't want to see her. Why is that so hard for you to understand?" She pulls her suitcase away from me and starts shoving clothes into it, messing up the packing system I sneakily implemented while she's been talking.

"Mom knows why you're so upset with her. But how can she fix it when you won't speak to her?"

Her jaw is tight. "Maybe it can't be fixed? Maybe I just want to live my life without her constant judgment about every choice I make."

I put down the sweater I was folding. "She's your mother. She'll always be your mother."

"Yeah, unfortunately I'm aware," she grunts as she tosses more clothes in the suitcase.

"Don't be like this Evie."

"Be like what?" She sighs. "I'm standing up for myself. All my life she's forced these expectations on me. I had to be as successful as Alex, as smart as you, as caring as Bea. I'm tired of being compared to all of you and constantly coming up short."

"You know why she was like that, don't you?"

Eve stops sorting clothes. "What do you mean?"

"She isn't critical of you. She's jealous of you. You're living the life she wanted. Doing anything you want, trying your hand at everything until you find what makes you happy. As far as she's concerned, you have it made."

She drops onto her comforter, slumping forward. "Really?"

"Yes." I step around the end of the bed and sit beside her. "Just promise me you'll think about coming tonight?"

———

By early evening, the last of Bea's belongings are on their way to the UK and she's sitting on our couch eating shredded cheese and watching game shows. She's desperate to get back to London and see Jamie, and it stings a little when she refers to London as "home".

After confiscating the bag of cheese and bundling Bea into the car with no context on where we're going, she's in high spirits again.

"This is exciting," she says as she tries to figure out what direction we're headed. She works it out quickly after we pick up several noodle dishes from Eve's favorite place. Fingers crossed we don't get food poisoning this time.

When we arrive, Bea settles on the floor of the dining room while I arrange the cushions I brought from the apartment. Judy was kind enough to let me borrow the old camping table with adjustable legs she had in the garage. It's older than Nolan, cracked and discolored, but I top it with the special occasion tablecloth I dug out of a box in Mom's new apartment, ensuring the overhang on each side is a little off, so Alex's gravy stain is front and center.

Dad is first to arrive, and he takes his place at the head of the table, setting to work, opening the food and distributing the paper plates. Mom shows up a few minutes later and sits in her usual place beside Dad. They talk to Bea about London and her pregnancy while I grin like an idiot because they're sitting next to each other.

"Is this an intervention?" Alex says, as he enters the room.

"No, it's family dinner." I grab his arm and pull him onto the cushion beside me. Mom smiles at her son, but her expression turns somber when she looks over at Eve's empty seat.

We wait for a few minutes, idly chatting, but the food is getting cold, so I give everyone permission to eat.

"Kit, tell me about that list you were working on," Dad says through a mouthful of noodles. "How much did you cross off?"

"All of it." I look over at my twin. "I ticked off every item."

"What was on it?" he asks.

"Really unpleasant experiences. Like conquering a fear, staying up all night to watch the sunrise and dancing in the rain."

"She got up on stage at Whiskey Double and sang karaoke." Bea sounds like a giddy schoolgirl.

Alex nudges my arm. "Are you trying to steal my thunder?"

"No chance of that." Mom laughs. "I've heard her singing in the shower."

"Well, thanks for your support, everyone," I grumble.

"What else was on the list?" Alex says.

Bea looks across the table, with a grin on her face and her eyebrows raised. "Skinny dipping."

Dad looks affronted. "Tell me you didn't do that, Katherine?"

"I did," I say proudly. "And I got caught by Fletcher, Nolan, and Gemma. I've never been more mortified in my life."

Mom reaches over and places her hand over Dad's. "Remember when we did that?"

Dad almost chokes on his beef and broccoli. "Elaine!"

"Yuck." Bea looks green. But it could be the baby.

"We'd been dating for three weeks and your father was house-sitting for Gran. Her neighbors had a lovely pool, so we snuck over and—"

"Okay, enough. Thank you." Alex screws up his face and I laugh at the turn this conversation has taken.

Dad pats the top of Mom's hand before she moves it away.

"As long as skinny dipping is the worst thing you did," he says.

My twin throws me under the bus yet again. "She spent seven hundred euros on a bottle of champagne in Paris."

I drop my plastic fork. "Bea, for shit's sake, stop ratting me out?"

Mom's eyes go wide. "You spent how much?"

I draw back in on myself. "In my defense, the exchange rate was pretty good."

"That's not the point. Why was a seven-hundred-euro bottle of champagne on your bucket list?" Dad grumbles.

"The list item was to spend money on something that won't last, and Danny and I were celebrating the coaching job. Oh, and we were in Paris."

He shakes his head and stares at his plate. "I knew those Larson boys were a bad influence."

"It's fine, Doug. She's a grown woman with a good head on her shoulders."

"Thank you, Mom," I say.

"It doesn't seem that way," Dad mumbles. "Seven hundred euros. You've got to be kidding me. I could make you a nice Tom Collins for less than ten dollars."

"Hey. I've got a good head on my shoulders, too, right?" Bea chimes in.

Dad scoffs, though he can't hide his grin. "Where's the ring, Beatrice?"

"Burn," Alex chides and Bea gives him the finger.

"What's all this?" a familiar voice says behind me, and we all look up to see Eve standing in the doorway.

Mom stands, smoothing her blouse as she smiles at her eldest daughter. "Evelyn. I'm so glad you're here."

Eve swallows hard and looks around the table. "We're a family, aren't we? I figured I should be here for the last meal in the house."

"Yes, you should." I take my sister's hand as she sits on the floor at the end of the table.

Everyone is silent for a moment, all watching Eve as she

heaps food onto her plate. It's too early to be excited about a reconciliation between her and Mom, but this is a perfect first step.

"Can you promise me there won't be any big announcements at this dinner? Our last one didn't go so well," Eve says.

"Agreed." Mom nods, and she looks at Dad. "We were just talking about Kit's bucket list activities."

Bea looks up at me, a wicked smirk on her face, and I know what she's planning.

"Don't you dare," I warn her, inadvertently making myself the prime focus of the table.

"What?" Dad's tone is wary. "Is it the champagne? I'm not happy about the champagne."

"You haven't told them about the tattoo, then?" Eve grins.

Mom's eyes are wider than I've ever seen. "Katherine, you didn't"

"Bea has one as well," I fire back.

"Eve has two." Bea points at her.

"Hey." Eve slaps Bea's accusatory finger away.

Mom exhales and looks over at Dad, who rolls his eyes.

"I don't have any." Alex folds his arms and straightens his back. So proud of himself.

Bea, Eve and I look at our brother, Eve groans, "Yeah because you've never done anything that Mom and Dad would disapprove of."

"Now, now girls," Mom tries to contain her grin. "Don't tease your brother for being responsible."

Bea's eyes dart to the gravy stain before we share a conspiratorial glance.

"He is responsible, Mom." I pat my big brother on the

shoulder. "In fact, he's so responsible, I'm sure he'd be happy to tell you how he ended up with that hole in his bedroom wall."

Eve steeples her fingers and clears her throat. "Or maybe, we should ask Spencer?"

ACKNOWLEDGMENTS

I never know what to write for the acknowledgments, and of course I left it till the last minute. I will start by thanking my sister, Nicole. You spent countless hours reading countless drafts and, as always, offered immense insight. Thank you for your continued dedication to my stories and sitting there while I meticulously explain every plot idea that pops into my head.

I also want to give a massive shout out to Jess. You are an absolute superstar, and this book would not have been possible without you. You gave me the feedback I needed to shape these characters and I can't thank you enough for your advice and friendship as we both navigate this ever changing hellscape known as writing.

To the entire SSP crew, who get more excited about my books than I do. Thank you for your constant support and for making my day job as fun as my author job. Also, a special thank you to Kirra (and Kirra's mum) for cheering me on and to Corey, for pointing out my spelling mistakes, getting me strawberry milkshakes and humbling me at every opportunity.

I'd also like to say a huge thank you to Sam. You have an insane amount of blind faith in everything I do and I appreciate your excitement at even my smallest achievements more than you know. I would say this to your face, but I'm awkward and don't like sharing my feelings.

Another big thank you to my parents, my in-laws and my friends for buying my books and asking when the next one is coming out. I can assure you that book 3 is being edited as we speak.

And to Marnie, my book best friend. Thank you for roasting the hell out of my work and making me a better author. I will finish my fantasy book one day and you will be the first to read it. It's actually coming along nicely.

As always, I could not do any of this without Callan. Not just for your baller design skills, but for your love, unwavering support, and for turning a blind eye to my insane number of book purchases. I love you more than ever.

Finally, to my new friends, the Writing Fridays crew. Kaitlyn, Demi, Mel and Tom. My little found family. It's always fun to toss ideas around, eat bagels and be very unproductive after 3pm with you guys. You make Friday the best day of the week.

ABOUT THE AUTHOR

Lauren Jones grew up in North Queensland and now lives in Brisbane with her graphic designer husband and two mini dachshunds. She started writing stories as a kid and thought time-travelling high fantasy was an easy place to start, she was wrong. Since then, Lauren has worked on her craft, gravitating toward contemporary fiction. She can be found in her little library, rearranging her books or having an afternoon nap.

To stay up to date on new releases you can follow Lauren on Instagram **@laurenjoneswrites** or sign up to her newsletter at www.laurenjoneswrites.com.au.

ALSO BY LAUREN JONES

Tell Me How It Ends

The Gossip Project